## CREATIVE TEXTS PUBLISHERS
## PO Box 50, Barto, PA 19504

Creative Texts Publishers products are available at special discounts for bulk purchase for sale promotions, premiums, fund-raising, and educational needs. For details, write Creative Texts Publishers, PO Box 50, Barto, PA 19504, or visit www.creativetexts.com

WHAT IF?
by Jerry D. Young
Published by Creative Texts Publishers
PO Box 50
Barto, PA 19504
www.creativetexts.com

Cover photo modified and used by license.
Credit: Rob Hurson

The following is a work of fiction. Any resemblance to actual names, persons, businesses, and incidents is strictly coincidental. Locations are used only in the general sense and do not represent the real place in actuality.

ISBN: 978-0692452837

# WHAT IF?

By
JERRY D. YOUNG

## CHAPTER ONE

-

Bethany waited anxiously at the GMC dealership. Her new vehicle was scheduled to be delivered any minute. It was one of the last ones off the assembly line, before production was ended. It had taken three months of searching to find it and she had almost given up hope.

But Gary Martain, owner of three GMC dealerships, heard about the search and lent a hand. He pulled some strings and got the rig assigned to this dealership so there would be no special delivery or other charges.

"Part of the service, Bethany," he told her when he called and told her when to expect delivery.

And suddenly there was the semi auto hauler with a full load of new trucks for the three dealerships. Besides the GMC Topkick 5500 chassis cab that would soon be Bethany's, two more vehicles were to be dropped off. Both were new standard pickup trucks. The rest would go to the other two dealerships.

Bethany and Gary inspected the rig thoroughly before handing it over to the dealership mechanics to do the dealer prep work before Bethany could take possession. While they were working on it, Bethany wrote a check for the total amount, just as she had told Gary she would.

"Now that it is almost in your hands, you going to tell me what you're going to do with it?" Gary put the check in his shirt pocket and smiled at Bethany.

"Going to make a motorhome out of it," Bethany replied. She stood and watched the mechanics going over the Topkick through the glass window between the office and the garage area.

Gary was surprised. "You know, there is a motorhome chassis available. It would be a lot easier to convert than the chassis cab. I think I can get my hands on one if you don't mind waiting a bit longer."

Bethany, her eyes still on the Topkick, shook her head. "The motorhome chassis cab is only available as rear wheel drive. I want four wheel drive. I'd actually prefer to have single tandem rear end, but the duals are okay. It'll be much easier and cheaper to do the sheet metal work on the cab than put a four-wheel-drive system under the motorhome chassis."

Bethany turned around and sat back down. She looked over at Gary. "Sometimes I want just what I want."

Gary nodded. "Sure. I'm the same. I just wanted to make sure you knew all your options." He thought Bethany's sudden smile lighted up the room more than the fluorescent fixtures overhead.

"Thank you. You've been such a big help on this. And haven't charged me an arm and a leg for all the special things you had to do to swing the deal. I appreciate it."

"Like I said. Part of the service," Gary replied. He was wracking his brain for a suitable way to ask Bethany to have dinner with him that wouldn't sound like he wanted something else for having helped out, sound patronizing, or be taken as too aggressive.

He didn't get the chance. Gary's lead mechanic came in with the keys to the rig and handed them to Gary. He gave them to Bethany and she was out the door without another word. Gary followed her out slowly. She was grinning as she closed the driver's door and buckled up the seatbelt.

"Be a bit of a rough ride, without any weight on the back, but you're welcome to join me for a bite to eat before I take this thing to the upfitters to get the work started on the motorhome body. I'd like to show my appreciation for all your help."

Gary didn't lose any time getting around to the passenger side of the truck. He climbed up and into the cab. Bethany waited until he was buckled in and then put the truck in gear and headed for the street.

Bethany had been right when she said it would be a rough ride. The city wasn't doing a very good job keeping the streets in shape, due to budget shortages, and despite Bethany's careful avoidance of all the rough spots she could, the truck still bounced around a bit. But the Topkick had the optional air ride seats and best cab/chassis mounts so the ride wasn't as bad as it might have been.

Pulling into a well known restaurant a short distance from the dealership, Bethany parked the twenty-six foot long rig out of the way and the two climbed down out of the cab. Bethany locked the doors with the remote and walked with Gary to the restaurant front doors.

Gary opened the door for her and was pleased when she smiled at him rather than chewed him out for being a chauvinist the way his last date had. Though this wasn't really a date. Not really.

It might not be a date, but the two had a pleasant talk over the meal. When she dropped him off at the dealership an hour and a half later, Gary realized that Bethany now knew most of his life story and he knew very little about her, except she wanted a four-wheel-drive motorhome and had the money to pay for it.

Gary did not see or hear from Bethany for two months. Then, when she did show up again he didn't recognize the vehicle at first. He did a double take when he saw Bethany get out of the cab of the motorhome.

He took a long look at the motorhome and then a longer one at Bethany as she came into the dealership. "Thought you might like to see what I did with the chassis cab you went to so much trouble to get for me."

"Yes. Yes, I'd like that very much," Gary said.

"Come on out," Bethany said and turned around to go back outside.

A little too late to get the door for her, Gary hurried out to walk beside her to where she was parked. As they made a turn around the exterior of the motorhome, Bethany pointed out feature after feature, including the rather subdued paint scheme. The motorhome was painted a light tan. Not unattractive, but nothing like the splashy paint schemes that seemed to be on most of the new motorhomes now being built.

Next, Bethany opened the side door and ushered Gary inside the motorhome and then joined him to give him the nickel tour. It only took a couple of minutes and the two were back outside.

More than a little curious, Gary checked the joint between the back of the cab of the truck and the motorhome body. "Did a really good job of merging the two," Gary said, looking over at Bethany. "And I like the way they cut away the cab to give access to the coach from the cab. I thought that might be awkward. More so than the regular motorhome chassis, anyway."

Gary was caught by Bethany's bright smile at the comments. "Feel like a ride?" she suddenly asked. "Haven't had anything since breakfast and it was a light one."

"Sure. But this time I pay," Gary said. He walked with her to the driver's side of the rig and opened the door. She climbed in by herself and he closed the door and then ran around to the other side.

"I'd better let them know where I'm going," Gary said, taking out his cell phone after he was belted in.

"Sure," Bethany replied. "I tell you I don't miss having to check in all the time."

Speaking only a few quiet words into the phone, he closed it and slipped it back into his shirt pocket. "Oh? You used to have to check in?"

"Oh, yes. Even though it was my company... well... because it was my company, I had to be available twenty-four seven. I was glad to get out from under it all."

"What happened? Nothing serious, I hope," Gary said, determined to learn all he could about this intriguing woman.

"Oh, it was serious, all right. A legitimate offer in the mid eight figures to buy me out. I loved the business. For a long time, I did. But I was ready to get out from under it and do a few things before I find something else to do. I started that business in high school and built it up over the years without ever taking a vacation. I plan on a great vacation that is going to last a couple of years."

Bethany's bright smile when she looked at him made Gary smile in return. "Sounds nice. I'm not one for vacations much myself. Too busy. I like what I'm doing. But I sure understand what you mean. It gets old sometimes, being the boss."

Bethany nodded and then they were at the same restaurant again. Another pleasant meal, this time with Bethany doing at least some of the talking. Gary was able to find out a few more things about Bethany.

She was thirty four, same age as he, and was allergic to seafood. Didn't have any close family left, had never been married, and didn't have any children.

"Where you heading after this?" Gary asked.

"Probably north. Thought I take a look around the Great Lakes. I'm sort of looking for some property to retire on. Something remote. I'm not much of one to socialize. Missed out on some things, I suppose, but it is the way I am." Bethany shrugged slightly. "I think I might like to write. For publication. I don't really have to work anymore, but I have to have something to do or I'd go nuts."

"I see. Real loner, then?" Gary asked.

Bethany nodded. "For the most part. I have my moments. You wouldn't want to see me in a karaoke bar. I'm addicted when it comes to karaoke. Can't sing worth a hoot, but I love getting up there and doing something very few other people are willing to do. Strange obsession for a loner, huh?"

"Not so strange," Gary said. "I've been known to hog a microphone a time or two at the Christmas parties. I'm actually pretty good, they tell me. I just can't remember the words to the songs, so I can't sing unless it is karaoke."

"Wow! Never would have expected it," Bethany said.

"Same here about you. I have a feeling you are better than you let on."

"Well… I'm better than I used to be. But that isn't saying very much."

"I'd like to judge for myself," Gary said. "This is karaoke night at 'The Lounge'. Would you care to go with me? I haven't been in a while."

Gary thought she was going to say no since it took her so long to answer. But she surprised him again. "I'd love to. What time?"

"Eight? We can get supper there first. They have a decent kitchen."

"I'll be there," Bethany said. "I think I'd better get you back to the dealership. I've heard your phone vibrate at least three times in the last ten minutes."

Gary blushed slightly. "Yes… Well… perhaps you are right. Probably something someone else can handle, but they want the boss to sign off on it."

The two got up from the table and Bethany insisted she pick up the tab again. There was no good way to protest without making a scene, so Gary simply nodded. Bethany stopped to pay for the meal with a credit card. Gary, attuned to such things, noted that it was a platinum American Express card. Also that she signed the receipt with a gold fountain pen. He had a hunch it wasn't just gold colored. Everything about Bethany was first class. And intriguing. "You want me to pick you up somewhere?" he asked before he got out of the cab of the motorhome back at the dealership.

"Nope," Bethany said with a grin. "I have Miss Daisy here to guide me." She patted the screen of the GPS navigation system incorporated into the new custom dash that was part of the upfitting as a motorhome.

Gary was out of the dealership earlier than he had been for months. He left before four, headed out to get a haircut and a manicure. He showered and shaved when he got home, and then took a nap. He wanted to be able to stay as late as Bethany was willing. Sometimes karaoke night lasted until closing time at two in the morning.

They didn't last until two, but they had a great time until a little before one when Bethany said she had to get some sleep before she left the next morning. "You wore me out dancing. I haven't danced in years. This was fun. Perhaps we can do it again if… when I get back to the city."

"I'll hold you to that," Gary said. "And you really misled me when you said you couldn't sing very well. You were a great!"

"And you weren't kidding when you said you were good. I think I sang better tonight than I ever have. And those duets with you… I've never done a duet. That was pretty cool."

"Yes, it was." Gary walked Bethany out to the motorhome.

"I had a really good time tonight, Gary. Thank you." She stood on tiptoes and gave him a kiss on the cheek. "Would it be okay if I called you… if I have trouble on the road or something and need dealer help?"

"Of course you can," Gary said. He was a little disappointed she'd tied the possible calls to business.

But then she said, "I might just call anyway, if that's okay."

"Absolutely!" Gary said. He let her hand slide lingeringly from his as she stepped up into the motorhome.

"Good-night, Gary."

"Good-night Bethany." Gary didn't dance over to his truck, but it was close. He felt better than he had in a long time.

The next morning, Gary drove by 'The Lounge' on his way into the dealership. The motorhome and Bethany were gone.

## CHAPTER TWO

-

Bethany waited until Gary drove away before she started up the motorhome and headed for the truck stop near the interstate she intended to take the next morning. She was smiling when she undressed and went to bed in the over-cab bunk of the motorhome.

After her morning ablutions and a quick breakfast made in the galley, Bethany went to the cab and started up the diesel engine and checked the myriad of gauges and indicator lights built into the custom dash. Everything was nominal so Bethany put the rig in gear and headed for the Interstate, the navigation system speaking the appropriate turns to take to get to the destination she'd programmed into the unit.

She turned her thoughts from Gary and concentrated on the road. Traffic was heavy, the rush hour starting about the time she got on the road. But the Topkick was more than powerful enough to handle the weight of the coach at full Interstate speeds, so Bethany was soon out of the hustle and bustle of the city and out in the rural area.

Bethany turned on the satellite radio and tuned in a news station to find out what was going on in the world. As much as she hated to hear it, she listened as item after item of news was bad news in some way. Natural disasters led the way, but human caused activities were right behind them. When the repeat started, Bethany tuned in a music station that had news breaks so she could keep up on anything that might be happening, while still having something entertaining to listen to.

She'd driven the unit enough now that handling it was second nature. And it handled well, anyway. Bethany would test out the off road capabilities in a couple of days, when she reached one of the multi-day stopping points she'd mapped out before starting the journey.

Bethany topped off all the fuel and water tanks, dumped the holding tanks, and stocked up on food before she headed into the National Forest for her off-road test of the new motorhome.

A week later, more than happy with the performance of the rig, Bethany got back on the Interstate. With traffic moderate, and having had a Blue Tooth unit installed, Bethany placed a call to Gary's dealership.

Disappointed that Gary was with a customer and couldn't take her call, she asked to be transferred to the parts department.

"Stefano. How can I help you?"

"I need to order some parts for a 2009 5500 series Topkick."

"You that lady got the chassis cab and put a coach on it?"

Bethany smiled. Stefano sounded impressed. "Yes. That would be me. I want to order two complete sets of electronics for it. A starter, water pump, pair of alternators, AC compressor, two power steering pumps, a dozen complete sets of filters. Three serpentine belts, two sets of injectors. Three fuel pumps… Let's see… What else? Windshield wiper motor and windshield washer pump.

"Uh," Stefano said, "You didn't… uh… have an accident… or something?"

Bethany chuckled. "No. Nothing like that. I just want to have spares. I plan on going off-road a lot with it and want to have the things I might need to replace handy."

"Oh. Okay."

"If there are any issues with the series, would you add what parts would be needed to fix the problem?"

"Yes, Ma'am! Of course. Uh… Fuses and bulbs?"

"My, yes. Of course. Only no bulbs. I replaced the factory set with HID units. Now that I know how well they work, I'll pick up spares. Ten complete sets of spare fuses, with extras of the most used."

"It'll take a couple of days…"

"That's okay. I won't be back that way for quite a while. I'll give you my credit card number to pay for them now, if you'll just hold them for me."

"That's not necessary," Angelo said. "I'd be glad to order them and hold them until you get back. I'm sure Mr. Martain won't mind."

"I don't suppose he is available now? He was with a customer when I called."

"Let me check."

Bethany listened to the hold music for a couple of minutes, but it was worth the wait. Gary was the one that picked up the line.

"Hi! Sorry I wasn't available earlier."

"That's okay, Gary. I needed to order some parts, anyway."

"Parts? Are you having trouble?"

Bethany laughed. "No. This is a very good vehicle. I just…" She didn't want to come right out and admit to being a prepper to Gary. Not yet. He might just be someone she could get close to.

"I just like to have spares on hand because I plan to be away from everything some of the time."

"Oh. Sounds like a good idea, especially if you get that place up north. How's that coming, by the way?"

"Good," Bethany replied. "I'm really pleased with the way everything handles. I contemplated several other units before I went with the Topkick. I'm glad I chose it."

"That's great! Love to hear from a satisfied customer. But how is your search for property going?"

"Oh, I haven't made it up there yet. I took a week to wring out the rig off-road at the National Forest. Just got back on the road, headed north, again."

"Oh. And everything was as you expected?"

"Sure was. And more."

"I don't suppose… Would you want me to bring up those parts? If you let me know where you'll be, I'll fly up with them and deliver them in person."

"You don't have to do that! Besides, I don't think you could get the things on a passenger plane. There are quite a few items…"

"I have my own plane. I can meet you anywhere you want. I'd be glad to do it." There was silence for a long moment. Then Gary added, "I'd like to see you again."

"Well… I wasn't planning on stopping…" Quickly she continued. "But yes. If you don't really mind… I plan to be in Lansing in three days. I'm taking it pretty easy, like I'm supposed to, to break in the drive train."

"Good for you. So, I'll meet you in Lansing. In three days. I'll call when I get there. Would that be okay?"

"Okay, Gary. If you really want to."

"Believe me, I do. It'd be a pleasure."

"Okay, then. See you in three days."

Bethany didn't realize she was smiling when she ended the call. On the other hand, Gary knew he had a big grin on his face. "Hot, diggity dog!"

Three days later Bethany was waiting for Gary at the General Aviation Airport in Lansing. She had no idea what kind of airplane he had, so when he showed up suddenly she was a bit surprised.

"Didn't mean to startle you," Gary said.

"It's okay. Just didn't know when you would get here. How was the flight?"

"Good. I love to fly. Any flight is a good one. Especially this one. It's good to see you again."

"The same here. I've been looking forward to seeing you again. Come on out to the rig."

"Need to unload the parts first," Gary said with a smile. Apparently the parts were secondary to seeing him. That made him feel good.

"Oh. Yeah. The parts. You need some help?"

"No. Got a guy out there waiting to help me. Could you pull the motorhome over to the gate?"

"Sure," Bethany replied. Gary went one way and Bethany the other.

A few minutes later and Gary was handing the boxed parts in to Bethany. "Come on in while I put these away," she said when Gary paid off the guy with the hand cart.

"I know you have a lot of storage space built in, but where are you going to put all this?" Gary asked.

"Only temporarily in here. I have a trailer commissioned to pull with the motorhome. It has storage for things like this."

"I see. Oh..." Gary's words faded away when Bethany decided to take a chance and opened up one of the built in cabinets to put in some of the parts

She was afraid she'd made a mistake when Gary quit talking as he looked at the gun rack in the cabinet. It contained several long arms and three handguns.

"You're a shooter?"

"Yes," replied Bethany, her chin going up a bit in defiance of anything derogatory he might say.

"That's great!" Gary said. "So am I. Quite the collection you have here. You mind?"

Relieved, Bethany nodded. Gary reached in and took out the Springfield Armory M1A. "Very, very nice! I'm partial to the PTR-91, myself." Gary said as he checked the chamber. He put the rifle back into the rack and took out a shotgun. "Mossberg 590A1." He put it back and looked over at Bethany. "You ever read any stories by TOM? Tired Old Man? On Frugal's Forums? You have the same taste in firearms."

"Not entirely," Bethany said with a smile. "He favors the Taurus 1911 clones. I have a couple of the Para Ordnance High Cap versions of the 1911. But yes. I have read his stuff. I'm a member there and on a couple more prep sites. I guess the cat is out of the bag now. I am a diehard prepper."

Despite his approval of the firearms, Bethany couldn't keep the hope out of her face that Gary would approve. Or at least not condemn.

"Well, well, well. We have something else in common besides karaoke. Very few people know it, but I've been prepping since 9/11. That opened up my eyes to so many possibilities. Bad ones. Part of the reason I have the airplane I do."

"And what is that? I didn't see when you came in."

"I have a Lake Seawolf amphibian."

"Wow. Amphibian. Opens up a lot of possibilities, doesn't it?"

"Yes it does. Rather like your four-wheel-drive wonder here."

Bethany smiled. "We'd better close this up. Don't want any curious eyes spotting my hardware this close to an airport."

"Good point." Gary stepped back and let Bethany close up the cabinet. She stacked the rest of the items on the bunk bed across from the cabinets and then led the way toward the cab.

"I ate at a nice place last night not too far away. You feel like some lunch before you head back?"

"Sounds good to me. I was up early this morning and didn't have much to eat before I headed up this way."

"Well, this place will make up for it." Bethany drove the motorhome skillfully, taking side streets to get to the restaurant.

As they enjoyed a leisurely lunch, the two began discussing their individual preps. It turned out that Gary was at about the same level as Bethany. He even had a small piece of property in the Missouri Ozarks, on one of the lakes, that was his go-to place in case of major trouble east of the Mississippi.

After the meal and trips to the restrooms, the two went back to the motorhome and entered the cab. "Well, I suppose I should get back to the airport and be on my way," Gary said, his reluctance obvious.

"Yeah," Bethany said, also reluctant for the visit to end. "Too bad. I saw a sign on one of the bars near here that tonight is karaoke night."

Gary perked up. "Well... I don't have to be back tonight. What say you take me to a motel and I'll spend the night here. We can go do karaoke this evening. After supper."

Bethany surprised herself. "Why not just stay here? We can stop and get you some toiletries. I've used all three bunks. They sleep great. You'd have your choice of the rear bunk...

after we move some of the stuff. Or the dinette makes into a bunk, too."

"Are you sure you wouldn't be uncomfortable with me here with you?"

Bethany shook her head. "No. I'm comfortable with you. I trust you that nothing would happen I didn't want to happen."

"Well then… sure. Let's find a superstore and I'll pick up a few things."

More than happy with the situation, Bethany used the GPS navigation system to locate a store nearby and then followed the voice directions right to it. "GPS navigation is great," Bethany said as she parked the motorhome and turned off the engine. "But I'm old fashioned. I like a map and compass, too."

Bethany nodded at the compass mounted in the custom dashboard. Then she opened a panel in the side console and showed Gary the group of road atlases and topographic maps inside.

"You don't leave much to chance, do you?" Gary asked.

"Not if I can help it," she replied as they walked toward the store. "I want to pick up a few things myself while I'm here," Bethany said. "I'll meet you back here in a few minutes. Okay?"

"Sure thing," Gary replied, glad that Bethany wasn't going to go with him to get what he needed.

A few minutes later he joined Bethany at the entrance to the store and they walked back to the motorhome, each one carrying a pair of shopping bags. "Find what you needed?" Bethany asked.

"Yep. You?"

"Yes." The two entered the coach portion of the motorhome and Bethany said, "It may sound a little corny, but I'd like to take a nap so I'll be fresh for tonight."

"I'd like to do the same. I think I'd rather move the things from the rear bunk rather than reconfigure the dinette. Is that okay?"

"Sure," Bethany said. "Let me park us out of the way, and then give me a minute in the head and I'll give you some privacy."

Gary nodded and sat down in the small dinette. Bethany put her grocery purchases away and went into the cab to move them. Gary waited as she came back into the coach and went to the compact head of the motorhome. When she came out she smiled at Gary and said. "All yours."

Without another word she climbed up into the over-cab bunk and pulled the privacy curtain across the opening. She fell asleep much sooner than she expected and didn't hear Gary when he came out of the head and went to the rear bunk. Quietly he set the automotive parts on the floor and lay down on his back on the bunk, his hands going to the back of his head. He, too, was asleep before he realized it.

Four hours later Bethany peeked between the two parts of the privacy curtain. There was no sign of Gary. "Gary?" she asked and then quickly dropped down to the floor. "Gary?"

She noticed that the side door of the motorhome was open a crack and she went to it. When she opened it wide she saw Gary leaning over, apparently inspecting the underside of the motorhome. He had wet hair, had shaved, and was wearing the new shirt he'd bought.

Gary looked around when the door opened. "Hope you don't mind. Washed the shirt and some other things in that all-in-one washer/dryer you have. That thing is slick. And I took a shower. Been looking the rig over in more detail. You've really got this thing tricked out for prepping."

Bethany smiled. "I thought about it a long time before I came up with the plan. Got a spreadsheet in the laptop with all the details, if you want to take a look. You can do that while I shower and change for the evening."

"Sounds great," Gary said, joining her inside the motorhome.

"As you know, that head isn't great big, though functional. So if you'd sit at the dinette facing forward I can get ready without embarrassing either of us."

"Sure thing," Gary said. "I did the same thing since you had the curtain pulled on the overhead bunk."

Bethany brought out her main laptop and set it up for Gary on the dinette table. She'd decided to leave her original one, now on a swing away mount in the cab, mounted where it was and get a new one for other uses. They were linked with a WiFi connection so she had access to the motorhome computer when she was using the new one in the coach.

Gary was engrossed in the computer when Bethany, showered and changed, came and sat down across from him in the dinette. "What do you think?"

"Amazing," Gary said. "Jerry D would be proud of this." Gary looked up. "You ever read any of his stuff on the forums?"

Bethany nodded. "I actually got a couple of ideas from his stories. His and TOM's mostly, but from some of the other stories, too."

"Yeah. So did I." Gary closed up the laptop and asked Bethany, "You ready to go?"

"Sure am. Let's go up front and we'll head out."

Knowing he would be flying in a few hours, Gary only drank soft drinks during the evening. Bethany decided to do the same. It didn't appear to affect either one's singing ability, and they each sang a couple of solo pieces and then three duets.

There wasn't much of a crowd, so they called it a night at midnight and went back out to the motorhome. Bethany drove them back to the superstore parking lot and parked well out on the empty section of the lot.

"I hate for the evening to end," Gary said when they moved from the cab to the coach. "But I really have to get some sleep. I do have to go back fairly early tomorrow."

"Six okay?" Bethany asked.

Gary chuckled. "Well, I was thinking more like eight. I don't have to be there that early. Just as long as I'm there before closing."

Bethany laughed. "Well, that sounds even better. If you'll excuse me for a few minutes I'll get ready for bed and then you can have the run of the place."

Again Gary sat at the dinette, eyes forward, while Bethany went to the head and changed for bed. She was in a robe, over a pair of pajamas, when she climbed up into the bunk. "All yours." She said. "I'll see you in the morning about eight."

Gary nodded and she closed the privacy curtain again.

It took Bethany a few minutes before she went to sleep, as she went over their conversations during the evening. She had a lot more in common with Gary than she thought would be possible with anyone.

Gary had much the same thoughts, though he was able to fall right asleep after he got into the rear bunk.

The smells of bacon cooking wakened Gary the next morning. He glanced at the heavy gold Rolex GMT-MASTER

II watch on his wrist. Just a few minutes before eight. Gary quickly dressed, and then went to the head before he stepped forward to the galley/dinette area of the motorhome.

Bethany was still in her robe and pajamas, standing at the small stove. "Thought you might like a good breakfast before your flight," she said, turning her face toward Gary.

Gary thought his heart would stop. He'd thought Bethany pretty, but this morning, hair tousled and in robe and pajamas she was absolutely gorgeous. He had to clear his throat before he could speak. "Yes. Yes, that would be good. You... You look beautiful this morning."

"Let's not go overboard," Bethany said with a laugh, capturing Gary's heart forever with her easy laugh, bright smile, and sparkling eyes. "You sleep okay?"

"Sure did. Like a log," Gary said. "Anything I can do to help?"

"Nope. Got it covered. "How many eggs?"

"Three?"

"Oh. Worked up an appetite singing last night?"

Gary laughed. "Yeah. Well, truthfully, I tend to eat more than is good for me. I could do to lose a few pounds."

"Couldn't we all. But three it is. Don't want you fainting from hunger when you're flying." Bethany cut a look over her shoulder. "I don't want to lose you."

"No chance of that," Gary replied, meeting her eyes with his own.

Bethany turned back to the stove and soon had Gary's plate of bacon and eggs, with two slices of pan toasted bread, and a mug of coffee on the dinette. When she didn't sit down to join him, Gary asked, "Aren't you joining me?"

"In a moment. I didn't want to disturb you. Need to get into the head. I'll be right back."

Gary smiled and took a sip of the coffee. A bit stronger than he preferred, but it was his favorite. Folgers. He'd only taken a few bites when Bethany rejoined him and took a plate from the counter to sit down across from him to eat her own breakfast.

"If you'll put the dishes in the dishwasher," Bethany said as they lingered over a second cup of coffee, "I'll get changed and we can get you to the airport."

"Can't believe you have a clothes washer/dryer and a dishwasher in this thing. Not to mention the ice maker."

Bethany grinned. "I like my luxuries along with the basics. Always hated doing the dishes."

"More power to you," Gary said and stood up.

Bethany stood as well and went to the back of the coach, closing the privacy curtain back there so she could change. A couple of minutes in the head and she was ready to go. She found Gary in the cab, looking over the custom dashboard.

"You've got more gauges and lights on this than I do in the Seawolf." He started to get out of the way for Bethany to take the wheel.

But Bethany asked him, "You want to drive it to the airport? Get a feel for it?"

"Sure! You don't mind?"

"I trust you. A car dealership owner probably knows how to drive his products. Besides, I'd like a chance to handle the Seawolf someday."

"Count on it," Gary said and settled into the air cushion driver's seat. Bethany joined him in the passenger seat and watched as he went over the systems. He took the time to adjust the seat and the mirrors to suit him and then started the diesel engine up.

"Thing just feels like it wants to run," Gary said after putting the transmission in gear and pulling forward, toward the parking lot exit. Before he got there, still in the wide open spaces of the huge lot, he stopped and put the motorhome into reverse.

"Note the rearview camera," Bethany said quietly.

"That's what I wanted to try," Gary replied. "Cool."

Bethany smiled. "Wait until you get ready to pass someone in traffic. The side view cameras are really great, too."

"Wow. That must have been what I was looking at and couldn't figure out what they were."

Very carefully at first, and then with more confidence, Gary got them out on the road and headed toward the general aviation airport. He was smiling broadly when he parked in the airport parking lot.

"I've been selling Topkicks for a long time. I think this conversion is as good a use for one as anything I've seen. It's a dream to drive."

Bethany smiled. "Glad you like it." Then she sighed. "I guess I'd better let you get to the plane."

Before Gary could react Bethany was sliding out the cab passenger door. Gary quickly left the cab and met Bethany in front of it. They walked together toward the entrance and then stopped before going in.

"Would you mind…" Gary began to ask, but Bethany stood on tiptoes and gave him a quick kiss on the lips.

"Thanks for such a nice time. And bringing the parts."

"It was my pleasure, believe me," Gary said, wanting to bend down and kiss her more deeply, but he held himself back. He had no intent to scare her away now that he'd found her. "Next time we'll fly somewhere and do the same."

Bethany nodded and then watched for a few seconds as Gary reluctantly went into the terminal. Even here the security was tight, so Bethany went back to the motorhome and left the parking lot.

She parked in an out of the way place, turned so she could see the runway. It was a good half an hour before she saw what she was sure was the Lake Aircraft Seawolf taxi out to the runway. She watched as it made the takeoff run and then leaped into the sky. Bethany sighed, put the motorhome into gear again and left the area, headed for the Interstate to continue her northbound trip.

That evening, parked in a campground, Bethany tossed and turned for a long time before falling asleep, thinking about how everything she had planned had changed when she met Gary Martain.

## CHAPTER THREE

-

Speaking to Gary every few days on the telephone, Bethany and Gary continued their courtship long distance, as Bethany continued her way northward into the LP and then the UP of Michigan.

She headed west then, to check along the shore of Lake Superior for likely spots for a bug-out location. She was determined now that any place she would consider would have to have lake or major river access for Gary's Seawolf. Every choice she was making now was influenced in some way by Gary's presence in her life.

But the reason for her trip came to the forefront of her thoughts one Monday morning as she was listening to the news. She'd been following the news on the off-shore drilling rig disaster in the Gulf of Mexico. But until she heard the speculation that it had been a North Korean suicide team in a mini-sub that had disabled the blowout preventers on the well a mile under the surface of the sea and then launched incendiary torpedoes at the rig, finally blowing themselves and the mini-sub up to finish the job, the thought had not occurred to her.

If it was true, and just the presence of the new news blackout on the subject indicated to her that it was, and then the things she was preparing for were becoming even more important to prepare for.

She called Gary and talked to him about the situation.

"You can come back here," Gary immediately said. "I have a good place here, and the place in the Ozarks."

"Not yet," Bethany said. "But thank you. I was kind of counting on that possibility when I called. What else do you think is happening? Or going to happen? I'm afraid it's going to be one of those mega-disasters that TOM and Jerry D write about."

"I don't know, Bethany," Gary said. "I'm afraid of the same thing. I had a discussion with one of the forum members on another board about some things that are happening. It got a bit of tin-foil hattishness about it, but the more I think about it, the more I think it is possible."

"What is it?" Bethany asked.

"Well... It is farfetched... but here goes. What if, say, that some of the secret programs that are whispered about from time to time are reality, not just wild speculation? Things like HAARP? Weather creation, modification, and control? Creating... or more likely, just triggering earthquakes where the forces of nature are just right? Volcanoes, too.

"What if the North Koreans, perhaps with Chinese help, are retaliating for the series of earthquakes and cyclones that area has endured recently? Perhaps in retaliation in turn of the great numbers of hurricanes that have been hitting the US over the last few years, under control of some type by the Chinese.

"Hurricanes that didn't follow the expected path. And appeared one after the other. Katrina, for example. And the deep sea quakes that have caused the tsunamis of late."

"Oh, Gary!" Bethany said, keeping a sharp eye on the road as she drove and talked through the Blue Tooth phone. "That's really out there."

"I know. But add in the rumors of the FEMA camps already set up. The government building new, bigger, and better bunker systems for the cream of the crop in government. Them buying out Mountain House freeze-dried food stocks. Canned butter and cheese. You probably know of how hard it was to find some of those things here while back."

"Yes. Yes, I do remember. I had to wait six months to get some things I wanted about that time."

"Huge orders of ammunition by the government for domestic use and shortages for civilians. Things are still somewhat difficult to get, though it's better now than last year. The bringing in and training of US military forces for use against domestic civil unrest under direct control of the President."

"I'm still listening," Bethany said when Gary's voice faded away.

"And there are the other weather patterns. The terrible winter in the northeast. The flooding southeast. The droughts out west."

"But those could all be natural," Bethany protested.

"Could be. What if they aren't? What if the major nations are already at war with these kinds of weapons? Weather and tectonic weapons. Based here or in space, maybe. That the powers that be aren't telling the populations of their own countries.

"I mean, there are the Illuminati, Bilderbergers, Tri-lateral Commission, the Round Table, the New World Order, the Security and Prosperity Partnership of North America (SPP), the UN's attempts to take sovereignty away from nations... I don't know. There could be more I'm not thinking off. "

"That's a lot to take in, Gary. Give me a few days to think about it."

"Of course. Hearing myself say it, it even seems even more incredible than when I was talking to that forum member about it."

"But if it is true..."

"Yeah. What if? I'm worried about this... you... If I might be so presumptuous, I want you to know you have a place in my shelter here or the place in the Ozarks. No questions asked and no strings."

"Oh, Gary! That is so nice! Thank you! Believe me I will take you up on the invitation if I think things are getting out of hand. Or… More out of hand. They already are out of hand, I'm afraid."

There was silence for a moment, and then Bethany made a snap decision. "Gary, what lake is your place on?"

"You mean in the Ozarks?"

"Yes."

"Table Rock Lake. Off FR-2150. North of that section of Mark Twain National Forest."

"I see," Bethany said. "I may just drift down that way… Take a look around. I need to go that way anyway, to pick up my trailer."

"That would be great, Bethany! I'll meet you there any time you say. Show you around."

"That's okay, Gary. It'll be a while before I get there. Let me look around on my own for a while."

"Well… If that's what you want. But if you want anything, just tell me, will you?"

"Of course. I think I'll go pick up my trailer. It should be finished now. On the way down. I'll talk to you again in a few days. Okay?"

"Certainly. I look forward to it. And Bethany…"

"Yes, Gary?"

"Be careful?"

"I will, Gary. I will."

Bethany ended the call and concentrated on the road as she came up on a heavy string of traffic.

Gary slowly lowered the receiver and hung up, feeling vaguely uneasy. He'd not really put everything together before, like he just did with Bethany. But it was worrisome. More so than anything he'd worried about before. It was just too intangible to get a real handle on. "Bethany must think I'm nuts," Gary whispered.

He quickly put his salesman's face on when the receptionist ushered in a potential customer.

Gary wanted to call Bethany several times during the next few days, but he didn't want to push. She'd said she would call. She would. On her own timetable. And that was the only one that counted in Gary's eyes.

He filled his time between customers and his duties at the other dealerships on the high speed internet in the office. Looking for confirmation of his suspicions or something, anything, to completely disprove them. It is almost impossible to prove a negative, but any reasonable explanation for some of the things he'd brought up with Bethany would ease his mind.

But the weather events just kept getting worse. Another offshore rig mysteriously went down with loss of all life and two more wells were pouring oil into the Gulf. The Gulf Stream had picked up some of the oil and not only the Gulf

Coast was getting hit hard with it, the Atlantic Coast of Florida was also getting it, to a smaller degree.

Already there were hurricanes building in the Atlantic. Where they natural? Gary and Bethany both wondered. Even if not created, were they being directed by humans bent on catastrophic damage and the huge expense of clean up and rebuilding in the Southeastern US?

And now reports were coming in that the Yellowstone Caldera was acting up. Even worse, in some ways, was the extent of tectonic happenings on the Kamchatka Peninsula in Far East Russia. Particularly worrisome was the activity at Ksudach Volcano. The two huge lake filled calderas were both showing significant activity.

Were either or both of the calderas to erupt as they had in past history, naturally or with help from human hands, the damage would be negligible for Asia, but the effects would cross the North Pacific and impact Alaska, Southwestern Canada, and Northwestern states of the USA. Would the Chinese, if they could, trigger such a blast, on Russian soil? Gary and Bethany had the same question on their minds as the story continued to develop.

Bethany, all thoughts of finding any property up north now gone, made a beeline, or as close as she could to one, toward Missouri and the Ozarks. She stopped at the custom trailer manufacturer's place and picked up her trailer, after giving it a good inspection. With things going the way they were, she wasn't sure she'd be able to have anything corrected if it showed up later.

But the trailer was fine. Just as she'd planned it out with the owner of the shop she'd picked out on the internet. Her recently customized GMC Sonoma High Rider four-wheel-drive-compact pickup truck rode securely near the center of the three axle trailer, behind the cargo compartment that made up the front of the trailer. As wide as the motorhome, at eight feet, six inches, there were cargo and tool boxes along the sides, too, with just enough room to get the Sonoma's driver's side door open and closed when it was in position. The trailer matched the styling of the motorhome perfectly.

A pair of RV propane saddle tanks like the one mounted on the Topkick motorhome were mounted to the outside of the frame, under the front body of the trailer. In addition, there were two one-hundred-pound cylinders on a platform rack on the front of the trailer. Beside them was a battery box with two large twelve-volt deep cycle maintenance free AGM batteries.

Two forty-two gallon waste water totes rode in racks on the front of the trailer, too. They would be used to hold the contents of the black water and gray water tanks in the motorhome until they could all be emptied at a dump station, or the contents buried, if need be.

Out of sight under the raised deck for the Sonoma were three diesel fuel tanks, carrying spare fuel for the two vehicles. Two insulated tanks with heaters run off an inverter connected to the batteries contained fresh water for the motorhome. Like the diesel tanks, the water tanks had twelve-volt transfer pumps installed. An array of solar panels on top of the cargo compartment kept the batteries charged when the trailer wasn't connected to the motorhome.

Besides the two spares for the motorhome mounted on the rear bumper of it, the trailer carried six more spares of the same tires and wheels for the motorhome and the trailer, which used the same ones.

Mounted on heavy tracks, two large cargo boxes rode behind the Sonoma. When it came time to load onto or unload the pickup from the trailer, the side panels of the rear of the trailer hinged down and the cargo boxes were slid outboard enough to let the Sonoma pass through between them. At the very rear, the counterbalanced ramps could be lowered or raised easily to get the Sonoma on or off the trailer.

The loaded trailer put the combination at the upper limit of total vehicle plus trailer weight limit of the Topkick 5500. But it was within spec, and the weight distributing hitch and brakes on all six wheels made for a safe package. Once she had a chance to cautiously practice with the trailer attached, Bethany learned that both she and the motorhome could handle the weight and length of the trailer safely.

When she stopped at the truck stop, she winced at the fuel bill after filling the motorhome's rear sixty gallon tank, and the three tanks in the trailer. "At least the twin fifty step tanks were still full," she muttered. She dumped the holding tanks and filled up the motorhome and trailer water tanks, and then pulled over to the propane fill station and topped off the tank in the motorhome and filled the two saddle LP tanks and the two one-hundred-pound cylinders. She winced again. "Sheesh! Good thing this is platinum," she said as she put the American Express card back into her wallet.

After a stop at a regular grocery store to pick up groceries, Bethany headed for home. She wanted to pick up a few things there before she went to the Ozarks to look for a piece of property. It was now a foregone conclusion that she would be settling somewhere near Gary's place on Table Rock Lake.

Three days later she was home, making carefully thought out decisions on what all to take with her. If, for some reason, she couldn't get back, she wanted certain key elements of her prep supplies with her.

Finally satisfied with the items and the way they were loaded in the motorhome and trailer, Bethany fired up the diesel engine of the Topkick Motorhome and headed southeast for the Missouri Ozarks.

They'd been talking every day or so, and Gary was anxious to meet up with Bethany on the lake. But her comments about scoping things out herself kept his offer to show her around unrepeated.

Bethany found a good campground where she could leave the motorhome and trailer and take the Sonoma to run around in. Two days later she had a lead on a piece of property that had to be fairly close to Gary's, if she'd understood his description of where it was. It was smaller than she wanted, but the real estate agent made a few quick enquiries and found out that the property adjacent to the one Bethany was considering was possibly for sale. For the right price.

"Right price, huh?" Bethany said, looking at the agent. Bethany stated an amount and told the agent, "If you can get it for me for that, I'll take both properties."

"I'll certainly do my best!" said the young man, eager to make his first big sale.

Bethany went back to the campground and settled in to wait to hear from the agent. She called Gary on an impulse. "Found a place, I think. Were you serious about flying down and help me look around?"

"Absolutely!" Gary replied, trying to keep the pure joy out of his words. "I'll be down there tonight!"

"Now Gary," Bethany said, chidingly. "It's already late. You will not fly down here tonight. Tomorrow, or even the next day is fine. There are some details I have to take care of first, anyway."

"Oh. Well, okay. But I'll come down tomorrow. Perhaps I can help with the details. Let me give you precise directions to my property and you can meet me there. Is that okay?"

"Sure. Sounds like a plan. Let me get a pen and my pad."

Bethany started smiling broadly halfway through the directions. She'd been right. She was close. Not next to his property, but only five lots down from where the lots she wanted were, unless she was completely off on the directions.

She took her time getting ready the next day. It would be mid afternoon before Gary could arrive. She went into Branson to look around. She was more than a little pleased when she found a regular karaoke operation in one of resort centers.

A few hours later she watched Gary taxi the Seawolf up onto shore on his property. She hurried forward and was giving him a bear hug as soon as he was out of the plane and had it secured.

"Wow. I'm really glad to see you, too!" Gary said. "Where's the motorhome? You rented a car... er... truck?"

"No. The Sonoma is mine. That is one of the reasons for the trailer I commissioned to have made. It's my running around vehicle when I don't want to drive the motorhome, especially with the trailer attached."

"Oh. Didn't realize." Gary looked back at Bethany. "Well? What do you think of my place? You look around some?"

"Sure did. Yep. It's a place. Not much to it except trees, grass, and the beach."

"Yeah. I plan..." Gary quickly said, intending to tell Bethany all about his plans for the property he'd been considering lately.

"I'm joking, Gary," Bethany said, putting a finger to his lips, her eyes twinkling.

"Oh. Okay. But I do have plans. Plans I'm going to start following through with. You've been keeping up with the news?"

Bethany's face fell. "Yeah. It's all bad news seems like. Depressing."

"True. Now, I need to find a bathroom and then we can go looking for property for you."

Bethany smiled. "Sure. Come on. The campground isn't too far away. We can go there, if you don't mind freshening up in the Topkick."

"Oh, no. That would be fine."

"Okay. Let's go."

"Some truck, for a compact," Gary said, putting an overnight bag in the back of the Sonoma, admiring the truck as he did. It was tricked out nicely for prepping, he decided after taking in the attributes of the heavily customized truck.

The two talked quietly about the world situation on the way to the campground. Just before they arrived, Gary said, "I'm selling two of the dealerships. I'm going to put the money into a shelter and cabin here, equipped and supplied for a long term stay. If you wanted, you could forgo your purchase and take a spot in my shelter if something happens. You'd be more than welcome.

"And I mean it, Bethany. No strings. We're becoming friends and I don't want to jeopardize that in any way."

Bethany glanced over at Gary for a moment, a softness in her look and voice when she spoke that touched Gary's heart. "Oh, Gary. That is such a tempting offer. And I agree. We're becoming friends. At times I want to take it further, but there are times I think about my independence and don't want the complications of a partner and marriage. I hope you can understand. I need a place for myself first. A home. Before I can consider anything else."

It pained Gary a bit, but he was learning about Bethany. And one of the things he'd learned and loved was her sense of independence. The accomplishments she'd made on her own. He swallowed the lump in his throat. "I understand, Bethany. I'll not speak of it again until you bring it up."

Her bright smile at him cheered Gary and he let the idea he'd come up with before coming down go back into the recesses of his mind. There would be a time in the future when the plan could be implemented. For now, just being around Bethany whenever he could was enough.

As Gary freshened up, Bethany put together a light meal, having learned of Gary's propensity to skip meals when he was involved in something.

"What's this?" he asked when he came out of the head. "I was planning on taking you out tonight."

"That's fine," Bethany replied, setting two plates on the dinette table. "But dollars to donuts you didn't have any lunch and possibly not any breakfast. You need something to tide you over until we go into Branson. I found a nice karaoke place where we can eat and talk and then do a few songs."

"Oh. Well, okay. That sounds good." Gary began eating.

Bethany smiled. He was hungry. Her cell phone rang and she stood up and moved to the rear of the coach for privacy.

Gary could see the excitement in her face when Bethany sat down across from him again. "Good news?"

"I'll say. But it is a secret for right now. I'll tell you about it when we leave."

"Well… Okay."

Bethany laughed at the expression on Gary's face. He didn't like waiting. But then her look changed slightly. But he was waiting for her. Patiently. "I won't keep you in suspense for long. Finish your snack and we'll be on our way. Unless you want to nap for a while before tonight. You know how we are when we get into karaoke."

"No, I'm fine," Gary said quickly. He wanted to know what the surprise was. Sleep could wait. He quickly finished the remaining fruit and cheese on the plate. He looked at Bethany expectantly.

"Okay, okay!" she laughed. "I'm done. Give me a moment to put things away."

Gary was up and put the plates, glasses, and flatware into the dishwasher while Bethany put the remaining food in containers and put them in the refrigerator. The occasional touch of hip to hip or arm to arm was comfortable for Bethany.

"Okay. I guess we're ready," she said a few moments later.

The two went out to the Sonoma and got in.

"Uh… not to be a back seat driver, especially since you have a nav system in here, too, but this isn't the best way to get to Branson. I don't really need to check on the plane, either," Gary said when the next turn took them down the road behind his property.

Bethany turned into an empty, heavily wooded lot a few seconds later. "Welcome to my new home place. Or soon to be, anyway. Confirmed the deal on the phone while we were eating."

"This is only a few lots down from my place!" Gary said, looking at Bethany in surprise.

"Yep. 'Tis. I thought you might be pleased. Actually, this lot and the one next to it. I'm buying both. I like plenty of space."

There were tears in Gary's eyes when he looked over at Bethany again.

"Why are you all teary?" she asked when she looked at him.

"Just… it means much to me that you want to be close."

Bethany leaned forward and wiped his tears away. Then she kissed him lightly on the lips. "Yes. I do. Perhaps closer, later, but that has to wait for a while."

"I know," Gary said. "Do you have plans for a house and shelter yet?"

Bethany straightened up and laughed. "Oh, you! I have some ideas. But it'll be a bit before I turn them into reality. Have to actually sign the deal and go through escrow before I can do much. I'll be working on plans the entire time."

"I'm planning on buying one of the turnkey systems from Radius Engineering," Gary said. "A bit of a wait, and expensive, but I just don't have the time to tie up keeping an eye on a builder."

It was getting dark and Bethany got them back on the road, headed this time to Branson for their evening out together. "I think I want to build my own. And a house. Both with long term self-sufficiency in mind. Won't have a working farm here, but I might buy one and become a windshield farmer. Do it on shares with an established farm."

"I hadn't thought about that," Gary said. "That's a good plan. Need an investment partner?"

"That might be arranged," Bethany said, without having to think about it. "I want something fairly traditional. Small beef and dairy herd, hogs, chickens. Horses maybe, for riding… and working, if things do get really bad. Grow our own feed for the stock and hay. Grains for the stock as well as human consumption. On site storage for everything. That's one of the things I picked up from a couple of Jerry's stories.

"Perhaps even get a farm large enough to do all that and be a truck farm operation, too, to help pay the expenses."

"Sounds to me like you've put quite a bit of thought into this," Gary said, watching Bethany as she drove. He loved looking at her.

"Well, a little, I guess. When I was growing up in the city, I dreamed of a rural life. I've discovered I'm not really cut out to be a farmer, but I am good planner and organizer. I like to consider myself a leader, rather than a manager, but that is for others to say."

"Oh, I suspect your employees all considered you a leader, not a manager."

"Well, perhaps. But moot, now. No more employees to lead."

"At least not at the moment," Gary said with a smile. "That will change, I expect, fairly soon."

"We'll see. We'll see," replied Bethany. "Here we are. Hope you like this place."

"Actually I do. I've been here before. Never done karaoke here, though."

Several hours later, laughing, the two came out of the place, arm in arm. "I had a great time tonight, Gary," Bethany said. She stopped by the Sonoma and stood on tiptoes again to give Gary a light kiss.

"So did I," Gary said, opening the door of the Sonoma for Bethany. "I haven't laughed so hard in a long time."

The two chatted companionably on the drive back to the campground. There had been no discussion about where Gary would stay. It was just understood by both that he'd share the motorhome with Bethany again.

And share again, they did, with Gary in the rear bunk and Bethany in her normal spot in the overhead bunk over the cab of the Topkick.

And again Gary woke up to the smells of breakfast being prepared. But this time the satellite TV was on and Bethany was watching it as much as she was the breakfast on the stove.

Gary chanced giving Bethany a kiss on the cheek. As he started the motion she lifted her cheek to accept it. "Bad news today," she said, using the pancake turner in her hand to point at the flat screen TV mounted on a swing arm on the wall of the motorhome.

"What's going on?" Gary asked, taking the plate with the stack of pancakes on it.

"Looks like another big hurricane is headed directly for the Gulf, right over the point the oil is still gushing. They've already stopped the drilling to relieve the pressure on the first well, so they can cap it. Had to evacuate that rig. If the hurricane is anything like it is shaping up to be, there's going to be crude oil on a lot more than just the shore lines of the Gulf."

"And China just had another big earthquake."

"Coincidence?" Gary asked, pouring the rich pure maple syrup over the buttered pancakes.

"No one is speculating. This hurricane has been building for three days. I don't think the administration is allowing any of the kind of speculation we've done about all the different situations."

"Probably not. Wow. These are good!"

Bethany turned around and said, "All prep items I'm rotating through. Even the maple syrup is reconstituted freeze-dried crystals. And the butter is butter powder with a bit of coconut oil added.

"You sure know your way around a prepper's kitchen."

"I have a few domestic skills," Bethany replied. "Just don't ask me to sew a button on a shirt."

Gary laughed. "I'll keep that in mind. What is on the agenda today? I don't have to go back until tomorrow. I thought I'd be showing you around the lake, looking for property, but you've outdone all I could have accomplished on that project."

Bethany sat down with a plate of pancakes and added butter and syrup. "I don't know. Oh. Yes I do. How about a ride in the Seawolf?"

Gary smiled. "You did say you wanted a chance to handle it. I think that can be arranged. I'll need to fuel up at the end of the trip for my trip back to the city."

Bethany wondered why he didn't say 'home', instead of 'the city'. "That's okay with me," she said. "Just as long as I get to try the controls. It does have dual controls?"

"Yep. So we'll do that, then. I hate to say it, but I'll need to turn in early. I need to be back at the dealership before closing again."

"No karaoke tonight then."

"I'm afraid not. But I'll take you out for dinner, if you'll allow me."

"Sure," Bethany laughed. "I just committed a tremendous amount of my hard earned money for the foreseeable future. You can definitely pay for dinner. Unless you want me to cook? I don't mind. Really."

"No. Better not get too domestic, I think."

"Good point," Bethany agreed. "Such things lead to other things better not contemplated yet."

"Exactly."

It was over a month before Gary was able to fly down again to see Bethany. He was amazed at the progress she'd made developing her property. She'd thinned out the commercial grade heavy tree growth, or actually, had a timber firm do it, cutting brush and mulching it and the unwanted tree waste that wasn't suitable as firewood as the process progressed.

Other than a few specific trees she wanted to keep for a very long time, the rest of her forested ground would slowly be transformed into a coppicing woodland, with suitable firewood trees, mostly ash and hickory planted in place of the odd lot of natural growth making up the forest at the moment as the trees were harvested for firewood and lumber.

She took seasoned timbers and lumber in compensation, rather than cash, and had the mulch and firewood stockpiled on the property. "Always thinking ahead," Gary had told her when she explained what she was doing.

That thinking ahead had turned into a firm plan of action. While she enjoyed the prep and PAW stories on the prep forums, she took nothing for granted and checked out in detail the recommendations that the writers often gave in story form. Even TOM's and Jerry's ideas were thoroughly researched online before she chose to use any of them.

Once she had the site plan done and approved, the well and septic systems were put in. One section of the forest that had been intentionally clear cut was converted to a large orchard containing both fruit and nut trees, with the most mature trees she could find, some of them wild trees that one fortunate farmer had on property he was reclaiming. She would have crops from the trees at least two or three years earlier than if she'd gone the cheap route and planted seedlings, or even young saplings.

The same farmer put her in touch with his brother, who had a farm in need of some investment money. Bethany met with the young family, but held off making a decision until Gary could come down and talk to them, as well.

Both made it clear that the property had to be turned into a post apocalypse world sustainable operation capable of feeding a moderate number of people besides the principle shareholders: the farm family, Bethany and Gary.

Bethany continued to check on the progress at the farm as she worked on her own place. Things were coming along nicely. Even Gary's place was finally getting converted to a bug-out location.

Taking a lesson from Bethany, he had the large lot logged, taking only specific trees, except in the area where the shelter, house, and out buildings would be. That area was cleared completely and planted with grass to keep the soil in place until final work could be completed.

Bethany oversaw that operation for Gary. He was having difficulty selling his second and third automobile and truck dealerships, due to the economy. Activity pretty much stopped when late fall turned into a very early winter, with lots of rain, then ice, and finally heavy snowfall. Not unheard of in the region, but disturbing none the less.

It seemed the weather all over the world was erratic and mostly terrible. Where storms weren't demolishing things, long periods of unending sun and heat were taking their toll. Climate change was now the catch word, having replaced global warming that didn't appear to be as relevant as previously thought; especially the human caused aspect of it.

Additionally, there were the continued series of tectonic events. Earthquakes and volcanic eruptions were occurring all over the world. Gary and Bethany continued to discuss the possibility that at least some of the events were indeed caused by human intervention using new techniques talked about in whispers.

Even some of the forums were avoiding the discussions, mostly accusation, actually, editing or removing posts and entire threads. That came about after three of the most vitriolic of sites suddenly were no longer online, and some of their supporters seemed to fall off the face of the earth.

Politically, the world was in just as much of a mess as it was nature wise. Every major power and minor was up in arms, sometime literally, at the announcement the US President made indicating that if the disrupted and restarted drilling to stop the oil flowing from the damaged well failed, a tactical nuke would be used to shut the well down.

There were immediate remarks that if the US used a nuke, then all bets were off and court was open for anyone having them to use them, for "defense of their shores and borders from natural or other potential disasters, not limited to direct attacks."

"You think they'll use the nuke?" Bethany asked Gary.

"I just don't know. I do wish we were further along in our preparations."

"They start the excavation for the basements and the shelter this Monday. And your guys say just another week and they'll start the prep work for your installation."

"That's good at least. Two months, perhaps?" Gary asked.

"No way. Concrete has to cure, I have a lot more concrete in mine, but it all takes about the same time to cure."

"Didn't TOM say something about something that makes the concrete stronger and set up quicker?"

"Oh. I think you're right. I'll check into it and get back to you. How are things going there?"

"Well, better. I've got the paperwork ready for one of the dealerships, and have a couple of legitimate inquiries for the other."

"Good. I miss you."

"I miss you. I'll talk to you in a day or two," Gary said.

He waited for Bethany to say good-bye and hang up before he did. With a sigh he went back to work. Selling vehicles in this economy was difficult.

Bethany did some research on the internet and then talked to her intended concrete supplier. There were additives to do exactly what TOM had written about, including making the concrete stronger, more crack resistant, and more waterproof, besides setting up more quickly so construction could commence much sooner than normal concrete. It just added to the expense, and required some special safety precautions.

Fortunately, the spring rains were fairly light, considering the terrible winter, and construction picked up quickly. With the well in and a solar pump supplying fresh water, and the holding tanks emptying into the new septic system, Bethany was living on site in the motorhome.

She was out every day, helping where she could, making decisions and clarifying things on the prints and drawings she'd done on the computer, and working on her own small projects around the property.

Bethany felt like she was in a race, one she couldn't afford to lose. Every morning she got up and watched the news, and then browsed the Internet before she would start to work, things were more involved and complicated. The rhetoric of the more aggressive nations was becoming more and more warlike.

Gary was down for the installation of the Radius Engineering shelter package he'd ordered. Even he was a bit overwhelmed at the sight of the huge hole in the ground required for the ECD-60 based shelter system, set up for twelve people. With the addition of the underground vehicle garage and access shaft, generator and support pod, spiral stair main entrance, and sloped emergency exit/entrance, the excavation was extensive, with dirt stockpiled in huge mounds for backfill. Only the periscope mast didn't take up additional room.

Another excavation, for the installation of a partially buried, partially earth bermed concrete Quonset style hanger for the Seawolf, with room for a second aircraft, was fairly large, but nothing like the shelter complex.

As summer came, Bethany counted her blessings. The major work requiring excavation and back filling was done at both places, just before a series of storms came through, dropping inch upon inch of rainfall in the area.

The work on the surface structures continued, between rains, with the finish work inside Bethany's shelter done when it was raining. Gary's more or less conventional bungalow was completed before Bethany's house and the rest of the out buildings were completed.

Bethany had gone all out. Though she was careful not to refer to the grouping of earth sheltered buildings as a compound, that was, in fact, what it was. All the buildings, including the huge garage, had a basement, and all the basements were connected with tunnels to each other, with three tunnels accessing the primary shelter. Even the large greenhouse had a bermed support structure at one end, with a basement.

The buildings were also connected above ground with either walls or tall berms incorporating fighting positions in case of an attack. There'd been no way to do what they wanted without some locals knowing about it, even with many of the work crews being hired from other towns some distance away. If the worst happened, Bethany fully expected to have to defend the place. She wanted to be ready.

The entire complex was surrounded with barrier fencing incorporating blackberry brambles and wild rose brambles as additional barriers to easy entrance. The gates were heavy and crash resistant, including the one opening toward the lake, where a structure much like Gary's hanger was built for the boats she intended to get. It, like the other structures, had a tunnel connection, though there was no basement, per se.

A short, but deep, canal connected the boathouse to the lake. A sturdy floating dock system was built for use during normal times. When things were calm, she intended to enjoy the lake, having been a frustrated fisherwoman all her adult life, never seeming to have time to do it. So she put in an order for a three boats, hoping there would be time for their production and delivery before anything happened.

Bethany was slowly making friends in the area, and had hired several people to help her do some of the physical work around the place. Greenhouse work, cleaning, taking care of the grounds, garden, and orchard. She was just as careful selecting the employees as she was of making friends.

It couldn't be said that she only became friends with people because of particular skills that they had, but the degree of closeness did depend a bit on the skill set the person brought to the friendship. Though preppers were a closed mouth lot, making it difficult to find out some one was, in fact a prepper, Bethany was a master at getting people to talk about themselves.

She cultivated those friendships carefully, as friends, not wanting to try and set up a mutual aid group. She'd tried that once. There were too many Chief's and not enough Indians. As the months passed, Bethany wound up with a small group of people she liked, respected, and felt she could trust. To a degree, anyway.

As winter set in, the final steps of preparation were taken, with deliveries of provisions and fuel for long term self-sufficiency delivered and put away, the fuel treated with PRI fuel treatment products. The in-house supplies would have to last between the time of the event, if there was one, and when the farm could start producing food again.

The farm project had come along nicely, with the additional work there completed shortly after the lake properties were. Gary came down after Bethany called him a few days before Christmas. "Things are ready to start using,

Gary. You want to spend Christmas here? I know you have commitments at the dealership, but…"

"Not enough to not come down for our first Christmas together and to celebrate the completion of our plans. I'll make arrangements to be away for the entire holiday season. I deserve it, and I want it. I'm even thinking of selling this dealership, too, and finding a business down there to operate."

Bethany was smiling. The times apart were getting harder and harder, with the times together short and sweet. She'd already decided to accept when Gary asked her to marry him. And she was sure he would, soon, especially if he actually moved here.

## CHAPTER FOUR

-

Christmas was a fun time in Branson when Gary came down. He and Bethany, both worn out from the stresses of getting things ready before something could happen, spent a lot of time seeing the sights.

Things around the world seemed to have calmed down. There hadn't been an earthquake, volcano, or flood in over two months. No place was having severe weather, the aggressive talk between nations was slacking off, and the well in the Gulf of Mexico was finally capped, without the use of a nuke.

Things were looking up, and Bethany and Gary intended to enjoy the time, without worrying about surviving a disaster. Bethany dropped a couple of hints, and Gary asked her to marry him.

She gasped at the ring he slid onto her finger while he was down on one knee. It wasn't that it was large, for it wasn't, she'd seen before.

Reluctantly, Gary went back to the dealership. He had a few things to accomplish before he moved to the lake. But the two talked every day, planning the wedding, having set the date for the coming June.

But that idyllic time was the calm before the storm—both literally and figuratively.

The entire middle of the US was being hit with the worst spring storm on record, with many places getting freezing rain, including the Ozarks. And things heated up overseas, almost simultaneously. North Korea, having had the success with the destruction of the drilling platform in the Gulf of Mexico, without any obvious retaliation from the US, began massing men and matériel on the border with South Korea.

China looked like it would support the action, massing troops just north of the border with North Korea. And anti-Japanese rhetoric was becoming common place in open sources in China.

Almost as if they were asking for trouble, Taiwan announced a new referendum on declaring their independence from mainland China. Days later China was building up its forces on the northern North Korea border, as well as the southern border.

Five countries announced within days of each other of their entry into the nuclear weapon club. Brazil, Venezuela, Iran, Japan, and Myanmar. All claimed to have weapons ready for use and warned enemies that they wouldn't hesitate to use them in a preemptive attack if provoked.

The UN was in an uproar, with accusations flying every which way, with counter-accusations coming hard on their heels.

As the recovery from the storms in the US started, three massive blizzards formed, one in the previously hard hit northeast US, and one along the Canadian border with Montana, North Dakota, and Minnesota. The third was barreling down the west side of the Rockies, affecting Idaho, Nevada, and Utah.

For the first time, the US accused the Russians and Chinese of weather modification warfare.

Both countered with accusations that the US had an earthquake and volcano triggering weapon. The US response was that Russia and China were the ones with tectonic weapons.

True or not, when China suffered yet another massive 8.0 earthquake, in the midst of a winter storm of their own, the Chinese leadership put the entire nation on a war footing, with not so veiled threats that the US was close to being destroyed.

Russia fell silent when the Kamchatka calderas, rumbling for months, suddenly erupted in an explosion that rivaled past Tambora and Yellowstone eruptions. Three days later heavy ashfalls began in southern Alaska, western Canada, and Washington and Oregon states.

Gary called Bethany and said he was sending a couple of people down with his belongings. He'd just collected for the sale of his last dealership and had converted most of it to preps, with enough left over to fund a business, if things got better.

They didn't. Three days later, when satellite reports of China fueling ICBMs and activating their Civil Defense system reached the President, the US went to high alert, with every communication outlet available broadcasting or printing instructions on how to create fallout shelter space and what to do in the case of nuclear attack.

Dozens of potential target cities in the US saw huge impromptu and unauthorized evacuations start taking place, despite pleas from FEMA for people to shelter locally.

Gary managed to get a call through, after a dozen tries. "I'm coming that way," he said. "My guys should be getting there today or tomorrow. Set them up in the bungalow, will you, if I don't get there first?"

"Of course," Bethany replied. "Anything special you want done?"

"Just try to get everything moved into the house before things get bad, if they do."

"I'm afraid they already are. Be careful, please. Now that I have you I don't want to lose you. I love you."

"I love you, too, Babe. Nothing is going to keep me from getting to you for this." Both had more to say, but the connection went down and they closed their respective cell phones.

Bethany secured everything at her place, including putting the Topkick and trailer in the garage, leaving the Sonoma out for use. Though she had replacement parts for the Topkick, there was no reason to risk it being taken down by EMP. The Cummins 4BT diesel in the Sonoma was impervious to EMP, even if some of the other electronics on board were fried.

The three boats, delivered over five days of the last week, were moved from the docks into the earth sheltered boat house.

Bethany went to Gary's and entered the hanger using her remote that Gary had insisted she take. She'd given him one for her place in return. With a NOAA NWS SAME alert radio clipped to her belt on one side, cell phone in a blouse pocket, and the Para Ordnance P-14 holstered on her hip, Bethany got the access doors to the hanger open and made sure all Gary would have to do would be turn the Seawolf around on the hanger apron, before they pushed it inside.

She'd just finished that task when a horn sounded from the front of the property. She ran around the bungalow, checking carefully first though. It was Gary's friends with his belongings. Her eyes widened when three identical GMC Yukon's, pulling tandem axle trailers, two box and one open bed, and two large rental trucks, also with box trailers, large ones, lined up on the street, waiting to pull onto the property.

Bethany opened the passage gate and went to talk to the driver of the lead Yukon. When she got close she recognized Stefano, the head parts man at the home dealership Gary had owned.

She looked into the Yukon. A woman was in the front passenger seat, and a baby in a car carrier was asleep in the back seat. There was a worried look on Stefano's face. "It's okay, isn't it? Mr. Martain said to come here with his gear. That we would be safe here."

"Of course. Let me get the gate." She hesitated a moment. "The others… are they going to stay, too?"

"Yes. All of us. Mr. Martain said it was okay. I'll call him and he…"

"No need. I know I can trust you. And I don't think you can get Gary now, anyway. The phones seem to be out. I'll get the gate."

The gate was an electrically operated two panel security gate controlled from the gate, a hardwired control in the bungalow, and a pair of remotes, of which Bethany had one. Not willing to give too much away until Gary got there, she went back inside the fence and used the controls there to slide the gates open, instead of using the remote.

The five tow vehicles pulled in, with their trailers, and the drivers and passengers all grouped around Bethany. There were six adults and four children, comprising three families. Bethany quickly got the women and children into the bungalow so they could use the facilities. The convoy had not stopped the last hundred miles and bladders were full. She led the men to the surface garage to use the bathroom there.

The bungalow was well stocked with food and Bethany put Stefano's wife, Angelet, in charge of the domestic side of things to get some food prepared for all of them. Bethany went back outside and directed the men, plus two of the women that came out to help, where to put the various things from the tow vehicles and trailers.

The group was well equipped to make the move, with hand trucks, dollies, and ramps. Everyone wore gloves. The two rental trucks both had folding lift tailgates, which made unloading them much easier, as they carried the heavy items.

Not entirely sure where Gary would want everything, and not ready to open up the shelter until Gary got there, some of the items went to the spacious earth sheltered surface garage. Bethany left plenty of room in the garage for vehicles.

Halfway through the unloading, while everyone was taking a break for food and water, Bethany heard Gary buzz the bungalow and ran outside to help get the plane into the hanger after he landed.

Stefano went with her, and the two stood and watched as Gary taxied up the new concrete approach ramp to the apron in front of the hanger. Bethany could see into the cockpit. There were at least two additional people with Gary.

Gary shut the engine down and climbed out of the Seawolf. There were two more people, one male and one female. Both lent a hand to get the Seawolf turned around, and then all of them pushed it back into the hanger.

No sooner had they cleared the apron when the sound of a helicopter filled the air. "He's with me," Gary told Bethany when a sleek looking Sikorsky S-76D in bright livery touched down on the apron.

The pilot had swung the craft around before he landed, so all the group had to do was roll the helicopter into the hanger in front of the Seawolf. Gary lowered the double set of rolling doors and the lights came on inside the hanger.

"Introductions later," Gary said as the newcomers looked at Bethany and Stefano. "How's the unloading going?"

"Good," Bethany said. "About half done. I'm putting some things in the garage, since I didn't know for sure where you would want them."

"That's good. Is the shelter garage open?"

Bethany shook her head.

"Would you open it up and go ahead and take down the Yukon's? We'll park the rentals in the surface garage. I'm going to put some stuff in your Sonoma."

Bethany nodded and ran off to take care of the task as those that had come with Gary began to unload the things they'd brought in the aircraft. Stefano went back to the vehicles to continue the unloading.

An hour later Gary was saying, "I don't know. If the Chinese starting fueling DF-5As shortly before the announcement, I surprised there hasn't been..."

Gary's words faded away when the alert radio on Bethany's belt sounded and an announcement came through. The one doing the broadcast sounded terrified. *Take cover! Take cover! Missiles in the air! Missiles in the air! Take cover! I repeat! Take cover! Incoming missiles! Incoming missiles!*

A bright spot appeared in the sky to the northwest, and the broadcast cut off. There'd been a slight squeal from the radio, but it was still on, with white noise coming from the speaker.

"HEMP," Gary said loudly. "Everyone to the shelter. Major, you're in charge." Gary turned to Bethany. "You go home and get into the shelter. I'll be over when I get these guys under cover."

Bethany wanted to argue, but simply turned and ran toward the Sonoma. It started right up. The gate was still open and she shot through it, having immediately to drive around a vehicle stopped on the road. A guy was looking under the hood. Bethany didn't stop. She didn't recognize the guy.

"Oh my..." Bethany said. There were several people standing around by her main gate. She sighed in relief when she recognized them all. Gary was going to get a big surprise when he got there.

Bethany triggered the remote of the gate. With the wiring to it from the house in conduit, underground, with only a short section exposed, the EMP hadn't damaged the motor or controls. The gate opened. Bethany tried the window button to lower her window, but it wouldn't work. She opened the door and told the group standing around to throw their belongings into the back of the Sonoma and follow her into the property.

"Can I bring my truck?" asked Jason Carpenter.

"It runs?" Bethany asked.

He nodded.

"Then sure." Bethany pulled through the gate, and to one side. As soon as Jason had his tricked out old Chevy pickup through, she closed the gate with the remote. The next few minutes were a blur to Bethany as she got everyone organized, and down into the main shelter. She was in the process of showing a couple of the people the ins and outs of the shelter when the intercom screeched.

"Bethany! Bethany! Help! Please! It's Annie! Please, oh, please let us in!"

Bethany ran all the way out to the gate, but came skidding to a halt when she could see what was happening at the gate. There was a standoff. Gary had a rifle held in the general direction of a dozen people. Annie and her two children were huddled together by the intercom box.

"You call it Bethany," Gary said when Bethany opened the passage gate and let Annie and the kids in past her.

Bethany had the P-14 out, holding it, like Gary, pointed at the group that looked aggressive. "Who stays and who goes away to find shelter?"

"We know you have shelter in there! I heard it from my cousin. He worked out here."

Firmly, the gun steady in her grasp, Bethany said, "Come on Marty. You and your wife. Jasper, you too. Evelyn, come on in." Standing aside so the named people could go toward the passage gate, Bethany motioned them forward.

"You got to let us in, Lady!" called a woman. "We'll die!"

"Go find some shelter, you guys. You aren't getting in here," Gary said, easing over toward Bethany. Bethany stepped back by the gate, getting some cover from the heavy column supporting the gate.

"You let us in or you'll regret it!" screamed another man. He pulled a gun and was pointing it at Bethany when Gary shot him. Bethany's P-14 went off at the same time and the man went down, dead on the spot.

"You'll be sorry!" said the woman, her hands, like the others, now up and away from their bodies. They all started to ease back.

"As soon as you turn your back, we'll be in there, you know," growled the first man. "And we'll kill you all and…"

He didn't finish the sentence. Gary shot him, twice, right into the heart. "Anyone that threatens us or tries anything after we go in will get the same thing. Now I suggest you go find some shelter of your own, before more of you die." Gary fired another shot, then another, over the heads of the group. They all turned and ran.

"Let me get the bike," Gary said, turning to Bethany. "Keep an eye out."

Gary went over to where he'd left the bicycle he'd ridden over on, one of the half a dozen Montague Paratrooper mountain bikes they had between them. He stopped at the man he'd shot that had pulled the gun. He picked the revolver up and put it in his belt, feeling in the man's pockets for more shells. There weren't any.

Gary rolled the bike through the gate and Bethany secured it. They both ran for the house. There was no activity behind them, though both kept glancing over their shoulders to make sure. They'd barely made it into the shelter when the intercom sounded again.

This time it was a calm voice requesting entrance. "It's Dr. Cooper, Bethany. Are you there?"

"It's my new doctor here," Bethany said. "I'm going to go let her in."

"Not alone, you aren't." Gary followed Bethany, again at a run, back out to the gate, being very watchful for anyone that might have or was trying to get over the outer fence.

Before she opened the gate, Bethany used the peep hole. She didn't see anyone, but still asked, "You alone out there, Jane?"

"I am. Except for a several hundred pounds of supplies."

Bethany quickly opened the gate and eased out, Gary still right behind her. The sight of the doctor surprised him. From her voice he'd expected someone much older and not the tall, willowy redhead. She had on jogging shoes, wore a heavily loaded LBE vest, with a PTR-91 slung over one shoulder and a pistol of some kind on the vest belt.

"You read one of Jerry D Young's stories?" Gary asked, taking in the loaded down game cart.

Dr. Cooper grinned. "He's an ugly one, but I like the way he thinks. Yeah. I read his stuff. You must be Gary. Nice to meet you."

"You, too," Gary said, taking the pull bar of the cart from the Doctor. "What do you have in here, lead? Good thing you have the dual wheels."

"Things I thought might come in handy in the PAW."

"Come on Jane. Let's get you inside," Bethany said, holding the self closing gate open. Before they could enter, there was a shout down the road. Dr. Cooper had the PTR-91 off her shoulder in a flash and up to her shoulder.

The man, and it was a man, had been running. He waved, but stopped running, bending over and putting his hands on his knees, obviously nearly spent. He had a huge backpack on his back.

"You know him, Bethany?" asked Dr. Cooper.

"Barely," Bethany said slowly. "His name... I only know his last name. Killany. He's a little strange, but he knows prep things. I think he has more in his head than all of TOM's and Jerry's stories put together."

Killany began a slow jog toward them.

"You want him in?" Dr. Cooper looked a bit impatient as she continued to hold the rifle up.

"Yes. Yes. I think so," Bethany said. The three waited nervously, scanning the surrounding area for possible trouble as the man came closer.

When he got to them, he again leaned over and rested. But only for a moment. "What's the buy in?" he asked, reaching into a belt pouch, which caused Dr. Cooper to lift the rifle again. "Couple one ounce Gold Eagles okay? I intend to pay my way if you'll take me in. If not, I need to get going."

"How far have you run?" Gary asked. Despite obviously being tired, Killany still seemed to have a bit more energy left, if need be.

"Headed this way yesterday, from Branson. Figured things were afoot and wanted to be in a position to get here on short notice. I see you've had some unwelcome folk attempt to enter."

"Yeah," Gary replied.

"Okay," Bethany said. "Come on in."

Quickly the four of them headed for the house, after Bethany secured the gate. Killany grabbed the handle of the game cart with Gary. "How far did you have to hoof it?" Bethany asked Dr. Cooper.

"Not far, fortunately. The HEMP killed my car. I was so sure it would survive EMP, but something got fried. It would restart, but not run more than a few seconds."

The group in the shelter looked at the four anxiously when they entered the shelter one after the other. None of them knew that there was more space, almost as safe as the shelter, in some of the basements.

But Killany seemed to know, as he said, "You can park me in a basement. No need to crowd here. They have at least a PF of one-thousand."

"How do you know that?" Gary asked, looking peeved.

Bethany just looked surprised. "You worked with one of the out of town crews, didn't you? Before we officially met. That's why you seemed familiar when we ran into each other in Branson."

"Yeah. That was me. Once I had the scope of things, I laid low. Don't mind working, but since I sort of just joined the crew unofficially I didn't get paid for the work. Well. I did. Knowledge gained that will probably save my life."

"You've planned to come out here in case of trouble since before I got the place finished, didn't you?" Bethany asked.

Killany grinned. "Sure did. Once the excavation was started, a simple, safe shelter could be created easily and quickly. As things progressed, less work would be needed, and the shelter quality was better. Fortunately your timing is impeccable and everything was finished. By the way, here's that gold." He dropped the two gold coins into Bethany's hand, which she held out automatically when he made the motion.

"And don't worry about extra provisions for me. I have some caches located around here and can replace anything I use here, after we can get out and about."

"We'll discuss it later," Bethany said. "Right now I want to get everyone settled."

"Okay. Which basement?" Killany asked.

Bethany sighed. "Garage. That wa…" Killany was already walking toward the right portal that was the tunnel to the garage basement. "…ay," she finished, looking at the pack on Killany's back.

"You're right. He's strange," Dr. Cooper said. "I've got some stuff that needs to be refrigerated."

For the next several hours, Bethany and Gary helped everyone get settled in for a long stay. They'd not felt any earth movement, but the remote reading radiation meter had begun to sound and the needle lift from the peg three hours after they entered the shelter. Gary checked the sound powered telephone system that connected all the buildings in each place. Everything was working so he checked the link to his shelter.

They'd run a waterproof cable down into the lake and then back out at his place to connect the two systems together. It had been disconnected and grounded to prevent EMP damage. The plan worked. Both places had internal communications, and could talk to one another without any trouble after the link cable was connected.

Two hours after the fallout started, an alarm panel annunciator sounded. So far it seemed the HEMP had not adversely affected any of the well shielded electrical and electronic items in the complex, for when Bethany turned on an outside camera mounted on one of the three antenna towers on the property, it showed three men and two women trying to get over the outer security fence.

"What do you want to do?" Gary asked. "I can suit up and…"

"No way. Everything is buttoned up tight. The chance of them getting inside any of the buildings is remote. And look at the radiation level. It's over six hundred R/hr already and still rising. They don't have much usable time left."

"Okay," Gary said. "I hope the guys in the other shelter aren't having the same problems."

"Your shelter is just as safe as this one. Even against fire. Look."

Bethany nodded toward the monitor again and Gary took another look. One of the men was in the process of lighting a piece of fabric stuffed into a bottle that had a liquid they couldn't identify. The man quickly threw the bottle and it hit the door of the house.

Fire flared up and the automatic sprinklers came on. The flaming liquid, still burning, floated away on the surface of the water and burned a small patch of grass. It seemed to incense the man that had made the Molotov cocktail and he threw what amounted to a temper tantrum, stomping, kicking the ground, waving his arms around and screaming.

Bethany decided to leave the speaker volume down. No need to hear what he was saying. She and Gary continued to watch for another hour as the group searched for a way in. Finally, one after the other, they began to collapse. A few minutes after the last one fell, there was no movement. Fallout began to accumulate on their bodies. Bethany turned the camera off.

The first three days in the shelters were adjustment days, especially for the children. Both Bethany and Gary had made provisions to have children in the shelter, so there were plenty of things to do, but the children all would prefer to play outside.

A week into the stay and everyone was into the swing of things. With both shelters at just over maximum planned capacity, things were a bit tight, but the square footage allowance per person was more than enough to handle the extra people without undue stress.

Killany's use of the garage as his shelter helped the situation at Bethany's, but neither Bethany nor Gary were willing to ask anyone else to use the relatively safe space in the other basements. While each had a PF of 1,000 or more, the shelter had a PF of over 1,000,000. With most of those in Bethany's shelter still relatively young, the less radiation they received, the better their long term survival chances were. It was especially critical for Bethany and Gary, who both wanted to have children. They wouldn't take any unnecessary risk when it came to radiation exposure, though both felt responsible for all those in both shelters.

A month into the stay, with the radiation well on the way down, everyone not asleep felt a heavy jolt. It rattled some dishes, but there was no discernable harm to any of the structures. Killany and Gary were checking every tunnel and building from inside when another, slightly stronger shake occurred.

Bethany was on the sound powered telephone with the other shelter. They'd felt the jolts, too, though with less intensity due to the type of construction of the Radius Engineering shelter system.

Major Tandy, whom Gary had put in charge of the other shelter, told Bethany, "Got the periscope up. I'm not seeing any additional damage. How is everyone over there?"

"Good, Major. I've got the external cameras on. I'm not seeing anything, either. Wait," Bethany said. "Did you hear that?" A heavy rumble had come from the speaker connected to one of the external cameras. A few seconds later a similar sound, only more intense came through the speakers.

"Yes. We got the sound signatures through the periscope microphone. It is a major event of some kind. Ask Gary to call me when he can."

"Will do, Major," Bethany said, signing off.

Gary and Killany were back a few minutes later after their inspection. "Major Tandy wants you to call him," Bethany said and Gary headed for the sound powered telephone. "Find anything amiss?" Bethany asked Killany.

"No, Ma'am. You designed and built well. I'll be going back to the basement now. Call me if I'm needed."

"Okay. And Killany... Thank you."

A shy smile appeared on Killany's face. "Sure thing, Miss."

Bethany had given up trying to get Killany to drop the Ma'am and Miss labels, but he continued to use one or the other whenever he spoke to her, which wasn't often. He stayed in the garage basement for the most part, coming into the main shelter to get his meals. There was a bathroom and shower in the garage basement, connected to the shelter systems, so he didn't even need to come into the shelter for those reasons.

"He is very annoying, you know?" Dr. Cooper said her eyes on Killany's back as she came over to talk to Bethany.

Bethany had to smile. Dr. Cooper had an insatiable curiosity, and Killany seemed to delight in frustrating her attempts to find out more about him, even his first name. No one in the shelter knew it, though a couple of the people that worked for Bethany did know him in passing.

"Yeah." Bethany said, hiding her grin as Dr. Cooper continued to look at the portal through which Killany had gone. "How is everyone's health and mood?"

"Oh. That. That's why I came over. Everyone is doing all right; except for that round of colds we all seemed to have gone through last week. Psychologically, things are pretty good, but not perfect. All the kids have adjusted, finally, to the isolation down here.

A couple of the adults are struggling a bit. But I'm talking to them every day, and gave both medications to keep them calm when they feel like they are going to panic. One of them is simply claustrophobic. If there wasn't as much room down here as there is, he'd be a basket case, I'm afraid."

Bethany nodded. "The other?"

"Due to their situation… I just can't go into details. She's having trouble coping. That's all I can say."

"I understand, Jane. But if there is something that could adversely affect us all down here, Gary and I need to know about it."

"I understand," Dr. Cooper said. "But for the moment, things are under control."

"Okay. I need to talk to Gary now," Bethany said, her eyes going over to her loved one as he approached.

"Sure thing," Dr. Cooper said, drifting away to join a group watching a cut-throat game of Monopoly.

"What's up?" Bethany asked, seeing the worried look on Gary's face.

"Bad news, if Bob is correct, and I think he is."

"One of the western calderas, isn't it?"

Gary nodded. "One or more. Bob thinks one blew and triggered another. The first one further away from us than the second, based on the difference in the shakes and the timing of the sounds. We'll know in a day or two. If we start getting ash, it was a caldera. This could be really bad. It's the middle of winter. With the nukes, and now possibly two super volcanoes putting ash and who knows what else into the atmosphere, we could be in for a long span of time before we can start growing outdoor crops.

"If the volcanic winter does occur and it lasts for longer than five years, we could be in a bind."

Bethany listened, calm outwardly, but her stomach was in turmoil. Five years of no crops, and probably very little meat production from the farm, and they would be out of food. A five year supply for thirty people had seemed like a great deal of food, and it was. But it would eventually all be consumed without resupply.

Their worst suspicions were confirmed a few days later. Ash had started to fall two days after the shakes and blasts. It was heavy. But nothing like a day later with the ash fall doubled in intensity.

"Has to be two different events," Gary said, speaking to everyone in the two shelters. The other shelter had hooked the sound powered telephone into their intercom system so everyone could hear.

"We won't be able to tell how long this could extend our stay, until the fall begins to lessen or, hopefully stop completely."

There were worried expressions on most of the adult faces, in both shelters.

"Our food and water…" asked Stefano, his words trailing off.

"Water we have covered. Between the wells on the property, which don't seem to have been affected by the shaking, and the lake, we're okay for many years, I'm sure. Food… Well, we have enough for at least five years."

Gary suddenly decided to shut up while he was ahead. The five year remark had brought relieved looks on just about everyone's face, except for Killany's, Bethany's, and Dr. Cooper's. Best to let them think that the time frame was such that they wouldn't need to worry about things too much. At least, not for a long time.

Better for just Gary, Bethany, Dr. Cooper, Killany, and Major Tandy to do the worrying for all of them.

While no one was put on short rations, every step available was made to conserve and eliminate wasting any of the stored foods. Once the radiation was down, the Bethany's greenhouse was once again put into production. A team had to go out and clear the ash from the polycarbonate roof panels and clear the area around it.

Ash was still coming down steadily, but with the bulk of it off the greenhouse, regularly sprinkling down the greenhouse, using the fire control sprinklers already installed, kept the roof and walls clear of the ash.

There was only faint sunshine coming through the ash clouds. Noon was only equivalent to bright twilight. The LED grow lights in the greenhouse allowed the continued production of some fresh food.

Though long distance communication was difficult, Gary was able to talk to those at the Farm on a regular basis. They'd only had minor problems initially, and everything had worked out. They like Gary and Bethany, had a couple of extra people present not initially planned for, but they were turning out to be a big help at the farm.

The two new custom constant production forage sprouters installed, but never used before the attack, were put into production, after a smaller one set up for producing the seed that the two production machines needed to sprout the forage finally began producing.

There was no attempt to clear any pastures or crop fields when spring came. Not yet. It would just have to be done again and again, until the ash fall stopped. But the effort was made, and then continued, to clear the two residential properties. Between stored feed and the fresh forage being produced, the animals would be okay for a long time. At least as long as people were around to take care of them.

Without needing to worry about radiation any more, except for inhaling some that might be mixed with the ash at the very bottom of the stack of accumulation, crews were put together to use the equipment Bethany had stored to clear the Properties.

In fact, inhalation of the ash was probably a more deadly possibility than any low level radiation that might be inhaled. Therefore it was an absolute that no one went outside without a respirator, at first, and then, as the weeks and months passed, P-100 filter masks and goggles, with the remaining respirator cartridges saved for future use, if needed, for other situations.

Unlike Jerry's stories, with the occasional use of Unimog U500s and Bobcat skid steer equipment, Bethany had gone with more conventional equipment. It was all old, but had been reconditioned when the county and state finally bought new road maintenance equipment and sold the old. The EMP had not affected any of it.

Parked in the forest here and there where there were small clearings accessible, if barely, to the vehicles, were six dump trucks, each with a trailer with a piece of heavy equipment on it. When the ash was laboriously cleared from them, the real work of clearing the Properties was begun.

It was a long slow process, but the accumulation of nearly five feet of ash on the Properties at the time they started, was moved to the other side of the road that paralleled the lake in this area. The air filters of the trucks and heavy equipment were cleaned every hour to keep the ash from getting into the engines as the fall of lighter and lighter ash continued.

Daily wash downs of the paved areas of the two properties allowed for some time outside for everyone, even the children, who naturally had to wear the masks while they played on the cleared areas. Tarp roofs were rigged to give them a play area with the least chance of any of them getting the deadly ash into their lungs. But time was limited and they were all monitored closely to make sure no one removed a mask while outside for any reason.

The road was opened between the two properties, though both groups preferred to stay where they started. But it did allow Major Tandy to get to the other shelter to perform the marriage ceremony for Gary and Bethany on the scheduled day. It was decided that he could be considered commander of the fleets; water, air, and land. Everyone agreed that a marriage performed by him would be upheld in any court, if there was ever one again, including the highest one, presided over by God.

They moved their belongings from the dorm rooms they'd been sharing with the other adults to one of the three bedrooms in the house Bethany had built, leaving the three in the shelter set up for couples available. All three had been used in rotation by all the married and otherwise paired off couples, to get some private time for two or three days at a time during the shelter stay.

Even with the construction of the earth sheltered house, the fine ash was hard to keep out, so everyone else chose to stay in the shelter for the time being.

The only way anyone could tell when spring passed into summer was the calendar, carefully updated every day. There had been a slight increase in temperatures the first few days of spring, but the ash was still coming down heavily then, and the temperatures started dropping, lower in summer than even the winter had been.

One day, dressed in heavy clothing, still wearing masks, despite the apparent absence of ash in the air, Gary and Bethany went down to the lake. It was only when they took a close look did they discover that the lake level had dropped by almost eight feet. The deep channel from the lake to the boathouse barely had enough water in it to float any of the boats. At that, what water there was was frozen solid, though the bulk of the lake itself wasn't.

"I thought it would be up," Bethany said, "With the ash fall into the lake…"

"Wouldn't have brought it up much, but I don't think it would have dropped it any. Something is wrong. We may have lost the dam. Though if we'd lost it completely, there wouldn't be any lake at all. I think it is time I went on a scouting trip in one of the birds."

"Oh, Gary! Do you think it safe? We haven't been able to talk to other survivors in the area. And though we can't see it, there is still some ash in the air, especially when the wind blows. And it is so cold. What if you go down?"

"We'd be careful, Honey. Take appropriate gear. And no, before you say something, you aren't going. You're already two months pregnant. I'm not risking you or the baby."

Bethany sighed. Though she'd been eager for children she wished sometimes that they'd waited. Times like these when she felt she should be by Gary's side, not at home, pregnant, and then tending to a baby. But Gary was right. She wouldn't risk the baby, even if she risked herself.

## CHAPTER FIVE

-

After long discussion with Major Tandy, it was decided that the Sikorsky S-76D would be the better choice for the reconnaissance flight. If they had to set down, they could do it most anywhere. The Seawolf, as long it stayed close to the lake, had the same option, but not if it had to range out some distance from it.

And Major Tandy put his foot down. Gary wasn't going with him. Oh, the Major wasn't going by himself by any means, but two of the three main leaders of the group were not going on the same jaunt.

There were plenty of volunteers to go with the Major, but the leadership decided on Killany, much to Dr. Cooper's disappointment, since it was her or him, since both were familiar with the area. Stefano Wilson, and Jason Carpenter, the arborist that Bethany had hired to care for the estate trees, were selected to go. Both ex military, with arctic survival training, they were the two best prepared for such a trip with the attendant risks.

They took two days to get ready, going over the Sikorsky from top to bottom since it had been sitting for months, even protected as it was in the hanger. The apron in front of the hanger was washed down carefully to eliminate any ash, at least on this end of the trip.

It turned out that the day of the trip, August fifteenth, was the first day of no sign of any additional ash. But it was only 12°F out. The Sikorsky was pushed out and Major Tandy fired it up, let it warm up as he studied every gauge and indicator on the dashboards. Killany climbed into the other pilot's seat and Stefano and Jason took the seats behind them. Then they were airborne, quickly disappearing in the sky as Gary and Bethany watched.

The two finally hurried back to the shelter Bethany had built, as it was home now for Gary, as well as Bethany. They were on the radio with the Major immediately. "Not a cloud in the sky. No ash that I can tell," the Major said when Gary made the contact. "It is beautiful out. Except, of course, everything the ash has killed. There are plenty of clear areas, blown clear by the winds over the last few months, and washed away by the few rains we had before it got so cold.

"But there are drifts I'd estimate to be twenty, even thirty feet high in places. Real ash dunes, if I may coin a term. That's what they resemble, sand dunes, only grayish black and bleak looking. No sign of anything green, except the isolated evergreen tree and they are more dusty gray green that the bright green they should be."

There was silence for a while. Then the Major again began describing what the four in the helicopter were seeing. "Lots of cars stalled on the roads. Most with ash piled up against them on one side or end, all the way to the roofs. Even the big motorhomes and travel trailers have a drift of ash against them.

"I don't think until we get some heavy rains that some of this ash is going to go away. Whatever the wind blows away here, more is just blown here from somewhere else. I'm going to have to be very careful not to land anywhere where there is ash accumulated.

There was silence for a long time as the Major flew down the lake, keeping over it for a guide in the amazing sameness of the partially ash covered terrain.

"Okay," he said finally. "I see the dam. Going in for a close look."

It was only a few minutes later that the Major was speaking again. "Still standing, but cracked like you wouldn't believe. There is water shooting through some of them, but only up high. Which is surprising... Unless... Unless the ash accumulation at the base of the dam is sealing some of the lower cracks. That's the only thing I can think of.

"I would have thought the ash would have made the cracks worse, eating on the concrete as it washed through. But apparently not. I think the lake will be okay. Especially if more ash keeps flowing down. We might want to expedite the process some way. Don't know how we could seal the dam... Something to think about.

"Wait! I see some activity by the dam! They are waving. The guys are waving back. Chimney!" The radio went silent, causing Gary and Bethany to look at one another in alarm.

"SOBs shot at us!" It was Killany. "The Major took a slug in the shoulder. Stefano and Jason are working on him."

"You're down?" Gary asked, gripping the mike so hard his knuckles were white.

"No. I took the co-pilot controls. We're headed back. Can you have Dr. Cooper meet us at the hanger?"

"Of course. You think you can get the helicopter back here and land it?" Gary asked the worry obvious in his voice.

"Assuming no more attacks, sure. I'm a licensed helicopter and fixed wing pilot."

Dr. Cooper had been brought over by Bethany and she heard the last thing that Killany said. "That Cro-Magnon can fly a helicopter and a plane?"

"At least she didn't call me Neanderthal." The humor was evident in Killany's voice.

"Sorry," Gary said. "I had the mike keyed to respond.

Dr. Cooper turned red, and didn't say anything for a few seconds. "See if you can find out how Major Tandy is and where he was shot. Anything so I know how to prepare for their arrival."

Gary keyed the mike and asked the questions Dr. Cooper had requested.

"From the looks of it, that I can see, and what Stefano and Jason are telling me," Killany said, "it's a small slug, lodged in the left right anterior scapula."

"If he says he's a doctor, too, I'm going to scream," Dr. Cooper said.

Gary had quickly released the key of the mike he'd pressed to respond, but it was obvious when Killany responded that he'd again heard Dr. Cooper's remarks.

"Don't worry, Doc. I'm not a medical doctor."

"Is that keyed?" Dr. Cooper asked, looking at Gary pointedly. Gary shook his head. "He's implying he's some other kind of doctor. The man's gall never ceases to amaze me," Dr. Cooper said. A motion of her head and Gary keyed the microphone again and held it up so Dr. Cooper could speak directly into it.

"No matter. Is he bleeding heavily?"

"No. They've got a compression bandage on it. He's awake and lucid. In some pain and a bit pale. But okay so far. We're about half an hour out."

It seemed forever to Bethany as she, Gary, Dr. Cooper, and three other people, with one of the stretchers from the medical stocks that Gary and Bethany had both stored, waited for Killany to land the helicopter when it showed up in the distance.

Dr. Cooper took a step back when Killany came in hot and flared out just before touching down.

"He just went into cardiac arrest!" Killany shouted. He'd killed the engine at touchdown and was already coming around the front of the Sikorsky with the rotors still slowing down. Dr. Cooper ran forward. Killany was dragging the Major out of the helicopter and had him on the cold ground on his back when the Doctor got to them.

He began CPR compressions and Dr. Cooper checked for pulse and then slipped a breathing mask she took from her bag over the Major's face and began to pump the bellows. Gary and the other three men had the stretcher ready.

Stefano and Jason, both with blood on the arms of their coats and their hands stood ready to help.

"I've got a pulse," said the Doctor after checking again.

Breathing hard from the exertion, the moisture in his breath freezing instantly in the cold air, Killany leaned back on his heels, and then rose to let the others slide the stretcher close to the Major.

Another minute, with Dr. Cooper monitoring him, the men carried the unconscious man over to the back of Bethany's Sonoma. The men slid him in and Bethany climbed into the cab and put the already running vehicle in gear.

Dr. Cooper was on her knees beside the stretcher as the others jogged alongside the truck. Those in Gary's shelter had the vehicle lift up and open, waiting for them. Bethany pulled inside, the doors were closed and they began to drop slowly.

It took a bit of time. When they reached the bottom and the others began to slide the stretcher with the Major on it out of the truck, he coughed and tried to sit up.

"Easy, Major," Dr. Cooper said. "You've just had a heart attack."

"What! No. I was shot… ouh…" He groaned and quit trying to sit up as he was carried at a fast shuffle into the main area of the ECD 60 shelter. A room was set up as a medical station. Two people were there. Annie from Bethany's shelter, and one of the men Gary had brought down. "We're nurses," Annie said.

Dr. Cooper ushered everyone out of the room, except for Annie and Clay Jennings. The door closed and Bethany, Gary and the others were left standing outside.

"I'm going to go secure the Sikorsky," Killany said, and turned around to leave.

"I'll go with you," said both Stefano and Jason. Reluctantly, Gary went with them. Major Tandy was one of his oldest friends and was almost like a father to him. Losing him would be a huge personal blow and a big loss for the group of survivors.

Killany was checking the Sikorsky carefully, front to back, top to bottom, looking for any other damage besides the one bullet hole in the windshield where the bullet had entered, down low, and gone up into the Major's shoulder.

"I can't find anything else," Killany said. "Let's get the bird back inside before things start to freeze up."

The four men turned the helicopter around and pushed it back into the hanger. Killany, with Gary's help, serviced the machine and set it up for storage again. As they walked toward the entrance to the shelter again, Gary said, "Mind if I ask you a question?"

"Of course not. Go right ahead." Killany suddenly grinned. "I may or may not answer, but you certainly can ask."

"I think I already know the answer... You told Dr. Cooper you weren't a medical doctor. Are you some other kind?"

"No big deal," Killany said, shrugging his shoulders. "I had some time one time, so I got a PhD. Actually, a couple of them. One in anthropology and one in civil engineering."

"How old are you?" Gary suddenly asked.

Killany grinned again. "I am a bit older than I look, I suppose." But that was all he said, changing the subject when he said, "I think we're okay on the dam. Despite the cracks, the structure seems solid. Unless someone intentionally uses explosives, a lot of them, or we get more big shakes, we should have a lake for many more years."

"Tell me. Why do you think those people shot at you?"

"Probably the local warlord. There were bound to be a few types like that survive. Going to be hard to survive long term, though. Without preparations like you have here, simply raiding, especially if they slash and burn when they raid won't be productive for very long.

"There aren't too many with the warlord intellect that will force long term cooperation to ensure future supplies of various commodities, most notably, food."

Gary nodded. "I'm a little worried about the farm. We're set up there pretty well, but I'd like to get a few more people involved. Primarily as a reaction force to do any fighting that might have to be done. That family is composed of farmers, not fighters. We have the installation set up to make it relatively easy to defend, just like Bethany's compound, but that only protects the building complex. The fields and pastures, once we can get them in production again, are going to be vulnerable."

"I know. I have a couple of ideas on that. I may need to do a bit of a walk-about here pretty soon. Check on a few things. A few people I think probably made it. They could be of help."

"Can't you contact them on the radio?" Gary asked. They were standing by the main entrance of the shelter now. "Any type of excursion is going to be very difficult. And very, very dangerous."

"Oh, I have a few tricks up my sleeve yet," Killany said. "I'll talk to you later. I want to go over to the other property and clean up a bit."

Gary didn't want to press it, since Killany seem not to want to discuss it in depth. So Gary went down into the shelter to check on the Major while Killany headed out to the road to go down to Bethany's compound.

Dr. Cooper came out of the medical room just as Gary entered the main part of the shelter. "How is he?" Gary immediately asked. Bethany came over to him and Gary put his arm around her.

"Doing very good, actually. He's a tough old bird. Turns out he's had a heart problem for some time now."

"I didn't know that!" Gary said, alarmed.

"It's not so bad, as these things go. His general health is very good. The heart problems he's had before were stress related. He's learned to cope, apparently. Getting shot kind of stressed him out, as you can imagine. If we can keep him away from stress for some time, he should recover nicely."

"The bullet wound?" Bethany asked.

"Oh. That. I was able to remove it with just a local anesthetic. No big deal. Barring infection, anyway and I have antibiotics for that yet. Wish there was an herbalist we could tag for help. The factory stuff is going to run out sooner or later. I'd like to start coming up with some natural remedies before I run out of commercial ones.

"By the way. Where's Killany?"

"Went back to the other shelter after we took care of the helicopter. He's fine. Just wants to clean up some."

"That man is a mystery to me. I intend to find out more about him. He's just too capable."

Coming from Dr. Cooper it was almost a curse. Gary decided to keep his mouth shut about the degrees Killany had told him about. Let Dr. Cooper find out on her own. Would probably be good for her and Killany both.

"I need to stay over here for a few days," Dr. Cooper said. "Can we make some arrangements for that?"

"No problem," Gary said. "With the ash seeming to be stopped, at least for the moment, I want to start moving people out of the shelter into the other facilities between the two places. There are two large houses, one smaller one, and the other two wooded lots. We need firewood. I think if we cut down some of the trees on those other lots, we can move in some mobile housing for everyone to have their own space."

"What about the owners?" Dr. Cooper asked.

"If they are still alive, and show up, we'll work something out. The only place that was occupied on this stretch was the Andersons. You know the ones. We found them on the first foray out."

"Yeah. I guess I'm okay with it."

"We'll talk it over with Killany, and then the Major when he's able," Gary said. "But I think most everyone is getting ready for some real privacy. We're all getting along, but I think everyone would like more open space."

It was unanimous. All those in the two groups were in favor of the idea that Killany and Major Tandy had agreed was a good idea.

Back in masks and goggles, the cleanup of the five lots between the two shelters began. Gary brought two of the Yukon's up and he and Stefano each took a team and went looking for portable housing and the means to get it to the lots while Jason and a crew began to cut trees for firewood, and remove the stumps to make room for them when the units were delivered. Another team, using the two rental trucks, went looking for septic system components.

The wells that Bethany and Gary had put in would provide enough water for everyone; they just needed additional pumping and storage capacity. The septic system crew would look for the potable water equipment, too.

Things were hectic for the remaining weeks of summer and then fall. The highest temperature of the summer was only fifteen degrees Fahrenheit. By November the temperatures were dropping well below zero again at night.

But the new housing got enhanced insulation and wood stoves for heat and cooking. There was pressurized water run to heat exchangers on the wood stoves, so all the homes had running hot and cold water.

Each home got a set of solar panels, storage batteries, and an inverter to provide enough power for some lights and small appliances. A generator and a fuel tanker were recovered and set up for a communal laundry in an independent unit that also included the home theatre system from the largest of the houses they had taken over.

When Christmas came around, the quiet celebration was held in the community building. It was thirty below outside, with winds blowing fifty miles an hour, according to the weather monitors in the two shelters.

With the help of the karaoke system that was part of the transplanted home theatre system for community movie night, Bethany and Gary were able to get people involved in singing Christmas Carols, lightening the mood significantly. Yes, things were tough, but life would go on, as long as those in the group continued to pursue that goal relentlessly.

Even Major Tandy was up for the party, having been slowly recuperating from the gun shot and the heart trouble. He wouldn't be flying anytime soon, but he was able to contribute to the leadership meetings again.

He was the only one that gave real support to Killany's announcement that he would be leaving for a while after the first. Even Dr. Cooper protested his leaving in the dead of winter. "Killany, you are an idiot! Temperatures are in the negative numbers every night. And the wind chills are brutal, day and night. How do you expect to survive?"

"I'll manage," Killany replied, his eyes steady on the Doctor's. "I'm pretty good in rough conditions."

"But..."

"I think if he can add something to the community, he should go," said Major Tandy. "You mentioned some guys that could help with security at the farm..."

"Yes. I know a couple of guys in the area that probably survived. They were ready for some of this, but not to the extent we've encountered. They are going to need a bit of help, long term, but they will contribute more than just a gun to the community."

"There is going to be a need for more guns, I'm thinking," added the Major. "When this weather breaks, as I'm sure it will in a few months, there are going to be some survivors in desperate need of supplies. That farm is going to be a prime target at some point in time. Once back in full production it will easily support our group, with plenty of extra for others. But only if it is kept safe, and those that know what they are doing are running it."

"What do you need, Killany?" Gary finally asked, accepting the fact that Killany was going, no matter what. Might as well give him the best chance of survival as possible.

"Not much. Just some of the emergency rations as a back up to my own supplies I'll pick up when I leave."

"How are you going to travel?" Bethany asked. "On foot is going to be very difficult. And slow. With the snow... the ash that remains… Even one of the Yukon's might not be up to the task. And there is the factor of having enough fuel…"

"I have the means. Something I put together for situations such as this. I just have to get to it to pick it up."

"Can we get you there in one of the vehicles?" Gary asked.

"Shouldn't be any problem. We only have to get to this side of Branson. I think one of the Yukon's will make it. The only problem could be the Highway 76 bridge. If it is blocked with abandoned vehicles there could be a problem."

"Won't know until we get there," Gary said. "When do you want to leave?"

"Tomorrow is fine. Won't take me long to get my gear back together."

Shortly after dawn the next morning, Gary raised one of the Yukon's to the surface and he and Killany, with Stefano along in the rear seat, left the Properties and headed on the roundabout trip to the west side of Branson, picking up Highway 76 from FR 2150. There were a few vehicles here and there, on FR 2150 after they got away from the Properties. Highway 76 had a few more.

All three men kept a close eye on the surroundings as Gary drove. There were no signs of anyone at all. No smoke. No tracks in the snow or ash. Nothing to indicate anyone had been anywhere close to the highway in a long time.

Though there were a few drifts of snow, and a couple of snow covered ash, Gary was able to get through or around all of them. Though it didn't show, Killany breathed a sigh of relief when they got to the Highway 76 bridge over a finger of the lake. There were cars stopped on it, alright, but only three and they were spaced out more than enough for Gary to drive around them.

It still took three times the length of time to get near Branson as it had before the attack. Killany directed Gary off the highway and onto town streets, finally motioning him to pull into the driveway of a rental storage company.

When Gary saw the gate had been pulled down, he looked over at Killany. "I hope your stuff is still here."

"It will be," Killany said quietly. "I made a few modifications to the door of the storage unit. I doubt anyone got in. But we'll soon see. Looks like we'll have to walk from here." There were still large drifts of both ash and snow around the long storage units.

All three men bundled up, as the temperatures on the sunny day were still only in the low twenties. Killany carried the portable jump starter as he led the way into the heart of the storage units. Stefano and Gary were both armed. They had to struggle a bit through some of the drifts.

Gary and Stefano both wondered about Killany's sureness his belongings would still be intact, for there were several open units, with things strewn about. Some of the doors hadn't been opened, they'd been torn clear.

But when Killany stopped, it was at a unit with an intact door. Mostly intact. A hole had been punched into the door and there were signs that something had been hooked to it. Someone had tried to yank open the door but failed.

"Went on to easier pickings," Killany said. "I figured anyone that would come in would do the easy stuff." He pulled a key from a pocket and unlocked the lock that was still intact. While Gary and Stefano lifted the door slightly, Killany, lying on the ground, reached through the resulting gap at the bottom of the door and moved something.

Gary and Stefano gave a heave and the much heavier than normal door rose, screeching loudly as it moved. "Got some stuff to go back to the Properties," Killany said, standing up and going inside. The bright sunshine illuminated the interior of the storage room enough to see easily.

There wasn't much to see at first. There were several things covered with tarps. Killany unfastened and threw back the tarp on the nearest item. Gary and Stefano saw what it was, looked at each other, and then both asked Killany, "What in the world is that?"

"NSU Kettenkrad, late model HK-101 version half track motorcycle," Killany replied, grinning. "With a few modifications of my own. Hand me the jump starter."

"Okay," Gary said. "That tells me the name. But what was it used for?"

"It was an artillery and support tow vehicle the Germans used in World War Two. Used a few of them as air craft tow vehicles, but most were used in the field. The Eastern Front. Though there were some in Europe as well as North Africa."

Killany lifted the engine cover behind the driver's seat of the thing, connected the cables from the starter unit and then turned to another of the tarp covered items. "I converted it to a twelve volt system," he said. "Uses an Opel four cylinder engine. The front wheel will steer it a little, but on harder turns the movement of the handlebars apply the track brake on the appropriate side to bring it around."

Stefano and Gary were helping Killany un-tarp what turned out to be a trailer, obviously for the Kettenkrad, as he continued to explain. "Has a lubricated track system. Usually had the driver and two passengers riding backward on the rear seat. Used for laying cable some, too.

"There was a special trailer for it for cargo purposes, but it was too small for my needs, and used wheels so I built one myself. Used ATV cart track conversion units.

Sure enough, when the trailer was uncovered, Gary and Stefano looked on in amazement at the trailer. A pair of Mattracks LiteFoot Trail-R-Mates supported the trailer. The cargo body, like the cargo box on the Kettenkrad, was covered with another tarp that Killany didn't bother to take off. "It's loaded with what I need," he said, "Including enough PRI-G stabilized fuel to get me to and from where I need to go, plus some."

Killany began to un-tarp some of the other piles. "Need to take the rest of this back to the Properties, if you will, and store it for me until I get back."

"Sure," Gary replied.

Being careful not to work up a sweat, the three men began to move the many totes that the tarps had covered to the Yukon. With the rear seat folded down, all the totes fit, but the polymer pallets they'd been stacked on had to go on the roof rack of the Yukon. The tarps were stuffed into the nooks and crannies left in the back of the Yukon.

When they were finished, Gary and Stefano went back with Killany. He got aboard the Kettenkrad and tried the starter. The engine groaned a bit, but turned over. Killany tried again and the engine caught. It was running rough, so Killany let it run for a couple of minutes until it smoothed out as he disconnected the jump starter.

He put the thing in gear, pulled forward and then lined up with the trailer tongue and backed up in low reverse. Gary connected the trailer and Killany put the Kettenkrad in low forward and headed for the Yukon, the other two men walking alongside.

"How fast will it go?" asked Stefano.

"Between thirty-five and forty miles per hour on good ground," Killany answered. "It has three forward gears and a reverse, with a transfer box for off-road and on-road, equivalent of six forward gears and two reverse."

Killany didn't take the easy track the men had made carrying totes. He rode up and over the compacted ash drifts, and just went through the snow drifts, the thirty-five hundred pound weight on the tracks giving more than enough traction. The trailer didn't seem to slow Killany down at all.

Stopping at the Yukon, Killany got off the Kettenkrad and retrieved his huge pack from the front seat where it had been moved when they loaded the totes. He secured it to the cargo box on the bike, after removing a folding stock PTR-91 from it. He set it in a rack obviously made for it. Pulling one corner of the cargo tarp up, he reached in and retrieved a pair of heavy insulated gloves and an arctic facemask.

"I'm on my way," he said, holding the face mask in his hands. "I'll be in touch from time to time. I have a Motorola HT-750 for around here and a Yaesu FT-897D for HF if I get out of range of the low band business band radio."

"Thanks for putting up with me." Killany held out his hand and Gary shook it.

"Well worth it, Killany," Gary replied. "You be careful. Do what you can, but don't hesitate to come back sooner if you need to."

Killany nodded and then put on the mask. He flipped up the hood of the heavy parka he wore, pulled on the gloves and then got back on the driver's seat of the Kettenkrad. He started up the halftrack bike and pulled away, the engine of the bike nearly silent, with the tracks of the bike making a bit of noise that the snow and ash seemed to muffle.

When Gary and Stefano got back into the Yukon and got it turned around, Killany had disappeared, with only the tracks in the snow to indicate where he'd gone. "That is some rig he's got," Stefano said. "Never saw anything like it. A halftrack bike. Sweet."

"Just a curiosity piece before. Now a really useful item, assuming he has the parts to keep it going."

"I bet he does," Stefano replied.

## CHAPTER SIX

-

Killany traveled at a moderate speed until he had assured himself everything was working the way it should and the trailer rode correctly. He'd only had a few chances to practice with the Kettenkrad after he'd rebuilt it, before he stored it away for future use.

Picking up US 65, Killany traveled north, right into the teeth of the wind. Only the protective shields he'd installed on the handlebars, his heavy gloves, insulated overboots, and the arctic mask kept him from having to stop to warm up. Five layers of clothing kept his body warm, but he would have to be very careful of his extremities and his lungs.

The miles rolled away under the tracks of the Kettenkrad. But Killany stopped early, at a good place to camp he knew about, rather than push on further and have to stop at a marginal spot.

He set up his tent and gear, and heated water for his meal. Killany ate heartily, knowing it was necessary to keep his caloric intake up because of the cold temperatures. Two cups of rich hot chocolate, with butter powder mixed in, was his bedtime snack. He stripped down to his long handles and slipped into the sleep system.

It consisted of a Gortex outer bivy, a heavy bag, an inner bag, and a silk liner. It took a minute for his body heat to warm the inside of the bag and he shivered, but that quickly passed and he was warm enough. As was his nature, Killany woke several times in the night and lay awake, listening for any telltale sounds of potential trouble. Nothing seemed out of place and he fell asleep again each time without any trouble.

Up at first light, Killany was back on the road by the time the sun had cleared the trees. The wind was much calmer and Killany was able to make good time without having to worry about frostbite or worse.

When he got close to Springfield, Killany left 65 and took side roads around the city. He could see the occasional smoke column in the city. It would justify a team coming up to make contact, but alone, it was too dangerous. At least when he was on a journey to get some additional help for the community that had taken him in.

He stopped early again that day, repeating the activity of the day before. He was getting close to his destination and wanted to make an appearance before noon. Roger Strotskey was not a man you wanted to slip up on unawares, even if you could. Killany knew he was one of the few that could, but he wasn't about to try it. It could be deadly.

So when he picked up Missouri road BB and turned left he slowed down and began to watch for signs of local human activity. He finally spotted the faint shimmer that indicated a heat source below, though there was no visible smoke.

Killany stopped and climbed off the Kettenkrad. He took his gloves off and pulled the HT-750 from inside his parka. Selecting a specific frequency, he keyed the radio and spoke a series of numbers. He waited twelve seconds by his watch and repeated them. Five minutes later he did the same thing.

Putting the radio away, Killany set up a windbreak with a tarp, poles, stakes, and cord from the cargo box on the Kettenkrad. He took out his single burner camp stove and began to heat water. He was on his second cup of hot chocolate when he suddenly said, "Come on around, Roger."

"Ah! Killany! I thought I'd finally got you."

Killany filled the cup Roger held out with hot water from the pot on the stove. Roger dropped a tea bag into the cup and squatted down the way Killany was, out of the wind that had again picked up from the north.

"How are you making it, Rog?"

"Good. At least for now. I thought I was prepped pretty well, but this is going on longer than I counted on. How about you? I see you got that old hunka junk going."

"That old hunka junk you're disparaging is going to get you somewhere safe and warm, with the potential of becoming the major seat of activity in this area."

"Really? Your place? But you only had that small shelter…"

"Yeah. I managed to hook up with someone that knew what they were doing. They are good people. And they are going to need some security help when things finally break open."

"I've been surprised," Roger said. "There hasn't been anything going on around here from right after the missiles began to fly. I was out and about after the fallout radiation dropped. There isn't anyone else left around here."

"Oh, I would beg to differ," Killany said. "Look." He pointed with his chin toward the east. "Here comes Dudley."

"Do Right is in this area? I didn't know that." Roger sounded more than a bit annoyed.

"Lay off the Do Right, Rog. You know he hates it. And the two of you are going to be working together."

"Aw! Man! Me and Do Right?"

"You and Dudley." Killany picked up the pot and filled the cup that the tall man with long red hair showing under the hood of his heavy cape held out, just as Roger had.

"Hello Killany. What's he doing here?" Dudley asked, barely deigning a look at Roger.

"Same thing you are, Dudley," Killany said. Like Roger, Dudley was dipping a tea bag in the hot water in his cup."

"Yeah. Hello to you, to D... Dudley." Roger helped himself to more water. "Thought you were still up at Fort Leonard Wood."

"No. I've been down here for a couple of years."

Roger's eyes widened slightly. "That's about the time I got here, too. What a coincidence."

"No coincidence," Killany said. "You're both in the area for the same reason I am. And the people I represent. It was... is a good place to be in times like this."

"That's true," Roger admitted. "You were saying, before Dudley showed up?"

"The group I'm with," Killany said, after a sip of hot chocolate, "is well equipped and well supplied. They have a working farm set up for the duration. You know as well as I do that when this weather breaks and people can travel again... those that are left, anyway, are going to be looking for any and all food they can find. And some of them are not going to care too much what they might have to do to get it.

"That farm is the key to the survivors in this whole area. Kept intact, under good leadership, it will allow things to come back to some form of normalcy. Eventually leading to rebuilding."

"Still on that rebuilding civilization thing, Killany?" asked Dudley.

"Still on that rebuilding civilization thing, as you put it, Dudley. It's important and needs to be done and you know it."

"Yeah. Yeah. Just razzing you, buddy. That still doesn't answer why Strotskey is here."

"Am I going to have to get between you two every time one or the other of you open your mouths?" Killany asked coldly when Roger started to get up, mayhem in his eyes.

Roger slowly squatted back down on his haunches. "No," he said slowly. "But Dudley there better just watch his Ps and Qs around me."

"You call me Do Right one time, and I'll have your guts for garters," Dudley replied, glaring at his long time nemesis. Roger was glaring back.

Killany shook his head, wondering if he'd made a serious error of judgment. "Okay, you two. Like I told Roger earlier, I need the two of you working together to keep that farm safe and sound. There will be compensations. You know good and well neither of you are going to find companions on your own out here, in a situation like this. And I know both of you were finally looking to settle down before this happened."

"Yeah, well… He'd just better not…"

Dudley's words faded as Roger spoke. "As long as he doesn't…"

"Now," Killany said, ignoring the exchange, "How long will it take you to get your things ready?"

"Couple of days," Roger said. "But I'm not sure my rig will make it. I've been out a couple of times. The ash and the snow… I thought my Dodge could take on anything. But that ash is treacherous, especially when it is wet. And even frozen, some of the stuff is several feet thick and still soft underneath the hard layer. Took me a day to dig out the first time I dropped through."

"Yeah. Same here. My Jeep isn't really set up for these conditions. Never did get around rebuilding it for here. It's still an open rock climber. It'd probably make it, but I'd be frozen to death in a matter of hours."

"We have vehicles available. The pair that set up the place knew what they were doing. We can come get your rigs when conditions permit. For now I want to get you there, acclimatized, and familiar with the farm and surrounding area. There are four ROKONs that can be used for local movement. We have some heavy equipment for putting in defensive positions.

"They are set up well on the home Properties, but we'll need to take the fight out from the center."

"Okay," Roger said. "But how do we get our stuff down there?"

"Yeah. I don't want to leave stuff behind. Me there to watch it, I don't worry. But if I walk away from it..." Dudley didn't look happy.

"I know what you are worried about. Unless you plan on taking everything including the kitchen sink, I have a way to get you and your gear to the farm."

"How's that?"

"The Kettenkrad will handle it all."

"But you're already loaded to the gills from the look of it," Roger protested.

"Yeah," added Dudley. "Bike and trailer both. If you can call that a bike."

Killany drank the last of the hot chocolate in his cup, and rinsed it out before putting it away. "Going to take a little work, but I have what we need cached here close. You guys still have skis' don't you?" Killany got under the tarp on the cargo box on the halftrack motorcycle and came out bearing a pick/mattock and a pick/axe, plus a D-handle round point shovel.

"Sure. You don't expect me to ski all that way, do you?" Roger looked amazed.

"In this weather? Are you nuts?" Dudley added his own comment.

"Give me some credit, guys. Come on." He handed each man one of the pick tools and carried the shovel himself, after slinging his rifle over one shoulder. The two men both slung their long arms and followed Killany toward the small watercourse that the road crossed a few yards away.

"Right here," Killany said a minute or so later. He pointed at a spot on the frozen ground just a few feet from the frozen water in the small stream, well off the road.

"Aw, man!" both men groaned. But both handed their rifles to Killany and lifted the picks up.

There was a lot of groaning and cursing for nearly fifteen minutes as the three men took turns breaking up the frozen surface of the ground. Two would use the picks and then the third would scoop out the frozen chunks of earth.

"That should do it," Killany said. "The rest will be easy."

"Easy? What is it? A bucket cache?" Asked Dudley.

Roger was poking around with the shovel. "Hey! This is dry sand!" He scooped out a shovelful and threw it clear. A couple more and the shovel thudded on something.

"Just clear around it," Killany said. I'll go get the Kettenkrad."

Dudley took over the shovel for a while as Killany dismantled the tarp windbreak and stowed it, and then started the Kettenkrad. He swung wide and pulled up parallel to the hole, and then backed up, putting the back of the trailer right at the edge of the hole.

"It's another trailer," Dudley said, astonished.

"Wrapped up in plastic," Roger added. The two men looked at one another and shook their heads.

"Only Killany…" Dudley said.

"Yeah. Only Killany."

Killany was retrieving a cable from the Kettenkrad. "Just a little more all around," he said when he looked down into the shallow hole, the top of a trailer identical to the one already hitched to the halftrack bike. "And slope this side.

The other two passed the shovel back and forth until they were well down the sides of the trailer. "Okay. Hook up the cable to the tongue."

Killany handed the hook to Roger and went back to start the bike again. The Kettenkrad didn't even spin the tracks when Killany put it in gear and drove forward slowly. Though wrapped in heavy plastic, and the tracks on the trailer not able to turn, Killany pulled the trailer out of the hole.

A few minutes later, the plastic cleared away, and the second trailer hooked to the first one, Killany shut down the bike again.

"Okay. Got a few supplies," he said, uncovering several six gallon plastic buckets that were under the tarp on the trailer. This going to be enough space for both of you to get the gear you can't safely cache?"

"Well… Yeah… I guess," Roger said slowly. "Half will do."

"Same here. Half. A full half," Dudley said, looking at Roger.

"You two take off and start getting things ready. I'll be by to pick you both up in two more days." Killany said.

"What are you going to be doing?" Roger asked.

"Sleeping, mostly," Killany replied with a grin.

"I'll have to come get you," Dudley said. "You'll never find my place."

"This place?" Killany asked, bringing a picture out from inside his parka, now partially opened to keep cool so he wouldn't sweat while he was shoveling.

"You have an aerial picture of my BOL?" Roger started laughing as Dudley sputtered.

"Not so fast, Strotskey." Killian handed Roger another picture. This one of his discrete little compound.

"But I only met you in Branson," Dudley protested. "How'd you find my place?"

"Rented a plane and flew around until I spotted it. Just used common logic to figure out the most likely spots, knowing both of you and your habits."

"Aw, man!" groaned Roger. "I really did think I had you on this." He looked at Dudley. "We only met in Branson, too."

"Well, water under the bridge," Killany said, taking the pictures back from the two men. "You both take off. I'll be around."

Rather dejectedly the two men walked off, each slinging their rifle into a comfortable position on their back. They didn't say anything to each other the entire time they travelled the same path. Then Roger cut away from the highway. A few minutes later Dudley did the same, only going south instead of north.

Killany sighed and went back to the cache hole, shovel in hand. He dug for a few more minutes and then removed two more six-gallon buckets, and two smaller buckets that had been a few inches under the six-gallon ones. Once he had them secured in the trailer, he got back on the Kettenkrad, started it, and headed for the camp spot he chosen nearby on the way up.

There was no sign of the buckets in the second trailer when Killany pulled through the opening in the fence at Roger's place. Roger was waiting and they soon had the totes and bags of his gear he was taking loaded up. There was easily half of the trailer space left.

"You have everything else secured or cached?" Killany asked Roger.

"Yeah. Except the skis. You mentioned skiing."

"Yep," Killany said. He went to the lead trailer and came back with a water ski tow rope. "Here you go. Carabiner it to one of the tow rings and we'll be on our way."

"Never occurred to me you'd just tow us…" Roger said, shaking his head. "But there is room for me to ride for right now…"

"You'll want the practice before Dudley sees you, believe me," Killany said with a laugh.

"You have no confidence. I'm an excellent skier."

"Yeah. We'll see."

"Uh… Don't go too fast, huh?"

"I won't."

An hour later, after only three falls, Killany stopped the halftrack bike near the cache point. "I'm going to go get Dudley. Shouldn't take long. You want a tarp?"

"Nah! I'm dressed for it. Go ahead. Don't know why I can't just go with you."

"You want Dudley to know exactly where your place is?"

"Crimeny no!"

"I'm sure Dudley feels the same way about you." With that, Killany shifted gears and took off down the road at high speed, the tracks of all three units lifting rooster tails of loose snow into the air. It had snowed the night before, dropping a good six inches of fresh powder on the ground. It would actually make the journey easier. Before this snow there were spots that the two skiers would have needed to walk rather than ski due to bare ground.

True to his word, Killany was back to pick up Roger within an hour. Roger was watching Dudley carefully. He seemed to be doing well being towed on the skis. "Geez. Glad I had the practice before he saw me make a fool of myself."

Killany stopped just long enough for Roger to uncoil his tow rope and get set. Then they were off, headed south. Killany, because of the towing, took it easy. It took them four full days to get back to the property, stopping early to set up camp, eat, drink something hot and climb into sleeping bags for much needed rest and to warm up. Even clothed as well as they were, it was a cold journey.

There was quite a crowd of startled onlookers when Killany pulled into Bethany's compound. He'd radioed ahead that they were almost there. Gary and Stefano had not really ever said how Killany was going to be getting around. Bethany and Dr. Cooper, both curious, were sidestepped the few times they asked. Then, with the regular reports that Killany was sending, the two women no longer worried about it.

"What is that thing?" Dr. Cooper asked when she first saw the men coming down the road.

"Can't remember exactly what he called it," Gary said. "But it is basically a halftrack motorcycle, with a tracked trailer." And then, surprised, Gary added, "With two tracked trailers. Pulling two men on skis." He shook his head. No wonder the two women, especially Dr. Cooper, were curious. Killany was always coming up with something unusual.

Killany pulled up and stopped. Roger and Dudley popped their ski bindings and walked up to the rear trailer and put the skis on it. Killany was waiting for them to join him so he could make the introductions.

"Okay," he said, "This is Roger Strotskey and Dudley Monahan. I'll vouch for their credentials and skills. Personalities... well, can't have everything, I guess."

"Aw! Killany!" protested Roger. "You'll give these people the idea we're some kind of misfits."

"Yeah, Killany," added Dudley.

Killany just looked at the two men for a moment.

"Okay. Okay. We're misfits. But we're harmless," Dudley said.

"Maybe not harmless," Roger said. "But not harmless in a good way."

"Give it up, guys," Gary said, chuckling. "Killany's opinion is good enough for me. Let's get inside out of the freezing wind. It's almost time for supper." Gary looked at Bethany.

"Won't be a problem. Got a pot of soup on."

"So you can join us," Gary continued. "I'd like to hear your plans about the farm. Stefano, would you let the Major know we'd like him to join us at the house?"

"Sure, Boss." Stefano hurried off, and the rest of those that had come out to greet Killany headed for their own homes. All took one last look at the Kettenkrad and then hurried to get out of the cold.

Dr. Cooper, Gary, Killany, and the two new men followed Bethany as she walked slowly to the earth sheltered house. Gary held the door open for her and she went inside. Dr. Cooper joined her, and then the men went inside.

"Annie," called Bethany.

"Yes, Bethany?" asked the young nurse. She and her children were staying with Gary and Bethany for the time being. In part to help the heavily pregnant Bethany with household chores, in part to keep an eye on her as Bethany was having some problems associated with the pregnancy. And finally, since she would have had a hard time on her own with the two children to take care of, under the difficult living conditions that existed in the other homes.

"Going to have a staff meeting at dinner. Could you prepare the dining room for me?"

"Of course."

"Here, now," Roger said, his eyes on Annie. "I'll lend a hand. Seeing as how I'm part of the cause for the meeting."

Everyone could tell the meeting was the last thing on Roger's mind. Annie blushed, but she didn't protest when Roger followed her to the kitchen.

Dr. Cooper and Bethany looked over at Dudley. He was muttering under his breath, staring at the door through which the two had gone.

"Don't worry, Dudley," Gary said, grinning. "There are several eligible ladies in residence, here and at the Farm."

"Really?" Dudley asked. "Cool."

As they all began to take off their heavy outer clothing, Dr. Cooper looked disapprovingly at Gary. Gary had learned how to avoid the good Doctor's few quirks and just ignored the look. He took Bethany's arm and guided her to the rocking chair in the living room that she favored since starting to show.

Before the rest could take seats, Major Tandy knocked and followed the sound into the house. "Hello Major," Gary said.

Dudley was suddenly standing at attention and saluting.

"At ease," the Major said quietly. "I'm retired."

"Yes, sir. Sorry, sir."

"Dudley," Killany said, "You're retired, too, remember?"

"Oh. Yeah. Sometimes I forget. I guess it did take me a long time to stop saluting you, too, didn't it."

Dr. Cooper gave Killany a hard look. He'd managed not to wince when Dudley spoke, but he had a feeling that the subject was not going to be completely dropped. Hopefully the Doctor and Roger and Dudley wouldn't get along too well and he could maintain a few of the personal details of his life private.

"Mrs. Martain," Roger said, stepping into the living room, "Annie asked me to ask you how many."

"Just the staff and you and Dudley. The Major just came in."

Roger looked over at the Major, and just like Dudley, quickly came to attention and saluted."

"He's retired," Dudley said, enjoying the fact that he was seeing Roger in the same predicament he'd just been in. And Roger hadn't seen it. "And so are you."

"Oh. Yeah. Did the same thing with the Colonel for a long time, huh, Colonel?"

This time Killany did wince. "Yes," he said, "You did. Dismissed. You too, Dudley."

Both men snapped to attention again and saluted Killany this time before making themselves scarce in the kitchen.

When the brass got together, retired or not, it was better for former noncoms to be somewhere else.

"Colonel?" Dr. Cooper asked an edge to her voice. Bethany and Gary stayed out of it completely, though they did watch the interplay with interest.

"Thought you might be service," Major Tandy said, looking at Killany much like Dr. Cooper was. "Why didn't you pull rank on me? You're the one that should be in charge."

"I'm not a rank puller, Major," Killany said, avoiding looking at Dr. Cooper. "I'm retired. It's a moot point for me. You're the kind of leader this group needs. I'm a..." He did look at Dr. Cooper then. "If you don't mind, I'd prefer to discuss this later," he continued, looking back at the Major.

Major Tandy didn't salute, but he did say, "Yes, sir," with respect.

"But..." Dr. Cooper said. She obviously wanted to know more, but refused to ask as Killany just looked at her without offering to continue.

"So, Colonel," the Major said, "How was the trip. You seemed to have gone and returned without undo trouble."

"Please, Major. Killany. You're the commander here, with Gary and Bethany Martain. At best, I'm just an advisor."

"As you wish, Si... As you wish. Though you aren't 'just' anything, I bet."

"Just what does that make me?" Dr. Cooper asked, more than a little peeved.

"It makes you a valuable member of the leadership team, in my opinion," Killany said firmly, his eyes on Dr. Cooper's.

"Yes. Well…"

Annie came into the living room then and announced that things were ready. Gary was up first and helped Bethany to her feet. Rather reluctantly, Roger and Dudley joined the others at the table after helping Annie bring the tureen of soup to the table.

There was only the clacking of dipper against tureen and bowls for a bit, and then Gary cleared his throat. "Please continue to eat," he said. "But I'd like to discuss the Farm and how we'll handle security and how Roger and Dudley fit into it."

"The farm is set up very well for close in defense against small to medium sized groups, given enough people are on the firing line." Killany pulled a large piece of bread from the unsliced loaf before he continued. "I believe we need to extend the defensive line further out, and set up some long range recce…"

Dr. Cooper looked at Killany questioningly.

"Reconnaissance. Long range reconnaissance to find potential problems before they find us. Between the two aircraft, we should be able to check the entire area every couple of weeks or so. I'm not sure of your fuel reserves, but even once a month for starters should let us spot anyone moving into the area, plus locate other survivors in the near area. There were people in Springfield, I'm sure. I saw the signs."

"You didn't contact them?" Dr. Cooper asked. She was holding her soup spoon just over the bowl when she spoke.

"No," Killany said. "I thought the risk was too high. I wanted to accomplish the mission I set out to do before taking that kind of risk."

Dr. Cooper didn't say anything else. She did take another spoonful of the soup.

"Though not their specialty, Strotskey and Monahan can reliably do the ground recce. Using two of the ROKONs for mobility under the conditions we're in right now. They can also train everyone on defensive tactics and details. More to keep anyone from doing something that will get them hurt or killed than increasing the effectiveness of our defense, although that will be the case, too.

"We need to have a plan to deal with those that begin to discover us. It is only a matter of time. The majority, given some help from us, will be willing to work with us to protect the farm, as it will become their primary source of quality food. Those that chose to try to take from us by stealth, or open conflict, we will need to deal with harshly. Just how harshly will have to be decided."

"Just whack them all, if they put up a fight," Roger said. He was on his second bowl of soup. "This is good."

"I don't think that will be necessary all the time," Killany replied, surprising Dr. Cooper with his response. "There will be desperate people out and about that might not believe they can get any help, so do it the hard way without even trying communication first. Not everyone out there is going to be a savage.

"Now, though we could put a few housing units at the farm, I think additional housing should be located here, across our road, and have a couple of bunkrooms and a community room for those working their time at the farm. Too easy for things to get out of hand at the farm if there are a lot new people that get together there and try to take over.

"Though there will be several there at once, if we keep the shifts rotated so no cohesive group can develop, until everyone discovers it really is in their best interests to keep the farm as it is, we'll be much more resistant to an internal take over from new people. And if we are to become the community supply house, we're going to need the people to expand the farm from what it is now."

Killany looked over at the Major. "What do you think, Major?"

"I think you're right. We will no doubt get some bad apples this way, but I think we can fish them out and not spoil the whole barrel. As for those that take up arms against us, then they get what they get. We already have a decent fighting force, though it isn't all at the farm."

"Dr. Cooper?" Killany then asked, again surprising her.

"I... I'm not sure... I don't like the talk of fighting. I know it may be necessary. I was on the verge of shooting someone when I first arrived. But I don't like the idea. We should make all efforts to bring people in peacefully. Offer them food, shelter, health care, and then try to get them to cooperate."

"I don't know," Bethany said, before Killany could ask for her opinion. "I think it better that they know well beforehand the circumstance under which they can become a part of our group. They can decide first to join us peaceably or try to take us on."

Everyone looked at Gary. "Ah. My turn. Yes. I agree with my dear wife. Things should be pretty black and white. You will follow the rules we set up or you won't be allowed to stay. We make it clear just how much food they will be getting, what services their work will allow them to purchase. And I think that we should set up a monetary system very soon so we can have it implemented before we take in any outsiders. Besides Roger and Dudley."

"You mean we might get paid, too?" Roger asked.

"Gold? Silver?" Dudley asked. "Surely not greenbacks."

Gary smiled. "No greenbacks. Silver and gold coins. We'll get someone to act as banker, start paying everyone that contributes now and set up a rate schedule for products and services we make available to them. Initially, with just a few exceptions, like the good doctor here, it will pretty much be just going back and forth between everyone else and Bethany and me, as the primary owners of the Properties and what they produce."

"Wait," Dr. Cooper said. "Why am I excepted?"

"You'll be charging for your services as soon as we set the monetary system up, since you deal directly with your patients. Much of the work is done as a matter of course; therefore most will draw a salary. Others, like Annie, will have a base salary, and then get paid for any other work she does for someone, such as helping around the house here.

"Those that cut and haul wood will be allowed to charge for it. Those at the farm will get a wage, with Frank and Colette getting salaries as co-managers of the farm. We need it set up before others get here, so they can see right off that if they work they'll be paid and they'll be able to purchase what they want, rather than be given some arbitrary amount of food, that they might or not prefer over other foods."

Dr. Cooper, Roger, and Dudley all three nodded their heads in understanding.

"I guess that would work. It feels strange though," Dr. Cooper said, "thinking of charging for what has become my contribution to the community."

"I think people will prefer to have options they can decide on, rather than have the decision of who does what made for them," Killany added.

"Now wait a minute!" Dr. Cooper's cheeks were suddenly flushed. "I'm a very good doctor. And I'm the only doctor. There isn't anyone else…"

"I'm not speaking of you specifically, Dr. Cooper," Killany said quietly. "There could be other doctors come into the fold. I think people should have a choice, not because you aren't good, simply because most people prefer to make a choice. No matter how qualified someone is in a field of endeavor, there will be some that prefer someone else to deal with. Some of the men here would quite probably prefer a male doctor. And if you were male, there would be women that would turn to a female doctor that joined us, just because she is a woman."

"I think I see what you're getting at, but I still feel like I'm getting slammed here."

"My apologies. What I've been saying wasn't meant to offend, only explain."

"Well… All right. Go on. What else?"

Gary spoke again. "We need to get things set up and just spring it on everyone at once. Give everyone basically a one month's wage or salary, for the work performed the past month, and put it on a cash basis from now on."

"You guys got enough gold and silver to do that?" Roger asked eyes wide.

"Don't get ideas, Strotskey," Dudley said.

"I'm not! It's just; I have some gold and silver. But it isn't much. And if the pay is low because there isn't enough to go around, and things are expensive, to get back the silver and gold paid out... Well... I'm just... curious. Just curious." Roger wouldn't look at Killany. He kept his eyes on the table.

"Well, Roger," Bethany said, her voice light, "We have enough to do the job properly, but not enough to just throw it around. It will be a balanced budget economy."

"We'll set the initial rates for all the basics and then let supply and demand set the rest, including the basics over time."

"That sounds good," Roger said. "Sorry."

"No need to be sorry," Gary said.

Roger breathed tiny sigh of relief and finally looked over at Killany. When Killany just looked back at him impassively, Roger relaxed.

There was silence for a while as everyone caught up on the eating they'd missed while talking. Annie brought in another loaf of fresh baked bread and set it on the table. "Dessert will be ready in about ten minutes."

"Dessert? You have a dessert?" Dudley asked. "I really messed up and didn't store enough comfort food. I haven't had anything sweet in weeks."

"Just apple pie, made from freeze-dried apples. Fresh baked whole wheat crust."

"My favorite," Roger said quickly. "I bet it'll be great if you made it."

Annie turned red again and hurried back to the kitchen. She didn't mind the attention. But wished Roger would do it in private.

Roger grinned over at Dudley. Dudley just looked sour and tore off a piece of bread to wipe out his soup bowl.

"Major, are you up for a trip to the farm tomorrow?" Killany asked. He'd only taken one bowl of soup and the one hunk of bread, though he did smear it liberally with the stored butter powder that had been mixed with a bit of coconut oil to make it into a spread again.

"Yeah. I'm doing fine. As long as I don't overdo it."

"Then, if you'll excuse me, I'm going to go start putting my gear away."

Looking disappointed, Roger and Dudley started to rise.

"Stay where you are, gentlemen," Killany said. "Enjoy the pie. When you're done, come on out and we'll get you squared away for the night."

Both men dropped back into their chairs with smiles on their faces.

"You know," Bethany said, "I don't think I've ever seen him eat any kind of dessert."

"You short on them?" Dudley asked.

"No. Not really. We do have to watch things or the children will gorge themselves on the sweet foods."

"There you have it, then," Roger said. "Killany would never take something that might conceivably short a child."

"Right. He'd starve before he let a kid do without something."

All eyes turned toward Dr. Cooper. "What?" she asked.

"Nothing, Dr. Cooper," Gary said. "Let's all enjoy the rest of the meal and let business slide until the next time."

## CHAPTER SEVEN

-

Taking one of the former county maintenance trucks with snow blade, Killany, with the Major as passenger, headed for the farm. The badly drifted sections of the road, both snow and ash drifts, had already been cleared, but the winds had been blowing strongly again, so the truck with the blade led the way, just in case. Strotskey and Monahan, with their gear, followed in one of the Yukon's.

After introducing the two men to Frank and Colette Winchester, Killany went into the house with them to discuss the changes being planned, while the Major took Roger and Dudley around the property, using three of farm's ROKON diesel powered two-wheel-drive motorcycles.

"We're going to need to put together a value list, or price and wage list, if you prefer. Wages for the various jobs being done, and the prices of the commodities and services the farm provides." Killany looked at the couple as they looked at one another.

They'd been a young couple when Bethany and Gary bought into the farm. They had matured during the buildup phase, and come into their own when the attack occurred. Both were now seasoned leaders, capable of not only running the Farm well, but the entire operation, including the security of the farm, once given the tools.

"I think we can do that pretty easily," Colette said. "We've been keeping the books just like we did before the attack, using pre-attack figures. All we really need is some kind of conversion rate between dollars and silver, and silver and gold."

Killany nodded. "That shouldn't be a problem. We can talk it over with the other staff and come up with something reasonable. There seems to be a more or less natural historical constant ratio between the two metals. It has varied, sometimes widely, but usually comes back very close to that ratio.

"Now, about Strotskey and Monahan. They know what they are doing. But they can tend to go overboard. Keep a pretty tight rein on them. Any major questions just do like we always do. Take it up with the full staff, and we'll hash it out."

"You really think its all necessary?" Frank asked. "There hasn't been any sign of problems."

"Don't forget about what happened to the Major. There are some people out there that are willing to shoot first and not even bother with questions afterward."

"That's right, Honey," Colette said. "We've talked about it before. Yes, we need to expand and that takes people. We'll be able to provide for a large number of people, but only if there is a low risk factor in working here."

"Assuming the weather ever changes," Frank sighed. "I know. I just hate the thought of having to fight other survivors."

"So do I," Killany said. "But when the time comes, if it comes, I have confidence that you will do what is needed. And Strotskey and Monahan are a big part of that. They are both very qualified noncoms, capable of leading a small fighting force each. With them as your key players and assuming we start to get a few additional people to fill out the ranks, we should be able to handle anything that comes along."

"Okay," Frank said. "We'll bring them into the fold. Make sure they have what they need to get the job done.

"Okay. I'm going to get the Major back. This weather is hard on him. The Yukon will be available to those two, primarily. Add it to your inventory."

"Okay Killany. Thanks. We'll get things squared away. Hopefully spring will actually be spring and not another extended winter."

"We can only hope and pray," Killany said. He shrugged into his heavy coat and left the house. He walked through the various buildings of the farm, speaking casually to many of those taking care of the greenhouses and the animals.

Things were going well, but everything would be much better if they could get at least enough good weather to get some feed and grain crops grown, harvested, and stored. When he went back to the truck to wait, he saw Strotskey, Monahan and the Major talking animatedly nearby, still seated on the diesel bikes.

Strotskey noticed Killany and waved him over.

"What do you think?" Killany asked them when he joined the group.

"Real potential here," Roger said. "Close defenses are just what you said. With some regular patrols and a few bunkers in key positions to control access from further out, the farm can expand production fields significantly and still be pretty secure."

"I agree," Dudley said. "Real potential. Those guys really picked a good spot for what they wanted."

"I've found Gary and Bethany to be a lot sharper about some things than you might think a car salesman and an executive business woman to be."

"Uh, any chance of getting some heavy metal or rock and roll?" Roger suddenly asked. "Fort Leonard Wood, maybe?"

"Would sure be nice," Dudley said.

"Not impossible," Killany said. "But not probable. We'll look at the possibility when the weather breaks. I don't think we'll need anything we don't already have before then."

Killany looked at the Major and noticed the pinched look around his mouth. "Time to get back, I think."

"Yeah," Major Tandy said, rather sadly. "I just can't take it like I used to."

"Okay, guys. Fit in. Do what you do best. Look after these people and this property," Killany reached out and shook first Roger's hand, and then Dudley's.

"Thanks, man," Roger said with feeling. "This is gonna be a good gig. Got some good people here, doing good things."

"Much as I hate to agree, he's right," Dudley said. "Always wanted to be part of something good. And things were getting lonely at my place." His eyes cut over to one of the women walking toward the main animal barn."

Killany smiled, as did the Major, and then both headed for the highway maintenance truck. Killany made sure the Major made it to Gary's shelter, where he was still living, unlike most of the other members of the group that had eagerly taken up residence in the other existing homes and those brought in after the attack.

Next, Killany went about unloading the Kettenkrad and trailer, storing everything in what had become his official home, the garage basement at Bethany's compound. He found Gary and, despite Gary's, and then Bethany's objections, transferred several cases of long term storage food to the group stocks.

"This isn't really necessary," Bethany said, her hands cupped under her swollen belly.

"Perhaps not, but I like to keep my independence. "I don't like to owe someone, even if it is only in my own mind."

"Well we appreciate it," Gary said. "We're holding our own, but the stocks are slowly dwindling. We have years yet, but the weather better change within a couple of years, or we're in trouble."

"I know," Killany replied. "Speaking of which, I may make another trip, this one quite a bit longer."

"Oh, no, Killany!" Bethany said. "You just got back. It is so terrible out!"

"I'm acclimated to it. I've proved to myself that the Kettenkrad will do what I need it to do."

"How long?" Gary asked quietly.

"Hopefully, just three months. Might be six, depending on what I find."

"What are you going to be looking for?"

Killany smiled the smile that so infuriated Dr. Cooper. "Oh, little of this. Little of that. Just whatever I can find."

Gary sighed. "What do you need?"

"Just fuel," Killany replied. "Have everything else I need. And I still have a few caches around with more things if I need them."

Bethany shook her head. "I wish you'd reconsider."

"I have, Bethany," Killany said. "I'm not doing this lightly. Yes, it could be dangerous. That doesn't really bother me. Not accomplishing my goal is what worries me. This weather is destroying many things that could be of great use to the group here."

"So this is a salvage run?" Gary asked.

"In a sense," Killany said, nodding. "More a long range recon, looking for things we can salvage, as it is obvious I can't carry much back in with the Kettenkrad, even with the trailers."

"Well, since you're insisting, we want you to go as well equipped and supplied as possible. Feel free to take anything from our stocks that will help you make it a safer and more productive trip." Bethany grimaced. "I'd better go lie down for a bit. Junior here is acting up."

Gary nodded at Killany and he returned it, as Gary saw to his wife's comfort and headed them to the portal to the tunnel to the main house.

Killany turned to the stacks of totes and began to sort through them, rearranging things in a group to take and a group to leave behind.

Three days later, in the early morning bitter cold of a March morning, Killany again fired up the Kettenkrad. With it and both trailers carrying maximum loads, Killany put the bike in gear and left, without any fanfare. Only Gary, Bethany, and Dr. Cooper braved the cold to see him off. And Dr. Cooper only quit trying to talk him out of the trip up to the point he started the halftrack motorcycle.

"The man is just sheer nuts!" Dr. Cooper muttered and turned to go back inside.

Gary chuckled and then helped Bethany back to the comfortable warmth of the earth sheltered house.

Killany, bundled up as he'd been on the first trip, was comfortable. The wind was at his back and the sun was shining brightly. Again he was headed north. He took it easy. It was going to be a long, slow trip.

Every other day Killany made contact with the Properties on the Yaesu FT-897D, using a Yo-Yo six-reel windup dipole antenna. He found he was talking to Dr. Cooper more than he had when physically at the Properties. She always seemed to be the staff member handy when he made the scheduled contact.

He kept her informed of his progress, and she filled him in on what was going on at the Properties. More information than he needed, perhaps, but Dr. Cooper seemed determined to keep him on the radio for as long as possible.

That is, until Killany mentioned he'd seen signs of people and he needed to cut the contact short so they couldn't triangulate on his location. After that, Dr. Cooper's exchanges were much shorter.

Again Killany was avoiding contact as he traveled. He was pleased to see that there were indeed other survivors, but wasn't prepared to let them know about the Properties for sure, or even his own presence. Though heavily armed and quite capable with the weapons he carried, it was better to avoid any confrontation than have a potentially deadly one.

He hunted occasionally on the trip, taking enough game with a suppressed Ruger 10/22 to avoid dipping into his precious supplies of quality protein. And every chance he had, he would dip the fuel tanks at service stations and fill the bike and the containers he'd emptied, treating the gasoline with PRI-G he carried with him to refresh it.

Killany kept a detailed record of the various things he found on the main roads he was traveling. It was disappointing to see so much canned food in delivery trucks ruined, and the other products that the mess from the burst cans had destroyed beyond use. But every roll of toilet paper, every pair of shoes, every sack of sugar and flour he found that was intact went into the notebook he kept handy in his pocket, along with a sharpened pencil.

He also supplemented his food stock from some of the finds. There were more than he expected. There had not been much salvage work done, with the suddenness and destructiveness of the ash falls, much more a hindrance than the effects of the nuclear attack. Only near communities did he find the signs of organized salvage along the interstates.

Killany avoided every town and city religiously, sometime even leaving the interstate if it ran through what had one time been a population center. He traveled for day after day, picking up Interstate 70 west, and then I-29 up to I-80 west.

The further west he went, the worse the ash was. Between that and the cold, Killany kept the tracks of the Kettenkrad well lubricated. He had plenty of spare track with him, and more at the Properties and cached, as well, but that was going to have to be a lifetime supply, hopefully a couple of generations. At least until industry had recovered enough to make more. Killany smiled at the thought. It was doubtful anyone would want to use the Kettenkrad once other means of transport were once again available.

It was late March, with no hint of spring when Killany hit the Utah border. Utah was his primary destination. There were a few stops he wanted to make, to find some important products that would be of use to the Properties and the group.

He was more than a little surprised he wasn't seeing more signs of life in the state. There were many well prepared Latter Day Saints Church members in Utah, along with non-Mormons that lived the prep lifestyle.

But the ash was deep here. Killany wasn't sure but his best guess was that one of the caldera eruptions that had occurred after the attack was Long Valley Caldera. It had covered all of Utah with ash before in ancient eruptions. Apparently it had again.

Killany had to be careful on some of the ash. Not all of it had compacted yet. The Kettenkrad was heavy, one of the reasons it had so much traction, but weight worked against it if ash was aerated to a significant degree. Any doubts and Killany found an alternate route.

He also avoided some of the steep sided cuts through deep ash accumulations in some of the canyons in the mountains. Huge accumulations of ash had been cut by the rivers running at the bottoms of the canyons, leaving unsteady cliffs of the ash that could bury Killany and the Kettenkrad and trailers forever.

Killany had some things to accomplish before he died. Again he found alternate routes. It took days of extra time to go around, but go around he did. It was simply the smart thing to do, since the Kettenkrad was more than capable of doing it.

Having left I-80 well before Salt Lake City, going south, it wasn't until he neared his first goal, Orem, Utah, that he saw signs of organized life. He stopped at the first sign of smoke in the distance and backtracked for a ways. He'd been watching for likely places to cache the bike and trailers, so knew where he was going. Up a side canyon, oriented so the canyon floor was swept clear of both ash and snow, Killany was able to find a place to hide his rig, without leaving telltale tracks behind.

He put on his pack, and hiked back to the point where he'd seen the smoke in the distance. It was snowing as he set up his tent, as it had been off and on all day. Killany stayed there for two days, waiting for the storm to pass before he broke camp and began the long slow shanks mare trip into Orem. If he got that far. Not far outside of town, Killany dropped a small, brightly colored bag with a length of orange survey tape tied to it to the ground and kept going.

There were some amazed guards at the edge of town when Killany appeared in the distance and walked toward them. The PTR-91 was slung over his back, though he carried a long collapsible staff, topped with a wicked spear point he'd made himself.

"What do you want?"

"Where'd you come from?"

"How'd you get here?"

Those were just three of the questions he was asked, as the two guards were quickly joined by several other people. No one aimed a gun directly at him, but just about everyone had one ready to do so.

"Here to do a bit of business," Killany said, allowing two of the people to take his spear, the PTR-91, and the Para Ordnance from the holster on his belt.

"Business? Nobody is doing any business! Man, there's been a war and a bunch of volcanoes and earthquakes. Where you been all this time?"

"In a safe place," Killany replied. "Is there someone I can talk to about Emergency Essentials? I'd like to make a purchase. A substantial one."

The men all looked at one another. "You've got to be kidding!" said one.

"You think there's anything left there, after all this time?"

"I'm counting on it." Killany's sharp eyes caught the look passed between two of the men at the back of the group. He smiled slowly. "Yep," he added. "I'm counting on it. And willing to pay cold hard coin for it."

"Let's get him inside," said one of the two men. The others jumped to obey. Killany wasn't abused, but he was handled none too gently when three of the men held him and two others stripped him out of his outerwear while one of the two men went through his back pack.

"You have excellent equipment," said the man after setting out everything on a table. "But I don't see any sign of anything that would purchase anything significant."

"Wait," said the third man searching Killany. "He's got a money belt on."

"Get it."

Killany made it easy, holding his arms up as one man lifted his shirt and another untied the cloth money belt. "Heavy," said the guy and passed it to the man that seemed to be in charge.

"Well, well, well. You do have some gold," said the guy. He looked into each compartment, pouring out the few coins in each one. There was a mix of quarter ounce Gold Eagles, one-tenth Gold Eagles, one ounce Silver Eagles, and old silver dimes and quarters.

"You really think you're going to buy much with this? Pocket change here."

"Oh, there's more where that came from. That's just personal money for buying meals, lodging, and such."

"I see. Take him over and get him some food and water."

As his arms were firmly grasped, the leader said, "I'll just hang onto this for a while. We'll talk again."

Killany acknowledged with a nod and went peaceably with the men after getting his outer clothing back on, using one released arm at a time. He knew he could get free, but he'd probably have to kill some of them, and he wasn't ready to do that, yet.

Inside what was obviously a communal hall, he was given a bowl of vegetable stew, without meat, though the stock obviously had been prepared with beef, a small whole loaf of bread, and a pitcher of milk was set on the table in front of him, as was a glass for it.

Killany ate with relish. The stew was hot and the milk was cold. He eased his chair back a bit when he was finished. A woman came in removed the dishes, hurrying back to the kitchen of the building.

Settling himself comfortably, Killany rested his hands in his lap and relaxed, letting his head go forward. He was actually almost asleep when one of the men touched his arm. "Let's go. They want to see you."

Again with a man on each arm, Killany was guided away, this time through an inside door in the building, down a short hall and into a small conference room.

"Sit down," said the man that had checked the money belt. He was sitting at the head of the table. He dismissed the two men that had escorted Killany in. "I'm Nathan. You say you want to purchase supplies. You implied you wanted to purchase a great deal and mentioned Emergency Essentials."

The other four men at the table were watching Killany with great interest.

"That is correct," Killany said, meeting each of the men's eyes in turn.

"Why would you think a resource like that would still have supplies available for sale?" asked the tallest of the four men.

"No reason not to have, unless the locals salvaged everything, and I just don't think that happened here. I think it would have become a community asset. Closely guarded, conserved, used only when absolutely necessary."

"If so," asked another of the men, this one short and stout, "why would we consider selling anything, much less a large quantity, of something that you admit yourself is an asset needing to be conserved until absolutely required."

"Many reasons. None of which I need to know. Entirely up to you. All I need to know is what you have to sell, and how much you want for it. I have nothing to barter or trade with. The things you might want or need, can probably be purchased with gold, just as I wish to purchase what I want, with gold."

"This isn't enough to buy more than a month's supplies for one man," said the third man at the table. He sat beside the tall one.

"I have more. Much more."

"We have gold to buy what we need." This came from the fourth man. The oldest of the four. "Why would we need yours?"

"So you can buy what you want and still have gold left. And, more importantly, you will be making contact with another group capable of helping you, if need be. And a group with a good genetic pool."

The five men looked startled. "You couldn't possibly know…" said Nathan.

"It's pretty easy to figure out," Killany said. "A closed society can run into genetic trouble pretty quick if the population is small and already fairly closely related. That goes for both humans and farm animals."

"We have no problems like that now," Nathan said.

"No. Of course not. Do you want to wait until you do before you start searching for alternatives? I'm giving you the opportunity to set up a trade route with a group that will soon be in a position to begin exporting food. Not a huge amount, but significant in that it will be foods you will have trouble growing here, under current and probable future weather patterns."

"If we were to sell you the things you want, what assurances do we have that we'd get equal value in return?"

"The deal will be in your hands. I'll give you twenty ounces of gold, in US Eagles, and when the time comes you deliver two semi trucks with well loaded double semi trailers of the items on the list that is in the money belt."

Nathan quickly checked the money belt again. The folded piece of paper had stuck in the pocket of the belt when the coins slid out. Nathan glanced at the list and then handed it to the elderly man. Nathan was studying Killany with intense interest.

"You have the gold with you?" Nathan asked as the list was handed from hand to hand around the table.

"Yes. Cached outside of town. When I leave, I'll leave the location with you. As I said, it is all your choice. You'll have the gold, if you agree, and then your conscience will be your guide to follow through or not."

"Travel is difficult," Nathan said. "What if we can't make it?"

"By the time you decide it is really what you want to do, travel will be easier, I'm sure. I don't expect anything in return for a couple of years."

"You're serious?" asked Nathan. Nathan wasn't the only one with an incredulous look on his face.

"I'm serious. Give me my things back, I'll write down the location of the gold, and you can go get it when I'm gone. If you agree."

"And if we just say yes and then don't follow through?" asked the elderly man, holding out a hand to stop the others from speaking.

"You won't say yes and not follow through. It isn't in you. Any of you." Killany looked around at each of the men. None of them said anything. "Yes or no?" Killany asked, "And I'll be on my way, either way."

"Wait outside," Nathan said.

Killany nodded and stood up. He stepped outside. The men in the hall came alert, but none tried to restrain him. They just watched him like a hawk.

Killany didn't have long to wait. Only a few minutes later Nathan came out into the hall, looked at Killany a moment and then said, "Yes." He handed Killany the money belt, heavy with the coins again.

"Very good. I'll see some of you in a few months." The men looked at Nathan, and when he shook his head, they stood aside when Killany headed for the community room.

"Someone will need to go with me for a ways," he said over his shoulder.

"I'll go," said the first guard that had spoken to him when Killany first appeared. There was silence between them as both dressed for the cold weather and then went outside. Killany's backpack had been returned to him, all contents intact.

The guard followed Killany until Killany stopped. He waited, watching curiously as Killany took out his notebook and pencil and wrote in it for a few seconds. Killany tore the sheet free and handed it to the guard. "Here you go. It's not far. Just be careful."

"You're just walking away?" asked the man after reading the instructions.

"I'm just walking away. See you sometime in the future, perhaps." Killany did just as he said he would. He walked away. He never looked back. He reached the campsite just before dark and set up his tent.

Giving it two full days to make sure no one was shadowing him, Killany finally went back to the spot he'd hidden the Kettenkrad. Everything was just fine. He spent the night there. The next day, one of the warmest on the trip so far, Killany started up the Kettenkrad and turned south.

It took only one day to get where he was headed. Mapleton. Whatever the vagaries of the wind caused it, Mapleton was buried under twenty feet of hard packed ash with two feet of hard snow over it. Killany traveled carefully.

This time there wasn't anyone around. There were signs of people having survived the worst of the ash fall. He didn't find any bodies and wondered if the people had moved somewhere else before it got bad, or perished with no sign under the ash.

But the place he was looking for was intact, more or less. The office had broken windows and was partially filled with ash and snow. The small warehouse area was still closed up, though the roof had collapsed partially, from the ash load, he discovered when he broke through the door. Carrying a bright flashlight, Killany searched the place. It didn't take long to find what he was looking for.

He smiled and then went to work on the outside loading dock vertical door. When he had it open he had to hack and shovel a way to the surface of the ash. Killany drove the Kettenkrad close and began to load the lead trailer with all the Power Research Inc. products he could find. PRI-G and PRI-D in sixteen ounce, thirty-two ounce, and one gallon containers. Killany took them all.

He was gone the next day, going north again, his task accomplished and with no wish to risk sinking in the ash. He skirted Orem again and stayed well away from Salt Lake City. It had taken at least one nuke, perhaps more. Next stop was Hyrum. Three days later Killany entered the small town. Like Mapleton, it was deserted, though not buried as badly. He found the Canning Pantry building without too much trouble.

But a blizzard was building and Killany decided to set up camp inside the building. He took the three days he was there to inventory the contents of the warehouse. Everything he expected to find there, he did. In huge quantities.

Unfortunately, Killany couldn't get any of the semi trucks running. But that wasn't a big problem. Not at the moment, anyway. He had one more stop to make before he could think about loading up and going home.

After the blizzard, Killany waited three more days for the winds to die down some. At least they were clearing some of the snow, pushing it up onto the existing drifts, but leaving open areas where Killany could travel without risking sinking into the deep snow.

Northward again, into the teeth of the wind once more, Killany took his time getting to Idaho. What was a few hours' drive before the war and the eruptions took Killany three days of slow travel. But he made it, and like Orem and Hyrum Utah, Montpelier, Idaho was deserted, as far as he could tell.

This would be a critical stop. The bulk of what he wanted, would be here, if it was anywhere. Walton Feed had been a major supplier of LTS foods and equipment before the war. Killany, Gary, Bethany, and most of the others he knew that had made extensive preparations had purchased from the company.

Killany was prepared to pay, and pay handsomely, for several truckloads of products from the warehouse. The place had been gone through, and some things taken, it looked like, but the warehouse still contained tons of supplies and equipment.

This time Killany made a concerted attempt to get a couple of the semi trucks caught at the loading docks when everything happened started, with limited success. One of them would run, but not well. But it wasn't the electronics, for the truck was an older one, with a mechanically fueled engine. After several tries, and a healthy dose of PRI-D in the fuel tanks, the truck began to run much more smoothly.

Again, after some hard work and much trial, Killany got a forklift running. He was able to load up all five semi trailers on the property with the things he wanted to get home to the Properties.

He sealed all the trailers up, and one at a time, moved them well away from Walton Feed. He wanted them to be intact in case someone else had the same idea he'd had, before he could get back to get the goods. In the process he found three more trailers, loaded them, and moved them to unlikely spots, too.

With the truck running fairly well, and the fortunate discovery of an Idaho DOT maintenance truck, much like those at the Properties, and the PRI-D to treat fuel Killany changed his plans slightly. After a week of work with an engine driven welder, Killany laboriously transferred the snow plow from the DOT truck to the semi.

Knowing he was pushing his luck, Killany took the semi on a bit of a jaunt, looking for more trailers, including an open deck equipment trailer. He found what he needed, after passing up a couple of trailers that might have done the job. But the ones he chose to take were in better condition, larger, and exactly what he wanted.

Another few days of jockeying the trailers around to get the two reefers loaded with more of Walton Feed products, and Killany was almost ready to head home. Several pallets of Walton Feed Super Pails were tarped and added to the equipment trailer he'd found, now attached to the semi truck as a third trailer.

Four pallets with four empty fifty-five gallon drums each were loaded behind the food pallets. All the pallets were securely strapped to the trailer. Using the Kettenkrad, he backed first one, and then the other, of the two heavily loaded bike trailers onto the equipment trailer. He secured the trailers and then loaded and secured the Kettenkrad.

After a day's rest, Killany hit the road, slowly. Very slowly. Once he picked up the Interstate, he stopped at the first truck stop he came to. Two days of hard cold work filled the sixteen fifty-gallon drums and the saddle tanks on the semi with diesel fuel that Killany treated with the PRI-D he'd salvaged.

The trip home was longer, and in some ways more perilous than the trip out. Always careful to leave a way to turn the truck and trailers around without needing to back up or disconnect and move them one at a time, Killany had to backtrack several times; looking for a route the truck could take. The snowblade was the only thing that let him get through some places. The ash would ruin it by the time he got to the Properties, he knew. But that was just a price that would have to be paid.

More than once he had to disconnect from the second trailer to use the blade more effectively with just the one trailer connected. It would have been easier to maneuver without the trailer, but he'd never have been able to move much with the blade without the weight of the trailer on the rear axles of the truck.

The truck had a sleeper, so Killany was able to rest well when he stopped each night, without needing to set up camp. Whenever he'd used up two pallets of fuel, he would begin looking for another truck stop to replenish his supply. Only once did he stop at one that had no fuel left.

He'd picked the time well to come out. Had he come much earlier, he would have needed to wait to get through the passes. Only the fact that temperatures were in the low forties and the snow had stopped was he able to get the truck through the highway passes that the Kettenkrad had taken without a bobble.

Killany turned off I-70 onto US 65, going south, nearly home on August 31$^{st}$. Two more days he was home. More tired than he'd ever been in his life, but satisfied that he'd fulfilled any perceived obligation he had to Gary and Bethany, Killany stopped the long assembly of vehicles on the road in front of Bethany's property.

There was a huge group of people waiting for him. Killany hadn't really mentioned to Dr. Cooper what he was doing when he gathered up the supplies, not wanting to be ambushed on the way back by someone that monitored their communications. So the long semi train came to a shock to all of the onlookers.

Dr. Cooper was the first in line to great him and welcomed him home. "You didn't mention any of this!"

Killany shook his head and smiled. Some things would never change.

"I take it you accomplished what you set out to do. Idaho, huh? And probably Utah." Gary said.

"You got it. It was a successful trip," Killany replied. "If things work out, we'll have enough to carry us through some more bad times, or trade away if things take a turn for the better.

"Now, since I blazed a useable trail, we need to put a team together to go back and get the rest of the items I laid claim to before the passes get snowed in again."

"You aren't going back!" Dr. Cooper exclaimed.

Killany nodded. "Have to. Can't let the opportunity pass. This good weather will not last. We have at least one more terrible winter to go through before any hope of better weather. But can we discuss it later. I'm ready for a hot meal, hot shower, and cool, clean sheets."

"Absolutely," Bethany said.

Gary asked, "Anything we need to unload immediately?"

Killany shook his head and headed for the garage and his basement apartment. He wanted as much rest and recuperation he could get before going back to get the things from the Canning Pantry and Walton Feed.

The next day the food stocks from the trailer were added to the community stores, with Killany taking possession of certain items he'd loaded up specifically for himself. Taking a few more days to rest up, but anxious to get going again, so they could make it there and back before the weather changed, Killany let others prepare the semi trucks for the trip. The trucks and several trailers had been recovered and made ready for use at the farm when the time came while Killany was gone.

Actually, quite a few things had changed while Killany was away. Gary and the Major took him around the Properties and the Farm to show him the improvements and get his comments.

"Any security problems while I was gone," Killany asked.

"No," Major Tandy immediately said. "Strotskey and Monahan really beefed up the outer perimeter defenses and only once has anyone tried to get inside them. They ran off without a shot being fired when they saw what they faced. But we're getting rumblings of rumors that there are some bad people out there somewhere. I think it is probably the same ones that shot me, down at the dam."

"I was afraid of that. And when the weather permits, they will eventually find us, if they don't already know exactly where we are. They might, already. One of the reasons I want this other trip over. I could be wrong when they decide to attack."

"We'll handle whatever comes up," said Gary. "Thanks to you, whether you are here, or not."

"Yeah. Well…"

Lastly they went across the road from the Properties to see what Killany had seen when he drove up, but in more detail.

There was a string of single, double, and triple wide manufactured housing units lining the road from beyond Bethany's original purchase to past Gary's original purchase.

"Already have five people that came aboard to work at the Farm or here at the Properties," Gary said.

"The ash? Power? Water? Septic?" Killany asked.

"All the ash was moved again. To that open area north of here, near the lake. We're going to make it a manure field. All extra dirt we get when we put in something, all manure from the farm, all the glycerin from biodiesel production, all vegetation remains, all go on it and get worked into the ash.

We'll have a huge amount of nearly perfect humus to improve the new fields we're working on.

"As to water, we got a drilling rig going, with a couple of people that knew the basics. Lost one drill bit, I hate to say, but we've managed to put in seven new wells. One more at the Properties, two here, and four for the new fields the farm will be using eventually," Gary explained.

"Septic is all from existing places around the lake that we dug up and re-used. Talk about a mess. But we got the job done. The houses are being torn down, the material to be used for additional structures elsewhere.

"Power is from a set of Diesel Prime Power Generators we found that were on their way to Texas for a drilling rig. They're over behind that berm for sound control. Have a couple of sets of tank trailers we're using to get fuel from wherever we can find it. Starting to run low on PRI products. That batch you brought in will tide us over for a long time.

"We know where more PV panels and equipment to hook them up with are. We just haven't had a chance to get and install them."

"That's right," the Major said.

"What about the silver and gold monetary system? That working out okay?"

"Yes. We kept it really simple. We're using the face value of the Eagles. Five, ten, twenty-five, and fifty dollar Gold

Eagles, one dollar Silver eagles, and then the pre-1965 silver dimes, quarters, and halves, also at face value.

"Not everything works out exactly, as a dollar's worth of dimes, quarters, and haves comes out to zero point seven one five to zero point seven two ounces, versus the one dollar an ounce of the silver Eagles.

"And if the gold eagles were straight line calculation, the one-quarter ounce gold Eagle would be twelve fifty, rather than ten dollars. But I think, as long as we simply use the coinage at face value, ignoring the slight discrepancies, we will be okay.

"I do think we should limit eventual external trade agreements to one ounce Gold Eagles and Silver Eagles. No fractionals. Straight fifty to one ratio. Private transactions, if people want to play the fractional discrepancy game, then more power to them. I think that the actual products for given coinage will be more important than trying to run up a fortune, playing the differential.

"Wages, salaries, and prices have been set according to what a hundred dollars average income will get you in terms of essential items like food, wood for stoves, and various services for now. As time passes, as long as we're consistent on our wage and salary payments, prices will work themselves out by supply and demand. For instance, your salary as a primary member of staff will be two hundred dollars a month."

"Sounds like a workable plan," Killany said. "Except for my salary. It isn't necessary. I'm not what you would call independently wealthy, but I have enough equipment, supplies and PMs for my needs at the moment. And I'll be doing some buying and selling on my own."

"But Killany…"

"It's okay, Gary. I get enough compensation in terms of a place to be while things are they way they are."

"Won't do you any good," Major Tandy told Gary. "Talking to Strotskey and Monahan has convinced me that Killany sticks to his guns, relentlessly."

Killany gave Major Tandy a side look, but didn't comment. "Roger and Dudley are right," he told Gary, looking back at him.

"Well…Okay. But if you change your mind, just let us know and we'll fork over whatever you say you need."

A couple of days later, a handpicked team, with Killany once again on the Kettenkrad, with both trailers behind, and six semi tractors left the Farm, on the way to pick up loads from Canning Pantry and Walton Feed. Two of the trucks had blades on them. There were extra cutting edges and the tools to install them on the blades so they wouldn't be ruined as quickly as the one Killany had brought back.

The two trucks with blades each had a ninety ten split of diesel and gasoline for the trip. They would continue to salvage fuel, but Killany thought it best to take some with them, all the same. The rest of the trucks pulled an empty trailer each, primarily to have traction on the rear axles of the trucks. With the route known now, the trip out took only a few days to get to the Utah border. Things slowed down after that, but continued at a steady pace.

Hitting Hyrum first, they used the forklift they'd brought with them, to load the four box trailers. Two more trailers, those that had been at Canning Pantry for loading when Killany found the place, were loaded up. With three loaded box trailers behind one semi, and the tank trailer and two loaded box trailers behind another, that team headed back to the Properties.

One of the new people that had shown up at the Farm was a diesel engine mechanic had come along specifically to try and get some more trucks running. It took him three full days, with everyone else helping where they could, but Patrick got four more trucks going.

Killany led the way the next morning, with six semi trucks following, pulling seven empty trailers behind them, plus the one tank trailer. Killany was beginning to worry about the weather when they reached Walton Feed. They barely took time to eat and sleep before loading up the seven trailers they'd brought, sending two of the new semis back to Missouri with three trailers each.

Killany and the other three trucks picked up the eight trailers he'd loaded and moved. Turned out the tactic wasn't needed, but Killany didn't begrudge the time and effort he's spent doing it. Things could have turned out different.

It had started to snow when they picked up I-80 east again, after coming back down into Utah. But they ran out of it not long after they crossed the border into Wyoming. The storm system chased them the entire way east, catching them again when they turned south on US 65 off I-80.

The roads had been clear, and the temperatures much warmer than the previous year, so the snow didn't begin to stick until the day after they were home. All three groups' last stop before getting on 65 had been at another truck stop. They all finished the trip with the same amount of fuel they'd started with, plus that in the tanks of the six new trucks.

## CHAPTER EIGHT

-

With few worries about the bad weather stretching out another year or two, everyone was more than happy with the weather as winter came early again, much more meekly than the previous two winters.

Oh, it was brutally cold for several days, and several feet of snow fell, but they were the extremes, not the norm for the entire winter. Lows stayed above minus ten, with highs up to the mid thirties a few times, with the weather actually beginning to change when late March rolled around again.

Bethany took little Jamie Ann out into the bright sunshine to celebrate the first day of spring. She'd been born that winter during the worst of the weather, but despite the complications that Bethany had suffered through, Dr. Cooper had delivered a beautiful, perfect baby to Gary's arms. He'd gently put her down on Bethany's chest as they waited for the umbilical cord to transfer the lung expanding, life giving placental blood to the crying mass of squinched up eyes, toes, and fists.

When Dr. Cooper was sure that the baby's lungs had expanded properly and the umbilical cord was no longer pulsing, she tied and cut the cord. Only then did Gary pick her up once more to hold for a loving minute before he gave her back to Bethany.

It had been a good sign for things to come. Four other births occurred, one after the other, that winter, keeping Dr. Cooper and Annie busy with the activity. Everyone stayed healthy. There was nothing that went around in the still close quarters, and shared habitations. Even Major Tandy was back at full strength and capability.

When the first rains of the spring began to fall, rather than more snow, everyone rejoiced. Things were returning to normal. If the weather continued to be no worse than marginal, the Farm would be able to get in some short season crops to boost feed for the animals, and supplement the food crops in the greenhouses.

The animals, for the first time in many, many months were allowed out to graze on the sparse grass that began peaking up out of the ash. The ash had compacted enough, and was wet enough, that the cattle didn't get much, if any, into their lungs as they grazed.

The hogs were only allowed out on carefully decontaminated ground to root to their hearts content so they, too, wouldn't ingest or breathe any of the ash that was still around. Those in the leadership roles were acutely aware of how lucky, due in part to the early, very strict requirements for masks to be worn, that they had been to have no more than three people with any lung problems. And those were relatively minor.

Things were finally suitable for a local exploratory flight. The Major and Killany would again take the controls of the Sikorsky, with Stefano and Roger riding as extra pairs of eyes. It was critical to know if there were any groups of people on the move, that could be a threat, as well as any that could use a helping hand from the Farm.

Major Tandy showed no signs of fear as they took off, though the flight was made at a higher altitude, and they didn't approach the dam at all. One of the main checks they wanted to make was at Springfield. There were definitely survivors there, but attempts to talk to them via amateur radio had been fruitless. No one local had ever answered.

The Properties did have regular contact with a few other groups, spread out over the Midwest for the most part. None were within range of physical trips without a very good reason, despite being somewhat closer than the trips that Killany had engineered.

The reasons would be addressed with the other groups, but not for some time. The small groups were going to be on their own for the time being. Flying east first, but turning south before they got to Branson, nothing much was seen. No signs at all of any groups on the move.

Turning west, they circled around and then went north, still without seeing anything but rather bleak landscape.

There were no shots taken at them as they slowly flew over Springfield and surrounding area. There were some acknowledgements, by people waving, even a couple of thumbs up, barely discernable to the men in the helicopter.

Major Tandy took them to the Springfield/Branson Regional Airport. After several passes, each one a bit lower, the Major finally set the Sikorsky down, as near to the fuel tanks as he dared.

There was no one around, or, if there was, they stayed well away from the helicopter and men. It took quite a bit of time to get one of the fuel trucks started, even with a fresh battery and some PRI-D for the fuel system. But Roger and Stefano each knew their way around vehicles and got the truck running. There was still plenty of AvGas in Gary's underground tank, but the group took advantage of every opportunity to add to their existing stocks.

Being extremely cautious, they loaded the empty fuel truck from one of the fuel tanks, and took it over to the Sikorsky. They refueled the bird, topped the truck off again, and Stefano and Roger headed back to the Properties with it.

Major Tandy and Killany took off again and took a zigzag course back, keeping an eye on the fuel truck while still checking things out on each side of the route the truck had to take to get to the Properties.

171

Back home again, the helicopter was serviced and parked. The AvGas fuel truck was parked out of the way, but close enough to the hanger to refuel the aircraft easily when needed. The fuel in the tanker would be used before the stored fuel was.

The flight wasn't the only exploring done that month. After much discussion, the decision was made to check the shoreline of the lake beyond what was visible from the Properties. It was the first time since Bethany had given birth to Jamie Ann that she left her in Annie's care and left the Properties.

The edges of the lake had frozen the first winter, though the middle of the branch of the lake they were on was deep enough to stay liquid, though it did ice over by a few inches during the worst of the weather. And the canal was finally thawed enough to get the boats out to the dock, now floating on water rather than ice.

Gary was reluctant, but Bethany insisted. She wanted a bit of freedom for a while, and wanted to enjoy the decent weather when she could, in case it turned bad again. The decision was made to take the Munson fifty-two foot landing craft that had seen only limited use before the war.

Bethany took the wheel of the Munson fifty-two foot PackCat and eased it out of the earth sheltered boat house down the canal and out to the dock. There, gear was loaded up, and those that were going got ready.

Gary and Killany, along with Stefano and Chester Bowman, one of the new people that knew the lake would be going. After a radio check to make sure the communications system was working, Bethany put the drives in gear again and pulled away from the dock. She took it easy, getting a feel for how the boat handled again.

She'd only used it twice after delivery and before the attack. But she had a knack for it and soon was comfortable enough to up the speed as the others watched the shoreline for signs of people or regular access to the lake from inland.

Staying in the middle of the channel, Bethany took them south, going slowly as the guys watched the shoreline on each side. There was the occasional lakefront property, but none had any signs of occupancy. Following the twisting course of the lake, all the way to Naked Joe Bald peak, without sign of anyone, Bethany turned them around and headed back to the Properties, opening up the Munson on the empty expanse of water.

She slowed as they passed the Properties and continued north. Again following the twisting path of the lake, they went as far as Cape Fair. There were boats here and there, some afloat, some sunken from the damage caused by the hard freeze on the lake edges.

When Bethany saw one particular boat, she turned the wheel of the Munson and eased over to it. "I wanted to get one of these before the war, but never had a chance. It'd be a good platform for fishing out in the lake, beyond the dock."

Bethany eased the nose of the Munson up against the pontoon party boat. "It's a Premier Boundary Waters luxury model party boat," Bethany said, holding the Munson alongside the aluminum pontoon boat.

"It even has the PTX third pontoon," Bethany said excitedly. Gary and Stefano transferred to the Boundary Waters to look it over. Killany was constantly surveying the surrounding area, on shore and off, with powerful binoculars. He didn't want to get caught unawares if there was someone out there that objected to their presence.

"Everything looks to be intact," Gary said.

Stefano was looking over the stern. "Pair of big Mercs," he said. "Won't know if they'll run 'til we get her back to the dock."

"That's assuming we tow her in," Chester said.

"The Munson will surely handle it," Bethany said, just a touch of doubt in her voice from the way Chester had spoken.

"Oh, sure. This beauty will handle it well. It's just, do we want to?"

"We want to," Bethany said firmly.

"Yeah," Chester said. "Just… I know the people that own her. Good people. I guess they didn't make it."

"I'm sorry" Bethany said. "I didn't mean to be disrespectful."

"Nah. You weren't. I'm just seeing my lake in a different light. Before it was all bright and shiny with people having fun and all... It's just different, now."

"I understand," Bethany said quietly. "But it will come back to that, someday. If we do our part, in a few decades, perhaps in just a few years, people will be back on the lake, not just for the clean water and fish that it provides, but for fun, too."

"I sure hope so," Chester replied. "Really. I don't have any problem using anything we find on the lake that isn't being used."

"Okay," Bethany said. "Gary, can we rig something up now or do we need to go get something?"

"Nah! We're good," replied Stefano rather than Gary.

It took a few minutes to check a few things out and then rig a towline. With Chester now on the Boundary Waters, named "Li'l Gem", to steer, Bethany gently eased away from the other boat, taking the slack out of the tow rope.

When it tensioned and the 'Li'l Gem' began to move, Bethany slowly upped the speed to an easy, but distance eating rate. As soon as they made it to the dock and had the 'Li'l Gem' secured, Stefano was taking the covers off the engines to check them out. Chester was right there with him, his melancholy mood gone completely now.

Bethany went aboard and began to inspect the boat in detail. She was grinning when she joined Gary and Killany at the boathouse a few minutes later.

"It's the loaded model," she said eagerly. "Just about the way I intended to order one, back in the day."

Gary chuckled. Killany's grin matched Bethany's. "You locate a nice, medium size luxury houseboat, I got dibs. I could easily see myself living aboard, on the lake, when the weather permits."

"I'll keep it in mind," Bethany said.

"You two and your toys," Gary said with a chuckle.

"I need to get back to the house to feed Jamie Ann," Bethany said, a wince of pain crossing her face. She was producing a great deal of milk and it was painful for her if she didn't feed Jamie Ann on a timely basis.

"I'm going to stay here and lend a hand, if I can," Killany said when Gary turned to go with Bethany.

As the weather continued to improve almost daily, the groups' avid fishermen began to take the 'Li'l Gem' out a ways from the dock into deep water to fish whenever they had some free time. But the trips were limited to only the parts of the lake where they could be seen by someone on the dock.

As the weeks passed, the Farm became the center of activity. The weather continued spring like, a normal spring, into the summer months, allowing those on the farm to get some crops in, and keep them growing into the fall. They were all short season crops and were harvested before the early winter hit.

This winter was shaping up to be much less severe than the last few. There was no really bad weather until late November. The first real storm came on Thanksgiving Day. It began snowing early in the morning. Both the Farm and the Properties were having simple celebrations. All the residents were truly thankful for the bounty of the land they'd received this year.

As people began to go to their quarters, the snow became much heavier. The next morning there was a foot of snow on the ground. But it was gone within two days.

At the staff meeting the following Monday, Killany brought up the subject of another reconnaissance flight.

"Why now?" Dr. Cooper asked. "Winter is coming on. You said there wasn't much chance of trouble during winter."

"That was the past. This weather we've been having is near normal. And we haven't been able to contact Orange Blue since before Thanksgiving Day."

Dr. Cooper frowned. "Orange Blue? You think that is a real crisis? Who calls their group 'Orange Blue'? Could be any reason they aren't talking. Radio problems. Fuel shortage for their generator. You name it, it could happen."

"So could an attack on their place," Killany replied calmly.

"Why are you so sure we going to be attacked at some point. You've found nothing to indicate it, other than the episode at the dam. And those people could have been defending what they thought was an attack on the dam."

Killany nodded. "True. I'd still prefer to do an over flight to check out the situation. Might be nothing. But someone might be injured and in need of medical care."

"Yes... That is a possibility, I suppose," Dr. Cooper said. "Perhaps I should go with you. See for myself."

All those sitting at the table were a bit surprised when Killany said, "I think it would be a good idea. Tomorrow morning at nine. Now, I need to take care of a few things if there isn't anything else we need to discuss."

"Nope," Gary said. "We covered it all."

The next morning it was a bit blustery, but well within the Sikorsky's capabilities with a good pilot at the controls. And the Major was a very good pilot, as was Killany.

Stefano joined Dr. Cooper in the rear of the helicopter. All four were armed, as usual, even Dr. Cooper. The Major wasted no time. Chances were the weather would get worse before it got better.

For the same reason, he flew directly to the location of Orange Blue. A man had come on the air one day during the daily contact between the Properties and the Farm, several weeks previously, 'to announce his presence in the area'.

No pleas for help or offers to join with anyone. Just communication for communication's sake. Killany had talked to him several times, finally getting Orange Blue's location, for future face to face visits, sometime the following year.

Orange Blue wasn't actually on the lake, but he was on one of the small streams that flowed into it. The sight of an antenna tower jutting up above the trees corresponded with the location that Killany had been given.

The Major made a circle around the site, with no response at first. Then, suddenly, causing the Major to dive away to one side, a red flare came up through the trees. It wasn't actually close, but the Major wasn't taking any chances.

Another flare came up, also red. "I think there may be a problem," Killany said. "Someone is signaling, not firing at us."

"I'll set us down in that clearing ahead," Major Tandy said. He was already heading the helicopter that way. The rotors barely cleared the surrounding trees, but the Major kept the helicopter perfectly centered and set the Sikorsky down.

"Keep it ready," Killany told the Major. With the rotors at idle, Killany, Stefano, and Dr. Cooper climbed down out of the helicopter and headed for the spot where the antenna tower was visible over the trees.

When a small cabin came into view, the three stopped. "Hello the house! Orange Blue! It's Killany! Are you all right?"

"Come on up," came a voice. It wasn't very loud, and sounded strained.

"Stay here, you two," Killany said and began to move forward, still staying behind cover until he was close enough to see a man sitting on the front porch of the small cabin.

"Orange Blue?" Killany asked.

"Yeah. Come on in. Killany?"

"Yeah." Killany slung the PTR-91 and stepped out into the open. When he got a good look at Orange Blue he called for Dr. Cooper.

"Need you up here, Doc."

"You got a doc with you? I'm Gridley Hornady, by the way. Orange Blue is just my moniker. I'd offer to shake, but it would hurt too much."

Dr. Cooper ran up and handed off her rifle to Stefano as she swung the medical pack she carried around in front of her so she could get into it. "My Lord! What happened? Who did this to you?"

Dr. Cooper was gently taking Gridley's right hand into hers. It was mangled, with crusted blood covering most of it. Killany was taking inventory of Gridley's other visible injuries as Dr. Cooper began to clean the hand.

Gridley's face was battered, covered in bruises. His shirt was ripped in several places, obviously caused by knife cuts, as the skin under the shirt was also cut, with dried trails of blood partially visible. The way he held his left arm against his side, either it was injured, possibly broken, or his ribs were on that side.

"Someone did a real number on you, Gridley," Killany said. "What happened?"

"Can we get him inside?" Dr. Cooper asked.

"Better out here," Gridley said groaning when Dr. Cooper tried to clean a cut at the base of his thumb. "I suggest you not go in, Doc. Killany, you might want to take a look so you know what you'll be dealing with sometime soon."

Killany carefully edged around Gridley and the Doctor, pulling a high intensity light from a pocket. His jaws were working, teeth grinding against themselves, as he controlled the urge to vomit. The inside of the small cabin was a slaughterhouse. Blood everywhere, three bodies, cut and shot literally into pieces.

"Quite a battle," Killany finally managed to say.

Stefano, before Killany could stop him had stepped forward and looked through a window. He gagged and turned away, managing to get around the corner of the cabin before he lost his breakfast.

"It was no battle," Gridley said through teeth clinched from pain. "It was a slaughter. Maybe I should start at the beginning."

"Yes, please," Killany said. "But on your own terms. Take all the time you need."

Dr. Cooper continued to work on Gridley as he talked, gasping from time to time as what the doctor was doing hurt him.

"They monitored our comms, Killany. They know about you. They're hurting, starving. The big guy, the one in charge, Delfontaine, looks like he's lost two hundred pounds. Just thick skin hanging off bone. They've been looking for sources of supply for the last six months."

"How do you know this?" Killany asked.

"A couple of them talked to me between beatings. Both of them were trying to atone in some way for what they were doing. Couched everything in terms of having to do the things they were doing just to survive."

Killany nodded. "I see. Go ahead."

"Delfontaine... he's a cop from Chicago... was on vacation, fishing down near the dam when everything happened. He just sort of took over, organizing the area. All for his benefit. Killed everyone that resisted. They even shot down some kind of helicopter."

Stefano looked over. "Only it didn't go down. That must have been the shot that hit the Major. Killany here took over. Pulled us out of it."

"They were sure you went down in the lake. Anyway, they made it through the first few months on what they could salvage, steal, and murder for. They couldn't venture far when the weather turned bad. But they were running out of supplies, living on fish for the most part.

"As soon as they could start moving around again, they started trying to raid. There just aren't many people around. They found some supplies to keep them going. Then I made the unforgivable mistake of contacting you. I was just getting so lonely here by myself. I'm sorry."

"We were on the air quite a bit, between the Properties and the Farm. They would have heard us eventually, even with the precautions we took." Killany shook his head. "It was inevitable. Don't think you caused the situation. What else can you tell us? What happened here?"

"We'll they'd been monitoring for some time, but everything they did hear was too far away for them to consider trying to get to. Until I contacted you. The fact that I was even alive, much less in good shape and able to communicate told them I obviously had the means to survive.

"So they came looking. And found me. Delfontaine is mean. Psychotic. Worked me over initially just to 'soften me up', 'for the real questions to come later,' he said. He really knows how to hurt a person." Suddenly Gridley groaned and bent over in pain.

"I'm sorry," Dr. Cooper said.

"It's okay," Gridley said, straightening back up. "No pain, no gain, huh?"

"Not in this case," Killany said.

"Yeah. Got to look at the best side of things. Back to the tale. Well, as he and his crew ate everything I had in the cabin, Delfontaine had his guys go to work on me while he asked questions. It was too much. I spilled my guts. Told them almost everything. Would have told them all, but they quit pounding on me to go get what I'd told them about after they finished everything in the house.

"Those seven guys ate four month's worth of my stores in a day. They just gorged until they just couldn't force anything else down. Then the talking started." Gridley shook his head. "It was disgusting. Horrible. Things they were going to do to the women and children when they found you. I never heard such things. I threw up and Delfontaine went berserk.

"That's when he went to work on my hand. Fortunately I was out of it after the first few minutes. When I came to, two of the guys were arguing with two others. Apparently the talk hadn't set well with them, either. The other three, including Delfontaine were outside somewhere.

"When he came back inside and heard the two saying they were going to break away and go warn you, he went beyond berserk. He carries this saw back machete on his thigh... The result is what you saw inside. The two managed to pull guns, and so did the others. One of Delfontaine's men got in the crossfire.

"It seemed to infuriate Delfontaine even more. He hacked him up, too. He turned to look at me... There is madness in his eyes. He's truly sick, psychotic. He swung at me with the machete, but he slipped on the blood and went down.

"When he got up, he swung again. That's the cut on my back. Only the chair took most of the blow. He was just so furious that he didn't notice. 'Kill him,' he said, and walked out the door. One of guys shot me and I went over."

"Shot?" Dr. Cooper asked. "Where? I haven't seen a bullet wound."

"Believe it or not, my belt buckle took the round. The guy was aiming to leave me to die with a gut wound. You know how terrible they can be. But the shock of everything put me out again. I finally came around, and with the back of the chair nearly sliced in two, I was able to bust it apart and get loose." Gridley shifted slightly and twisted his belt, exposing the buckle that had been hidden under his tattered shirt tail.

The large, elaborate, western buckle had a significant dent in it. "I think it was small caliber. And I got really lucky."

"Yeah," Stefano said, staring at the belt buckle. He was pale, but seemed over the incident. "So, we have four murderous maniacs out there to deal with. I think our guys can handle that."

"No. Not four. At least twenty, unless someone else has died."

"What do you mean, Gridley?" Killany asked. "You said there was this Delfontaine plus six, now minus three."

"Delfontaine had four other teams out looking for other survivors. To get enough provisions to make a march north to the Farm. They've been gone for a day. They might have hooked up again. They got enough from me to feed twenty to twenty-five people for a week. They'll be looking for your place now."

"We'd better get back," Killany said. "They could be getting close already."

"No. They don't know exactly where you are. I stuck to the story that I didn't know where you were, exactly."

"You said you caved," Stefano said.

"I did. But only on myself. I couldn't turn over on you guys. Not with women and children… The way they were… And I don't know exactly where you are, so I was able to make it believable. I know you're on the lake, and the farm isn't, but that's all I know. But I managed not to even admit that. But they know the Farm is north, not too far from the lake, just by the conversations they overheard between us."

"You're a tough one," Killany said. "He about ready to travel, Doctor?"

"In a few more minutes," replied Dr. Cooper. "I want to splint his arm before we try to move him."

"I don't want to be a burden," Gridley said. "I feel responsible for what might happen to your group."

"Don't," Killany assured Gridley. "We knew something like this would develop. We've made preparations for such an event. Having advance notice of what we're facing is a big help."

Killany's handheld radio broke squelch. "Everything okay?" asked the Major. "It's been a while. I don't want to waste fuel if it's going to be much longer."

"It'll be a few minutes. Go ahead and shut down, but keep a really good eye out. There could be hostiles in the area."

"Will do."

"What all do you want to bring with you, Gridley? We'll start getting things packed up."

"There's a cache out behind the cabin. It's buried under the middle of the wood pile. It's the only one I didn't give up. They took all my other supplies, and all my hardware, except what's in the cache. I was hoping to break away and get to it, but it never happened."

"Stefano and I'll get it out," Killany said. The two headed around to the back of the cabin. The pile of firewood, just piled, not stacked, was huge. The two men looked at each other, sighed, and began to toss firewood to one side, creating a larger and larger pile as the first one slowly shrank.

Gridley hadn't been kidding. It was only when they had moved over half of the pile that they found the set of totes and cases wrapped in plastic. A few minutes later they had them unwrapped and moved around to the front of the cabin.

"Thank you," Gridley said. "I would never have been able to get to it in the condition I'm in. You've probably saved my life."

"By the way, how'd you manage to keep the flare gun?" Killany asked.

"This?" Gridley asked, picking up the pen flare launcher lying beside him. "One of them dropped it when they were going through my gear. It got kicked over in a corner when one of them was working me over." Gridley put the launcher down and picked up a red stained leather case.

"They simply didn't see it. About the only thing they did miss. I planned on using it as a weapon if they came back, but when I heard the helicopter, I decided to take a chance. I'm glad I did."

"He's ready," Dr. Cooper said, putting things back into her medical pack. "I'll get him back to the helicopter. Can you get my rifle?"

"Sure," Stefano said. He slung it over his shoulder with his own, and picked up one of the totes. Killany picked up another and the four headed back to the Sikorsky. It took five trips to get Gridley's things to the helicopter, but when everything was loaded, Major Tandy had them in the air.

## CHAPTER NINE

-

Killany and the Major didn't waste any time after they landed back at the Properties. Leaving Gridley in Dr. Cooper's and Stefano's care, they headed for the Farm. In a matter of hours the Farm was made as ready as possible for an attack, and those with extensive firearm experience put on a rotating schedule at the forward defensive points.

Everyone else able to use a weapon was assigned a position in the close in defensive positions, doubled up so one could eat and rest while the other stayed alert. With the defenses as ready as possible, Gary and Killany took to the air, Gary in the Seawolf, with Stefano as observer, and Killany in the Sikorsky with a spotter as well.

Both flew to Gridley's place and split, Gary going east and Killany west. Flying a simple search plan, they flew back and forth over their assigned areas, looking for any sign of a group on the move.

For two days they kept up the search, but the weather turned, grounding both the helicopter and amphibian. Those on the defensive lines began to grumble about being there, in the cold, and snow, when it started.

But Killany was insistent and the Major, having seen Gridley, was as well. One or the other of them was always on the perimeter, encouraging everyone, trying to keep their spirits up as the snow continued and the temperatures dropped well below freezing.

Three days of the bad weather, with snow almost two feet deep, Killany and Major Tandy finally pulled the forward defenses back, putting those people in the rotation for the close in positions to give everyone a decent break. It was a chance, but neither man thought Delfontaine would try an attack with the weather the way it was. It was just too difficult to move effectively or quickly.

That all changed the fifth day. The snow had stopped the day before and a warm wind began blowing, melting the snow quickly. Killany and Major Tandy were out on the outer perimeter, checking the conditions of the fighting position, discussing moving people out when the concrete of the fighting position sparked when a bullet ricocheted and then the sound of a shot was heard.

Both men dove backwards and scrambled into the small bunker. Killany and Major Tandy regularly went armed, usually with just a side arm, but had taken to carrying a rifle, as well, during the last few days.

Killany pulled his radio free of the pouch on his belt and called the Farm, warning them of the attack. Major Tandy fired a shot, and then another. "We got a bunch of them, Killany! They're spread out. They'll get around us if we don't do something."

"You stay here. I'll go over a couple of positions and try to keep them from flanking us."

"Too dangerous…" The words were barely out of the Major's mouth when Killany slid out of the back of the bunker and began to run, going to ground every few steps to take a shot or two.

Major Tandy quickly began firing, trying to draw fire from Killany to himself. He sighed in relief when Killany made it to the next fighting position. But Killany didn't stop there. He kept moving, this time firing as he ran. The Major picked up his own rate of fire, switching out to a fresh magazine when the one in the M1A ran dry.

He ducked when another bullet chipped the concrete ledge a few inches from his face. The Major didn't see Killany go down just before reaching the second fighting position. But when he was able to begin shooting again, he heard Killany's PTR-91 firing as well so didn't think about Killany anymore. He was too intent on trying to take down the men trying to flank his position to worry about Killany.

Killany and the Major, with Roger and Dudley's help, had trained the residents of the Farm and the Properties well. Only a few minutes after the radio call, every suitable vehicle was approaching the perimeter line.

When the attackers saw the approaching group, they turned tail and ran. Roger and Dudley were in the lead, on a pair of the ROKONs.

Major Tandy climbed out of the bunker. "Track them!" the Major yelled at the two men when they got close. "Don't try to engage further! Just track them!" He looked over toward where he expected to see Killany standing, ready to lead a force to go after the attackers.

But Killany wasn't to be seen. "Killany!" Major Tandy ran toward the other bunker. When he got close, he saw Killany. He was stretched out on the ground, the PTR-91 still up on its bipod, with Killany's cheek against the stock, four empty magazines on the ground beside him.

"Medic!" Major Tandy yelled, going to one knee. He carefully felt for a pulse in Killany's neck. There was one, but it was faint. And his fingers came back bloody. One of several people at the Farm that had first-aid training, enhanced by attending Dr. Cooper's more advanced courses over the previous months, ran up and dropped to her knees beside the Major.

Carefully, they turned the unconscious Killany over onto his back. The wound was immediately obvious. A bullet had entered Killany's right shoulder, inches from his neck. Blood was oozing slowly from the wound and there was a small pool on the ground.

Then both noticed the blood on Killany's pants, just above the knee. A tiny hole in his pants, with a blood ring in the cloth around it, indicated another wound.

"We have to get him to Dr. Cooper," said the woman. "Fast." She had her kit open and was applying a pressure bandage to the shoulder entry wound. Major Tandy was on the radio, calling for one of the pickups to come over. Then he pulled his knife and slit Killany's pants.

The medic pointed with her chin at another bandage in her kit and the Major quickly applied it, wrapping the ends around Killany's leg. He tied the bandage off over the pad, to keep some force on it to control the bleeding, slight as it was.

It was only a few minutes and Killany was in the bed of a pickup, with the medic riding with him, on the way to the Properties. They were on high alert, with guards roaming the area around the new facilities.

Dr. Cooper was ready for Killany when he was brought into the new clinic that the doctor had set up in a small manufactured housing unit brought to the expanded Properties. Annie was there to help.

Gary and Bethany, waiting to hear about Killany's condition, stayed in contact with the Major. His follow up report was disappointing. Despite the ROKONs, Roger and

Dudley lost track of the gang. They'd picked their approach well, for it was also provided for a rapid escape.

"The only good thing," said the Major, "is we got three of them. One of them is alive. We should be able to get some information out of him when he comes around."

"Is he injured?" Gary asked.

"Yeah. Minor. Bullet grazed his skull. Knocked him out. May have a concussion, and will definitely have a headache when he wakes up. But Barbara Ann say's he should be able to talk when he comes to on his own."

"Okay. Let me know what you find out. We're going to stay on alert here until we know for sure we have the threat neutralized."

"Very good. I'll contact you when we know something. Out."

Gary put the radio back in his belt case and took Bethany's hand in his.

"I'm worried," Bethany said. "Killany has done so much for us. He's a good man. Doesn't deserve this."

"I know, Sweetheart. I know. He's a remarkable man. Mysterious in many ways. Drives Dr. Cooper to distraction at times."

Bethany chuckled. "I think the good doctor has feelings other than distraction for Killany."

"You really think so?"

"I sure do. But Killany seems immune. Which surprises me. He is so perceptive about most things." Bethany put her head on Gary's shoulder and the two waited in silence.

It was another hour before Dr. Cooper came out of the treatment room. She gave Gary and Bethany a tired smile. "He's going to be all right. As long as we can avoid infection."

"The bullet?" asked Gary.

"I got it out. It entered, hit the shoulder blade and glanced off, almost exited, but traveled under the skin for several inches. It was about midway down his right side. No major nerves or arteries hit, fortunately. He's a lucky man. A couple inches to his left and he would have taken the bullet right in the neck. It would have killed him for sure.

"The wound in his leg is minor. I got that bullet out as well, though it was harder to do. It had lodged in the bone. He'll always have a problem with it, but it shouldn't be debilitating."

"Can we see him?" Bethany asked.

"No," Dr. Cooper, said. "He's out and I want him to stay out for a while. You know how he is. He'd want to go back out there. Or at least get on the radio and try to run things from here. I won't allow it. He's bullheaded and doesn't know what is good for him sometimes."

"Uh. Yes," Gary said. He took Bethany's hand as they both stood up. After a glance at one another they left so the doctor could go back to Killany's bedside.

It was another hour before the Major called Gary on the radio again. "Afraid we didn't get much from the guy. He just said we were in for something terrible and clammed up. I decided not to let some of the guys have him, the way they wanted. The least thing they wanted to do was water board him. He's secured for the moment."

"Not even how many of them there are?" Gary asked.

"No. He's really scared and that's keeping him silent. I think he believes if he tells us anything we'll just kill him."

"Okay. I guess just keep an eye out and people on alert. I don't see them attacking again soon, now that we're on alert, but you never know. And Dr. Cooper says Killany should be okay, barring infection."

"That's good. We need him," replied the Major. "I need to go. Want to check the perimeter again."

"You be careful, Major Tandy. We can't afford to have you out of action, too."

Gary went to check the Properties defenses, the way the Major was the Farms. When the attack occurred, half of those living at the Properties expansion area were dispatched to the Farm to lend a hand. The threat of an attack on the Properties seemed slim. It was the Farm that had the resources that the gang wanted.

And that seemed to be the case when another attack came at the Farm, this time in the form of long range sniping from at least three points. The Major immediately sent flankers out to try and find the snipers, without endangering themselves. But though they found the spots the snipers had used, there was no sign of the snipers. They'd just fired a few shots, until a response began and then had withdrawn.

Despite their best efforts, those on the Farm were unable to catch any of the snipers, as they continued to move and fire harassing shots all through the night. As daylight approached, a much more intense action took place, with massed fire coming from beyond even the positions the snipers had been using. It was obviously not aimed fire, just volleys that kept the defenders' heads down.

Major Tandy was ready for the attack he expected to occur immediately after the volley firing stopped. But no attack came. When nothing else had happened by noon, the Major called Gary.

"They are just harassing us. I don't see how they can keep it up. But they are tying us up. People are getting tired. I think we should go after them in force. Either take them out; if we can, or run them off far enough to be sure they can't come back this winter. From the looks of it, we're going to have another storm soon. If we can get them out of the area, I don't think they'll have the resources to stay and continue the fight."

"You don't think that is too risky? We're well protected the way we are. I don't want to lose anyone. Killany's injuries are enough."

"We are going to have to take some risks, Gary. No way out of it. Better on our terms than theirs."

Bethany was listening in and sighed. But she nodded. "Okay, go ahead," Gary told the Major. "I'll send over some more people to beef up the security while you are out."

They signed off and Bethany said. "I'm worried. It was one thing to have direct confrontations, the way we did when this started. But this… this… continuing situation… I'm afraid we're going to lose people."

"I know. So am I. But if we can push them back far enough, they might not survive the winter. Gridley said they were desperate. If what they are presenting is the best they can come up with, we have a good chance of chasing them off."

Bethany put her head on Gary's shoulder and took his hand in hers. "Give me a minute. But then I'd like to go check on Killany."

"So would I. Dr. Cooper wasn't very forthcoming this morning at breakfast."

"She stayed up all night, monitoring his condition," Bethany said. "Okay. I'm ready."

The two stood and left the house, going over to the medical trailer. Dr. Cooper was in the small office that was part of the facility. "How is he?" Bethany asked.

"That hard headed fool is as okay as possible. But he's refusing to take the pain medication. He wants to get up, but, fortunately, he is physically just too weak. Even his tremendous constitution isn't up to walking around after injuries like he has."

"Can we see him?" Gary asked.

"Yes. But don't let him con you. He needs to be in here for quite some time yet. And don't tire him out too much. He needs rest as much as anything. That's why the pain medication is so important. He's hurting, trying to hide it, and it just makes things worse."

"Okay. We won't stay long," Gary replied.

The two went to the small room Killany had been moved to and Gary knocked on the open door frame before they entered. Killany's eyes were closed and Gary started to back out of the room. But Killany's eyes opened and he spoke.

"I see she finally relented about someone seeing me. What's going on? Did we get them? She just said things were under control. Annie wouldn't tell me anything either."

Despite the pinched look around Killany's mouth, and the pain obvious in his eyes, Gary thought knowing what was going on would be better for Killany than not knowing. At least he should be able to relax.

So Gary explained what had happened the last few hours.

"They keep harassing? That doesn't seem logical," Killany said, a distant look shadowing his face. "I was fully expecting a hard push to just overwhelm our outer defenses. Take some hostages and parley a deal of some kind, if they couldn't just overrun us. With twenty desperate people, they might have succeeded in getting inside our outer perimeter.

"It just doesn't seem…" Killany looked startled suddenly and he looked at Gary, near panic in his eyes. "How many attackers were there?"

"Major Tandy didn't say for sure. We killed those two, and the one we caught isn't talking about anything at all."

"You have to get me out of here," Killany said urgently. "I think we have a big problem."

"But we're containing the situation. Major Tandy is going after the group as we speak. I sent everyone we didn't need over to the Farm to fill in the holes in the defenses, with the teams going out after the gang."

"If there wasn't an overwhelming amount of force projected, there is a reason," Killany said. He was trying to swing his legs around, to get out of the bed. But even before Gary moved to prevent him, Killany fell back onto the bed with a groan. "Ah, man! That hurts!"

"Look. We've been concentrating on the Farm," Killany said after a few deep breaths to control the pain. "And I'm sure the Farm is what Delfontaine wants. But what if he is going to try and come in the back door?"

"Our defenses here are better than the Farm," Bethany protested, her thoughts going to Jamie Ann.

"Yes. Your two properties can't be touched. But the rest of the people. We have families here. If they aren't inside the shelters they are vulnerable. I'm not sure we could hold out if they captured some and threatened to do to them what Gridley implied."

Gary began to look worried.

"The back door. The Lake," Killany continued. What if the original attacks are just diversions? What if they are coming up the lake?"

"But you said that Gridley said he didn't tell them that," Bethany said. She was holding Gary's arm tightly in both hands.

"No. But if he's got any brains at all, he'll wonder about it. And if he's done any triangulation on the radios we've been using, he could have a pretty close idea where we are." Killany was adamant. "You need to get ready for an attack on the Properties, Gary. If I was able, I'd go out to survey the situation. Meet them on the water, if I could. Unless they have managed to get a bunch of boats going, which is unlikely, they could be concentrated on just a few.

"Our boats… your boats… are all fast and maneuverable. Some sandbag defenses and I'd have a chance…"

"You aren't going anywhere, Killany." Dr. Cooper was in the room, ready to ask Gary and Bethany to leave, since they had been in for some time.

"Gary?" Bethany asked.

"We're doing it."

"You may not have much time," Killany said. "I'd go with you…" His eyes cut to Dr. Cooper, whose own eyes were flashing. "But I'm stuck here for a while. At least," he added, "get my hardware in here where I can get to it in case they break through. And I need a radio."

Killany was talking like it was a sure thing now, and the feelings Gary and Bethany were the same.

"I'm not going to give you a weapon," Dr. Cooper asked.

For the first time since they'd all teamed up, Gary pulled rank. Without even trying to talk it out, Gary said. "I'm pulling rank, Doctor. I'm sorry. But I won't leave him here, vulnerable, unarmed."

Dr. Cooper's eyes flashed again. But she saw the appeal in Killany's eyes when she looked over at him to protest again. Her shoulders slumped and she sighed. "All right. I'll get them and get them ready." She turned and left the room.

"Go," Killany said.

Gary and Bethany ran out, Gary pulling his radio from the pouch on his belt. He gave out instructions to everyone with a radio to notify everyone else to head for the Properties shelters. When they got to the house, Bethany ran inside to get Jamie Ann to take her down into the shelter.

"Okay, people! Listen up," Gary said, addressing the group that was still forming. "We could have a problem. That gang may be coming up the lake, and…"

"But they are fighting over at the Farm!" protested someone.

Gary shook his head. "It has been determined that those attacks are only by a few people. The rest of the gang is out there somewhere. We think it could be the lake. "We're going to take the boats out and see if we can find and drive them off."

Then Gary began to give out assignments. The majority of the women, mostly those that had little or no firearms skills were assigned to the shelters, in charge of taking care of the children.

Most of the rest were sent to the lightly staffed outer defensive points. A select handful followed Gary to the boathouse, after first going to one of the storage buildings to get a large bundle of empty sandbags and half a dozen EZ-Bagger sandbag filling scoops. Three people ran off to get a couple of the maintenance trucks, with three more going to the dock to keep watch on the lake.

They'd used many sandbags to prepare some of the fighting positions, so already had a large pile of sand stockpiled to use as fill. The six EZ-Baggers were put into use as others carried the filled bags to the trucks.

When one truck had enough bags to get started, Gary took the truck down to the dock with half the crew. The bags were moved to the boats, and fighting positions quickly built. The pace slowed slightly, as handling the bags was heavy work, but within an hour and a half, Gary was satisfied with the result.

He was in the process of assigning people to the three boats when Bethany ran down to join him.

"You're staying with Jamie Ann," Gary said.

"I'm not arguing, Gary. I'm going. I have the most experience in the Munson and the Nautica. Simply tell me which one I'm driving and let's get this situation resolved."

Gary wanted to argue. He really wanted to argue. He wanted Bethany safe. But she wouldn't hear of it, he knew. "Okay. The Munson. You'll be safer there. We put sandbags around the control station on it, too."

"Okay." Bethany shifted her rifle to a better position on her right shoulder and the bag of magazines on her left, and then boarded the Munson, going immediately to the control cabin.

Gary finished the assignments, and everyone took their places. Gary took the forward gun pit in the Munson. Jason Carpenter took one of the side positions, and one of the women took the other. Stefano was on the roof of the control cabin in a prone position, with Gary's Barrett M82A1 .50 BMG.

The Nautica 41' Cabin RIB had a prone position sandbagged on the foredeck with two kneel down positions in the rear. Sandbags also protected the helm position in the cabin. Bethany's Vigilance VR-1 .338 Lapua sniper rifle armed the man in another prone position on the roof of the Nautica cabin.

The 'Li'l Gem' pontoon boat had fighting positions at each corner, and the helm, like the control cabin of the Munson, was armored with sandbags.

"Let's go. Everyone keep a sharp eye out," Gary said into the radio. Bethany put the Munson in gear and led the way from the dock, turning south without guidance from Gary. She eased the throttles forward, picking up a pace to cover ground, but not run up onto something unexpectedly.

She slowed at each bend, easing around them cautiously, the others following suit. They were in one of the wider areas of this branch of the lake when Gary saw a houseboat moving slowly upstream. He almost missed it. It was running slowly along the western shore.

"There!" he yelled as he pointed. "Get us close enough to check for other craft. And make sure it isn't some innocents in the wrong place at the wrong time," Gary said into the radio.

Moving at moderate speed, Bethany led the three boats toward what turned out to be a relatively large houseboat. There was suddenly no question as to whether it was innocents or the gang. Rifle fire sounded and bullets began to hit the water well short of the Munson.

"Pull up, Bethany!"

Bethany slowed the Munson quickly and the others did likewise. After a minute or so to allow the boats to settle down on the calm water, Gary gave the order, "Snipers! Target the helm!"

When the .50 BMG and .338 Lapua semiauto rifles began to sound, the houseboat suddenly surged forward. It wasn't nearly as fast as the Munson, Nautica, or Premier Boundary Waters "Li'l Gem, but it was fast. The gang didn't turn tail. It was still headed north.

"Go!" Gary yelled. Bethany had the Munson up on plane in the matter of a few hundred yards. The Nautica and 'Li'l Gem' flanked her.

Though Gary radioed everyone to hold their fire, as at the speed they were going, and the movement of the boats, there was no way to take aimed shots, those on the houseboat didn't have the same restriction apparently.

Small spouts of water popped up, mostly in front of the boats, as those on the houseboat continued to fire. It didn't take long before the houseboat began to approach the more narrow waters north of the wide spot.

Instead of taking it, the houseboat was turned and headed directly for the Munson, more fire coming from the open bow and from the upper deck of the boat. "Open up!" Gary ordered, beginning to fire himself, despite the slight pitching of the boat.

Incoming rounds began to hit the forward hulls and sandbag fighting positions. Those on the houseboat had no such protection, and despite their much heavier fire, they began to drop, one after the other.

In seconds the Properties small fleet shot past the houseboat, the Munson and Nautica going along one side and the 'Li'l Gem' down the other, as everyone still able on all four boats continued to fire.

All four boats turned, and began another run. The Barrett and the Vigilance were both concentrating on the helm of the houseboat. Their many shots finally connected. The man at the helm went down, and the houseboat swerved before another man took over.

The swerve was enough to bring the houseboat into contact with the Nautica, but the tough inflatable tubes of the RIB simply absorbed the impact and the Nautica bounced sideways without damage.

The Nautica hadn't escaped all damage. Several bullet holes in the tubes were leaking air, but the rigid body of the boat was up on plane and the leaks in the tubes were of no danger to the boat. Bethany had repair materials stored. It would only take a few hours to repair the tubes if nothing worse happened.

This time when the houseboat turned, it wasn't to continue the fight. It bore away, headed south at its highest speed. Gary had his fleet continue the chase. He wanted the threat ended. Letting the group go, as a whole, wasn't an option in his mind.

The three faster boats drew closer. There were significantly fewer people shooting at them, but there were still bullets impacting the boats. Everyone able, poured fire into those firing from the rear of the houseboat, on the main deck and on the upper deck.

One rolled off the upper deck, and then two fell off the lower deck, all dead when they hit the water from bullet wounds.

"Get those on the upper deck!" Gary yelled into the radio and then proceeded do so himself. The fire from the upper deck was becoming more dangerous as the small boats approached. They were almost to the point of being able to fire down into the sandbag emplacements from above.

But as splinters flew and bullets impacted boat and flesh, the danger from above was eliminated. The heavier weapons were now firing at the stern waterline of the houseboat, trying to disable the engines. They were finally successful and the houseboat slowed suddenly. It threw several of those on the houseboat backwards, exposing them to more gunfire from the three boats.

Slowly the houseboat came to a near stop, only the very slight current of the lake pushing it, slowly turning in the wind.

A couple more shots rang out, but several rifles were fired at the shooters and those two fell silent. There was an eerie silence, broken only by the quiet sounds of the engines idling on the three smaller boats.

"Ease up, Bethany," Gary said. "I'm going aboard."

Bethany almost didn't do it; for fear that Gary would be killed or injured at the very end of the battle. But she knew this needed to be ended now. Bethany held the pusher bars on the front of the Munson against the side of the houseboat. The other two boats were also pulling alongside, all guns pointing at the houseboat.

Gary climbed out of the protection of the sandbags, as did one each from the other boats. All opted to leave the rifles behind and went with handguns drawn. Gary was barely aboard when a figure rushed out of the inside of the houseboat, machete raised high.

Gary reflexively raised his right hand, to protect himself. The machete knocked the pistol from Gary's hand. It landed in the Munson, with Gary falling on top of it on his back. Delfontaine couldn't hold his balance, either, and fell on top of Gary. He was raising the machete again, to take another swipe at Gary, this one again aimed at his head. But five guns sounded and Delfontaine fell to his side, clear of Gary.

Covered in blood, that Bethany couldn't tell was his or Delfontaine, Gary quickly bounced up and kicked the saw back machete clear of Delfontaine's hand. "Are you hurt!" Bethany asked.

Gary shook his head and bent down to pick up the pistol. There were sudden shots inside the houseboat and Gary leaped back aboard. But it was over. There wasn't a single survivor of the gang. All had been killed. But there was a price.

The call for a medic from the Nautica had Gary going over to it, now tied to the houseboat. Gregory Sampson lay bleeding behind the sandbags of the fighting position on the foredeck of the Nautica. They had not eliminated the threat from the upper deck of the houseboat in time.

Gregory had taken three rounds high in his back, any one of which would have been fatal, said the medic. The medic left Gregory and began to treat some minor injuries two other people had suffered.

Those on the 'Li'l Gem' were retrieving the bodies of the men that had fallen off the houseboat during the fight.

"What do we do with the bodies?" Asked someone.

"I guess we add them to Boothill," Gary said. Those killed at the beginning had been buried in an out of the way spot in the forest some distance from the Properties.

"All of them?" asked the same person.

"Yep. Let's rig a towline to the Munson. No need to transfer all of them to our boats. Do a head count."

"Gary," Bethany called, "The Major is on the line." She held up the microphone of the radio in the control cabin of the Munson.

Gary climbed back aboard and joined Bethany.

"Yes, Major?"

"What's going on? I just got back. When I called on the other frequency they told me you were out on the lake."

"Yes," Gary said. The Major could hear the fatigue in Gary's voice, even over the radio. "Killany, when he heard about the battle there... that there were only a few showing themselves and were just keeping our forces tied up, suggested that Delfontaine might be coming up the lake to attack the Properties. To get hostages to make the Farm give up."

"What happened? Is everyone all right?"

"No. We lost Gregory Sampson. Got some small injuries. But I think we got all those that were on the houseboat the gang was using to come up the Lake in. Hang on. I'll get you a count."

Gary stuck his head outside. "What's the count?"

"Twenty-seven," Stefano said.

Gary whistled. "Twenty-seven here," Gary told the Major.

"More than Gridley thought," said Major Tandy. "Thirty-nine, all together. We managed to sucker in the group that was harassing us. With the two original dead, and the prisoner, we've got twelve over here. It was an ambush and they fought back. Not a one lived, and we didn't lose anyone. I think it's over."

"Good," Gary said. "We'll meet up tomorrow morning." Gary handed the mike back to Bethany, went outside and leaned over the railing for several seconds while he emptied his stomach into the lake. Bethany was there with a wet bandana for him to wipe his face and lips. She handed him a canteen and he rinsed his mouth, spitting the water into the lake.

"I'm okay, now. If we never have another situation like this, it will be too soon for me."

The next morning, Major Tandy joined Gary, Bethany, and Dr. Cooper in Killany's small recovery room. Gary and the Major told their tales. Dr. Cooper looked sick. Killany just nodded. "That's good. I think that will end the problem for a while. You guys did great. Just shows you how little I'm needed around here."

"It was your heads' up that saved us," Bethany said. "If you hadn't figured out what they were doing, we would have been caught almost unprepared here."

"We weren't unprepared. Just not prepared for the kind of attack Delfontaine was intending."

"I think we should leave him alone for awhile," Dr. Cooper said. "He still needs plenty of rest."

"Okay. We'll be checking on you," Bethany told Killany.

"Yeah. I know."

Gary, Bethany, and the Major all laughed. Dr. Cooper just looked annoyed.

## CHAPTER TEN

-

The winter turned out to be as severe as the previous winter, but wasn't as long, and it broke when it should. When spring rolled around, Killany was up and about. He was out on the houseboat, still tied up at the dock, bloodstains everywhere, when his radio broke squelch.

"We need you up here, Killany," said the radio operator.

Killany, barely using the cane he carried, hurried up to the house and then around front. He began to grin when he saw the semi trucks parked on the Properties' road. Two had pairs of fifty-three foot box trailers, and a third had a fuel tank trailer with an equipment trailer behind.

There were three vehicles on the equipment trailer. Two SUVs and a pickup truck, all set up for off-road use.

Seven men were standing around. The sentries on duty were there, half surrounding them, their weapons ready, but pointed at the ground.

"We're looking for a man named Killany," said one of the men, looking around with interest.

"Here he comes," Bethany said when she saw Killany approaching.

When he came up he addressed the oldest of the seven. All the men were bearded, and the man that Killany addressed had liberal amounts of gray in both hair and beard. Killany recognized him from the trip to Orem. It was Nathan.

"Well, Nathan," Killany said, not offering his hand, as Nathan had made no move to do so. "I see you decided to honor the agreement."

"What agreement?" whispered Dr. Cooper to Bethany.

Bethany whispered back, "I don't know. Something Killany set up, apparently, on one of his trips."

Nathan was frowning at the Doctor and Bethany. "May we discuss our business? In private?"

Killany managed not to smile at the outraged looks on both Bethany's and Dr. Cooper's faces when the import of what Nathan was asking sunk in.

"Yep. Come along," Killany said. "You might as well join us, Gary." He looked at Bethany. If you'd have someone get the fellows some food and drink?"

"Yes. Yes. Of course. We're still civilized here." Bethany said archly.

The younger men looked a bit uncomfortable, but Nathan frowned again. "This way, Nathan," Killany said. He led Nathan and Gary to his basement apartment.

"Cup of coffee?" Killany asked.

"Yes. Please," Nathan said, more relaxed now.

There was silence while Killany prepared the coffee. Only when each man had a cup did Killany speak again.

"You brought the four trailers. I'll assume they contain what was on the list. I don't have to inventory them before we conclude our current business, do I?"

Nathan's frown was back. "Of course not! We are honest folk! When we agree to something, we honor our agreements."

"Yes. Of course," Killany said. "Now, about future arrangements…"

"You have a dozen women ready to go back with us?" Nathan asked. "That is fair trade for what we have done."

Gary was beginning to look more than annoyed. He was getting angry. He didn't like what he was hearing, especially with Killany taking it so calmly.

"Oh, I think you might have misunderstood what I was suggesting, Nathan. I said nothing about having women available to go back with you. I said you had a potential genetic problem you would need to take care of fairly soon. You and the others obviously agree.

"Our milk and beef cattle, hogs, and chickens are all quite healthy. We have a small surplus with which you can breed your current animals to diversify the bloodlines." Killany took a sip of coffee.

"But the human genetic pool. You implied…"

"I implied nothing," Killany said, making his voice hard. "I said you would be opening up trading routes. Meeting and mingling with other people. The genetic pool will take care of itself when young men and young women are allowed to socialize."

"But that is not…"

"I know it is not. But it is your choice. Help the entire gene pool, or allow your own to dry up and die."

"I must talk to the council. This is not what we expected."

"Oh, I think you expected this very thing. You just don't want to deal with it. Now, if you have a list of what you want in the way of stock and seeds, we'll get it ready for you. We even have a stock trailer you can use."

Nathan rose, but he stopped and drank the coffee left in his cup. "I will contact those at home and give you an answer."

Killany walked with Nathan until he was on the sidewalk headed for the trucks.

"Going to fill me in, now?" Gary asked.

Killany grinned. "Guess I should. Since I just offered up some of the Farm's stock." Killany told Gary about his trip, the stop in Orem, and the conversation and events leading up to Nathan and crew showing up.

"So, you essentially forced them to open up and start dealing with outsiders?"

"More or less. It was much more voluntary than Nathan lets on. They know and understand genetics. They are going to need outside blood at some point, even if it means losing a small portion of their population when the flow is outward, rather than in."

"Things can sure get complicated, can't they?" Gary asked.

"Yes. They can. But some things need to be done to make sure the species survives, as strong and healthy as possible. The years ahead are going to be tough. Not just the weather or potential raiders. The current population has many obligations to future generations."

Killany filled their cups again. "Look, Gary, I'm not out to force marriages or anything like it. But people need contact with others, for many reasons, not just genetics. There are tremendous amounts of information available to future generations. It needs to be available to everyone, not just small groups here and there with their own 'specialty' if you will."

"Okay. I get your idea. But I wish you'd filled us in before they showed up. You saw Bethany and Dr. Cooper…"

Killany grinned. "Yes. Fortunately I don't have to deal with either one if I don't want to. Speaking of which, there is something I want to bring up at the next staff meeting." A knock came and Killany added, "But it will have to wait."

A stiff faced Bethany opened the door to the apartment to let Nathan in when Killany said, "Come in." Nathan was just as stiff faced.

"So. What's the word?"

"We will take a load of your stock to mingle with ours. Also seeds. But there will be no mingling among our groups. Now, what will we have to pay to get the stock? All of your gold back?"

"No, actually," Killany said, looking over at Gary for a moment. Gary gave a tiny nod and Killany continued. "Just a like number of stock and seeds back for us to use to diversify our own bloodlines and crops. We will be doing this with several groups, so no one that has viable stock and seeds will lose that viability."

Nathan looked a bit startled. "There are other groups? We've contacted only two others, besides yours. And they are further away."

"Well, it is not your concern. Only what deals and exchanges we do between our two groups."

"Yes. Well. If you could start the process, we would like to be on our way."

"Oh, you have time for a celebration of your delivery, don't you?" Killany asked, as if he'd just thought of it.

"I think not. We'd prefer to be on our way."

"Okay. But you're going to miss a great party," Killany said with a wink at Gary that Nathan couldn't see.

"I am not a party person, thank you."

"Why don't you ask your boys? They might be of another mind."

"They will do as I say."

"Okay," Killany said. "I'll get right on that stock. If you'll excuse me."

"Yes. Of course. We have what we need with us. We don't need your hospitality. There was no need to ply my men with expensive delicacies."

"Don't worry about it, Nathan. We share what we have with who we choose. They look like well behaved young gentlemen."

"Yes. Well. Excuse me."

Nathan let himself out this time and Gary looked over at Killany. "I suppose I'm going to have to ask Bethany to help put a party together on short notice."

Killany actually laughed. "Yes. If you don't mind. My injuries are bothering me. I think I'd better take a little rest before this evening after I contact the Major and get that stock rounded up. Slowly. Thoroughly, with very accurate counts, and all the bloodline paperwork complete and in order."

"Man! You do push it! Nathan will be furious."

"Yeah. Be good for him. Get his blood stirring a bit."

Gary headed out of the apartment and Killany headed for the shelter radios, using the tunnel system, something he hadn't done in months.

After a long conversation with Major Tandy, Killany went back to the basement apartment and actually decided a nap might be a good idea.

"A party? For them? Are you out of your mind?" Dr. Cooper half shouted. "This is Killany's idea, isn't it? Where is he?"

"He said his wounds were bothering him. He's taking a nap."

"Oh. Well… Still…" Dr. Cooper sputtered.

Gary looked at Bethany. "There is a good reason. I'd rather discuss it later. It will take a pretty good effort to put a party together."

"Yes it will. And you and Killany will both owe me," Bethany replied. But she stood on tiptoes and gave Gary a kiss on the cheek.

"I'd better be able to figure out the reason by the time the party is over or Killany is going to hear from me, nap or no nap," Dr. Cooper said. "I'll help, Bethany. No need for you to do all the work."

"Okay. Thank you."

Gary shook his head and left while the leaving was good. He went out to supervise the unloading of the trucks. He had plenty of help, he discovered, including at least half of the unattached females currently in residence.

Despite Nathan's best efforts, his men were engaging in animated conversations with the young ladies, as they carried boxes and totes of the Emergency Essentials products to one of the storage buildings for distribution and storage later.

Bethany and Dr. Cooper found it much easier to get the party organized than they expected. While everyone was allowed time for leisure activities, everyone still had to work hard, especially in the spring and fall. Planting and harvesting were intense days. But everyone that was asked to help agreed eagerly. Especially, the two noticed, the women. Word had spread that the seven strangers, all male, were here.

Killany made an appearance a little after five, to give Nathan the bad news. "Sorry, Nathan. We just couldn't get it done today. Early tomorrow and we'll have the stock ready, with all the bloodline papers, and feed for you to get them home. I'm afraid our guest facilities..."

"We have what we need. There is no need of hospitality, as I said."

"Okay," Killany said. "But consider yourself and your men invited to the party, at least. Bad enough having to camp out."

"Bah!" Nathan near spat out as he turned on his heel and marched off toward the trucks again.

Killany caught a glimpse of Bethany and Dr. Cooper headed in his direction. They hadn't spotted him yet and he made sure they didn't, going back to his apartment immediately. He decided a late entrance to the party might be better than getting there early, as was his wont.

As he'd expected, Nathan's men, despite Nathan's wishes, had joined the quickly set up party. Killany had to admit it didn't look hastily set up. There was food, plenty of it, along with not only water and juices to drink, but some of the Farm's stock of root beer, ale, and wine. There was no hard liquor in evidence, for which Killany was pleased. He'd have to give Bethany and Dr. Cooper kudos for that fact, above and beyond what he'd intended, anyway.

Another thing he'd expected was the announcement the next morning by two of the women, one from the farm and one from the Properties, that they were going back to Utah with Nathan and the others.

It was only when the small convoy was already on Interstate 70 going west that it was discovered by Nathan that one of his men wasn't along. He came very close to turning around and going back to bring the man back by force. But when he thought about the probable outcome he decided to let it go. Killany had been right.

Jeremiah Albush was brought to the staff meeting the next morning after breakfast by Karla Sweeny. "Jeremiah wants to stay," she told the small group. I want him to stay. He's a good guy. A farmer. He'll be a big help, I promise."

Jeremiah stood with head down, as if waiting for a sentence.

"Totally up to him. And you, apparently," Gary said after a short consultation among the staff while the two in question waited outside.

"Oh thank you! Thank you!" Karla said delightedly.

"Thank you, Sir. I will be an asset to the group. I promise you."

"Don't thank me. Thank Mrs. Martain and Dr. Cooper. They okayed it," Killany immediately said.

Both women gave Killany a sharp look. It had been unanimous decision.

"Oh. Thank... Thank you," Jeremiah said, looking at Bethany and then Dr. Cooper. It was obvious he wasn't used to having women in positions of authority over him.

With other business taken care of, Killany brought up the subject of the houseboat that Delfontaine's gang had used. "I'd like to buy it from the community," he said.

"Buy it?" asked Gary. "It's yours if you want it."

"You know me. Pay my way. A couple ounces of gold, just to get something on the books?"

All nodded, except Dr. Cooper. "Why would you even want it?" Dr. Cooper asked sharply. "It's bloody. Shot up. I understand the engines are inoperable."

"Yes," Killany said. "It'll be a challenge, I admit. But I plan to do a little more exploring of the lake this summer. I simply don't believe we are the only ones making it on this lake. It has hundreds of miles of shoreline. I think there are people out there that could use our help. And provide help to us, as well. I figure to have the boat ready by early July."

"But you can't just go traipsing off alone again," Dr. Cooper said, her eyes on Killany.

"I've got the wanderlust in me, Doctor. It is not something I can control very well. And I thought I might take a small team with me. For safety sake, for one reason. And a couple more people that might be of help to someone struggling to make it. Actually, I planned to ask the medical personnel if one of them would consent to go along, with an extensive medical kit."

"That would be asking a great deal of the medics. I've done my best to train them for emergencies, mostly trauma care. I'm the only one that has the experience needed for a trip like that."

"Okay. I'll keep you informed of my progress on the houseboat and let you know when we leave. Welcome to the team." With that, before a stunned Dr. Cooper could respond, Killany was out the door.

"But…" Dr. Cooper sputtered her surprised eyes on the closed door Killany had gone through.

She whirled back around to look at Bethany, Gary, and Major Tandy. All three quickly wiped the smiles off their faces. "If he expects me to go along on this trip, he's out of his mind!"

Dr. Cooper rose and stomped after Killany. Fortunately, he had prepared for such an event and was nowhere in sight. The Doctor hunted for him most of the morning, but when she discovered that the Kettenkrad was gone, she gave up. There was no telling when he might return. He'd disappeared several times over the months, usually for just a few days, usually coming back with some wild game, or a report on a possible resource he'd found on the lake not too far away.

When Killany showed up a week later for the staff meeting, Dr. Cooper started to say something to him when he entered. But he spoke first. "Good news. Found a couple of engines to replace those in the houseboat. We should be able to leave the middle of the summer. Give us a couple of months to look around before we have to head back."

Killany gave Dr. Cooper a direct look. "You have a list of things we need to do on the boat to make it easier for you to treat any patients we might run across?"

"I'm not..." Dr. Cooper's words faded away as Killany looked at her. But she stiffened and started to tell him again she wasn't going. But she just couldn't bring herself to do it. She wondered for days why she hadn't just said no. After a week and a half of wondering she just gave up and accepted the idea that she was going. For whatever reason.

She even found herself cooperating with the small team of workers that Killany was paying out of his pocket to cleanup and repair the damage to the houseboat. Fortunately, the lower hull hadn't taken any rounds, and was sound as the day it was made. Most of the other holes were plugged and sealed with epoxy.

A couple of places were shot up so bad, such as around the helm, those sections were removed and new materials put in place. Though Bethany had fiberglass repair materials stored for the Nautica, Killany had found his own to use.

The most difficult task was the replacement of the engines. Not only had the engines been damaged, but the stern drives, as well. Everything had to come out. That meant bringing the stern of the houseboat up onto the lakeshore so the stern drives could be removed.

While that work was being done, Dr. Cooper supervised the conversion to a medical treatment room one of the four staterooms the twenty-two by eight-eight foot Thoroughbred State Dock houseboat contained. That left three more bedrooms, two on the port side and one on the starboard.

The two bedrooms on the port side were made into three person bunkrooms, while the one on the starboard side, next to the medical room, would be Dr. Cooper's room. There were three bathrooms off the center hall that connected the rear deck space with the open kitchen, dining, and lounging area.

The water slide that went from the short upper sun deck to the water line was cut away, and the area under the sun deck enclosed and another bathroom added. It would be Killany's quarters. They were at the rear of the houseboat, with an enclosed helm station forward. The area between the helm and Killany's quarters on the second deck was open.

True to his word, two days after the Independence Day celebration on the Fourth of July, Killany was at the helm, easing the refurbished houseboat away from the dock at the Properties. Standing on the bow deck, waving to the group on shore that had shown up to see the newly christened 'Wanderlust' leave, was Dr. Cooper, three other women, and three men, all but the Doctor eager volunteers for the mission. At least a couple of them would have gone even without Killany's promise of generous wages.

Dr. Cooper was wondering again what she'd let herself in for. She'd almost backed out once, when she thought about leaving all the ones behind that might need her medical care, but the Major and Gary both assured her that either the Seawolf or the Sikorsky would only be hours away if she was needed. Though there was a great deal of shoreline, the lake arms were convoluted and there wasn't that much distance from one side of the entire lake to the other.

When no other excuses came to her, she decided to just see where the adventure would take her. That was what she was thinking now, after suppressing the initial thought.

While it was summer, a near normal one, it was on the cool side of normal, at least on the cold water of the lake. Someone usually had a fishing pole out, and the group ate fish at least every other day. They had plenty of the new biodiesel the Farm was finally making, and the houseboat's generator had come through the battle without a scratch, so all the appliances worked, including the large refrigerator freezer unit.

Even with the supplies they'd brought with them, and the regular fish catch, Killany stopped every couple of days and went ashore after game and to look around at likely spots that might have survivors.

But nothing turned up the first month, though they did find numerous useful items at various locations on the shore that they mapped for pickup by the Munson landing craft before wintertime.

Several of the houses and businesses on the lake showed the signs of long abandonment and the effects of the terrible weather. Others structures had fared better, but there was no sign of anyone having been there since the attack. There were some remains here and there, that Killany insisted be buried near where they were found.

The wildlife population had been hit as hard as the human, and there were only occasional signs of animal depredation of human remains, but there was some. The slow recovery of the wildlife was one reason that Killany had always gone far afield in his pursuit of game. He wanted the area right around the Properties and the Farm to have the best chance of large scale recovery before they were hunted again. At some point it could be vital to have game close. Hopefully the weather had stabilized, with reasonable summers and winters. Enough for the animals to survive and flourish.

It was August fifteenth when they found the first signs of human activity on the lake. There was house, well back in the trees, but the dock area and beach area were clean and well kept, and there were three canoes, two kayaks, and five various jon boats and small V-hulls, all equipped with oars or paddles.

There were two children fishing off the end of the dock when Killany brought the slow moving 'Wanderlust' around the bend and into their sight. Both jumped up, their poles clattering on the dock boards.

Killany continued to ease the houseboat forward, but kept well away from the shore. Everyone except Dr. Cooper was armed and ready if those on shore became aggressive, but after a bit, someone stepped into view and yelled out to the houseboat.

"Who are you and what do you want? We have a dozen guns on you! You try anything and we will fire."

"Peaceful mission," Killany said. He turned down the PA volume a bit and continued. "I'm Killany. From the Properties and the Farm. We're surveying the lake to find people that might need help or have something we could trade for."

"You the government?" yelled the man back.

"No. Just private individuals looking to make it, just like you. We have a doctor aboard if you have any medical issues you'd like attended to. We have some silver to buy things with, and a stock of items for trade, if you'll let us tie up at your dock."

The man disappeared for a moment, but was back in the sunlight a few seconds later. "Come on in, but I'm telling you, you try anything, you'll all die."

Killany idled the houseboat up alongside the dock when the small boats were moved out of the way. With the bow of the 'Wanderlust' almost touching the bank, the stern was still well out past the end of the dock.

"Leave the guns inside," Killany told his crew before they went out to secure the boat to the dock.

Three men came down with the man that had done the talking, all with guns held level at their waists, ready for any dangerous move that Killany or the others might make.

Killany came down from the upper pilot house and stepped onto the dock. Dr. Cooper was right behind him.

"I'm Killany," Killany said, holding out his hand. He hadn't brought his rifle, but he did have on his pistol. "This is Dr. Cooper. My crew behind us."

"Richard Lee," said the leader. He finally took Killany's hand and the two men shook.

"First off, is there anyone sick or in need of medical help?" Dr. Cooper asked, stepping up beside Killany. Everything else can wait."

The four men looked at one another, without speaking. But they communicated something between them for Richard said, "Yes. Mandy is pregnant. Got a couple of young'uns got some scrapes and cuts from falling out of a tree. And Michael back here has a broken arm could use some attending. It's healed, but gives him lots of problems."

"I have what I need. Have them come aboard. The children first."

Killany leaned forward as Dr. Cooper went back aboard. "She's kind of pushy. But her heart is in the right place. She is a good doc."

Richard smiled. "Got one like that, myself. She isn't a doc, but she does pretty good with herbs and stuff. But it isn't the same, I guess. Peter, go up and get them two rascals."

Richard turned back to Killany. "Good kids, but they venture out too much on their own. They were after some bird eggs and knocked each other out of a tree."

"I see. We've got a couple at the Farm like that. Do you have a radio? Have you picked up any of our radio chatter?"

"No. Radio gave out when it all happened. We've been a ways up and down this arm of the lake, but we haven't found anyone."

Peter returned, nearly dragging two children, ages, at best guess, ten and twelve. The boy was probably ten and the girl, twelve.

"I'll take them in to Dr. Cooper," said Twilla. She was working with Dr. Cooper in the quiet times, getting trained as well as Dr. Cooper could with the resources she had.

"Why don't you come aboard? We'll have some coffee and we can hear each other's stories," Killany said, gesturing toward the houseboat.

"I don't think I should. It isn't right, me drinking coffee when the Missus and the others can't have any." Richard had a firm look in his eyes.

"Tell you what," Killany said, "you have one of yours take up a pound to the others and you and I can discuss what's happened and where we want to go from here."

"Is it… Is it real coffee? We're doing some dandelion coffee, but it sure isn't the same."

"Real coffee," Killany said. "We ration it, but we'll spare a pound for you folks," Killany said. "Reed?"

Reed, already at the kitchen to make a pot of coffee pulled out one of the precious pound brick bags of Folgers coffee and handed it to Richard.

"Oh, my," Richard said, handling the coffee gently. "Peter! Take this up to Sally and ask her to brew up a pot."

Peter handled the package of coffee as gently as had Richard. "Now," Richard said, "What do you want to know?"

It was about as Killany thought might be the case. Richard and his family were locals, living close together when the attack came. They'd gathered here, where Richard had a deep root cellar. They'd all received enough radiation to make them sick, having come out a bit too early after the attack.

One child had died from the radiation, and two adults had died from getting too much ash in their lungs working outside while the ash fall was still coming down. Between all the families, they'd had enough food put by to get along; with the fish they caught and ate almost every day, filling in all the holes.

They'd had little success hunting early on, but were getting some game now. And their huge garden was doing very well. The previous year had been the worst, with only a little production from the garden, and their canned goods about gone.

"Can't say some of us adults didn't go hungry some nights, but the little ones always had a full belly," Richard said. His gaze had been far away as he'd told the story. He focused on Killany. "What about you? How'd you and yours make it through?"

Without going into any details about exactly what the Farm and Properties had in the way of facilities, Killany gave a quick sketch of the time from the nuclear attack until they'd docked here.

"Some story. It's not good having to kill people."

"I know," Killany said. "But it was kill or be killed. And worse for our women and children."

"Yeah. That is what scares me now. We'd be hard pressed to resist a group like that. I'm not sure what I'd do if I thought we were going to lose and the women and children were likely to be hard used…"

Killany nodded. "It's a hard choice, when it comes to that. We intend to see it doesn't. We have the personnel and equipment to keep things peaceful, if we know something is going on. If you'll accept a radio from us, we'd like to stay in touch. You can be our eyes and ears up this way. And we'll do everything in our power to keep you safe if something does come up."

"Yeah. I'd like that. It's good to know there are some good people out there besides us." Richard drained his cup and pushed it away. "Don't want to abuse the hospitality. You gave us some coffee for just us. I'll have my share of it."

"As you wish," Killany said. "You feel comfortable with doing some trading? Don't know what you need or have, but we've brought some things we thought might be in short supply."

"Yeah. I trust you." Richard looked over at a smiling young woman, her belly swollen with the life growing inside her.

Dr. Cooper was handing the girl a large bottle of pre-natal vitamins. "Take one a day. And if there are any problems, you send someone to get me."

"I'm giving Richard one of our radios with a solar charger. They'll stay in contact."

"Oh." Dr. Cooper said. "Good. Who's next?"

"I guess that's me," said a man standing out on the foredeck. It was Michael, with the bad arm.

"Come on back." Dr. Cooper led the way back to the medical room. It wasn't long before she came out. "I'm going to need some help," she said. "I need to re-break his arm so it can heal properly."

Killany and Richard went to join her. There was fear in Michael's eyes, but he went through the painful process without crying out. "Okay," Dr. Cooper said. "I'm going to cast it, and give you something for the pain, but just for when it gets really bad. Keep it strapped to your chest, except when you bathe."

A white face Michael nodded. Killany and Richard left to let Dr. Cooper and Twilla to finish treating Michael.

"She knows her stuff, doesn't she?" Richard asked.

"Yep. She's the best."

"Uh... None of my business, but you and her..."

Killany chuckled. "No. She's not too fond of me, actually."

"Oh. Okay. She'd make a good wife, I bet," Richard said.

Killany, unaware that Dr. Cooper had stepped out of the medical room to get something from her room, said, "Yes. I think she'd make a fine wife. Dr. Cooper is everything a man could want."

It shocked her no end, but Dr. Cooper quickly and quietly got what she need from her room and went back to the medical room.

She avoided looking at Killany when she came out with Michael a few minutes later. "I'd like to take a look at everyone, if you don't mind," she said, addressing Richard. "I might be able to catch something in the early stages."

"Yeah. You sure? We don't have much to pay with."

"Not a problem," Dr. Cooper said. "This is humanitarian aid."

"We don't take charity. We'll pay," Richard said firmly. "I'll go get the others."

"Thank you, Doctor," Michael said. He was still pale and stumbled a bit going outside. Richard lent a hand and helped him onto the dock.

Dr. Cooper was staring at Killany, but quickly looked away when he seemed to feel it and turned to look at her. A few minutes later a string of people, twelve in total, came down to the houseboat.

Dr. Cooper and Twilla worked the entire afternoon. When things were winding down, Killany had the crew bring out the trade goods they'd brought. Mostly basic items difficult to make by hand.

"Afraid we don't have much," Richard said, looking at the selection wistfully.

"We could use some fresh vegetables," Killany said. "Twenty servings of vegetables, and you can have twenty items."

Dr. Cooper gave Killany a sharp look. He'd furnished all the trade goods. Some, she thought, would trade for a lot more than a single serving of vegetables.

"Really? The garden is doing pretty good..." He turned to his family. "One item each."

The girl that had fallen from the tree whispered to her mother and pointed at the packet of reusable sanitary pads.

"We have more," Dr. Cooper said, seeing the look. "And patterns to make more out of scrap cloth. Do you have a good sewing kit?"

"Only one needle left," said the mother.

"Killany? Do you have a sewing kit?"

"Sure do," he said, moving a couple of items to uncover the small wicker basket.

"That's worth more than vegetables," protested the mother.

"Deal is a deal," Killany said. "Twenty items, twenty servings."

The woman looked at Richard and he nodded. She picked up the pads and handed them to the girl and took the sewing kit for herself. "We'll make a pattern from one of these," she said. "I've made patterns before."

After each person had taken something from the selection, there were still five picks left. "Ammunition? I don't suppose you have any twenty-twos? I don't see them out here."

"Some things I won't put out unless asked for," Killany said. He disappeared for a few minutes and when he returned handed Richard two fifty-round boxes.

"Four more items," Killany said.

"No. It's too much. We'll give you the vegetables for what we've selected. We still have to pay the doctor for her services." Richard looked over at Dr. Cooper.

"Really. I…" she said, but Richard cut her off.

"I insist."

"Very well. Whatever you think it is worth… A couple of servings of vegetables?"

"Not enough," Richard said. He took an old leather coin purse from the front pocket of his worn jeans. "We've been saving this for emergencies. Silver coins. Real. See? All before 1965. I saw a program before the war that silver coins would still have value. They're from the kids' coin collections I put together for them over the years."

Killany could tell Dr. Cooper really didn't want to take them, but she finally said, "Okay. We're using silver coins at our places. "Would a dime for each person be okay?"

"How about four quarters for everyone?" Richard asked. Since they were bargaining now, he felt no compulsion not to try and get a better deal.

Killany hid his smile when Dr. Cooper looked exasperated. "Okay. Of course. Four quarters."

Richard handed them over. "See? All before 1965."

"I see," Dr. Cooper said. "Thank you."

"No. Thank you!" Richard said. "I guess we should go back to the house and let you people be on your way. We'll bring down the vegetables right away."

"Okay, Richard," Killany said, holding out his hand. Richard shook it firmly. "Good doing business with you."

"Yeah. Same here. Stop back anytime. Just to socialize if you want."

"Might just do that," Killany replied. He let the crew take the fresh vegetables and put them away. He went back up to the upper pilot house and started the engines. A few minutes later he backed the houseboat away from the dock and turned it up the lake again.

It was getting late and he found a good place a mile or so from the Lee family's holding to drop anchor for the night. They seldom put ashore at night, preferring the security of some open water between them and the shore.

As they sat down for a supper of fresh vegetables and freshly caught fish, Dr. Cooper asked Killany, "Why, Killany? You could get a lot more even from some of our own people for what you've brought along, than you took for those trade items."

"You ask me that and you didn't want to take anything from them for your medical services?"

"That's different," Dr. Cooper protested. "It was just my services. Even the medical goods are mostly what you provided. I'm not out anything much."

"Yes. But people, most people anyway, don't like the idea of charity, no matter how bad things are, as long as they are making it day to day. They need the things much more than I do. I'll get more return in the future than what little I let go today.

"There will be times, you will see, when I'll be striking what you will probably think are outrageously unfair deals with people that can afford the price."

Dr. Cooper frowned. "I guess I should have known there was an ulterior motive."

"Yes. I thought you knew me better than to think there wasn't an ulterior motive."

The reply bothered Dr. Cooper, but Twilla was asking her a medical question about one of the Lee family and she didn't have a chance to pursue the conversation.

The further east they went, the more people they found. Three more extended families, and a group of five unrelated men, all but one group hanging on by the skin of their teeth. A couple of times Dr. Cooper received no offer of payment for checking people over and doing some minor medical work. Killany gave away a few things, including a radio at each place so they could keep in contact with the Properties and now with the other groups.

At the other places, Dr. Cooper took what was offered without protesting. And Killany did more trading, doing exactly what he said he would do when one of the families, packing a real attitude according to Twilla, wanted more than Killany was offering.

She saw him go hard and watched as he convinced those in the group that it would be in their best interest to take what was offered, at the requested price or he'd take his 'toys' and go home. They forked over gold coins they'd denied having at first.

Mid September Killany turned the 'Wanderlust' around and headed them home. He kept the speed up during the day, but they continued to overnight away from the shore. Someone was there to wave at them at every place they'd stopped. Killany sounded the air horns whenever the children waved, delighting them no end.

It had taken two and a half months to get to where they turned around, but it took only a week and a half of steady running to get back to the Properties. Just as there had been when they left, there was a group on the dock, this time to welcome them rather than wave goodbye.

Dr. Cooper and Killany were the last two off the 'Wanderlust'. Bethany and Gary were watching closely as the two approached.

"From your radio reports, I take it things went well?" Gary asked.

"Yes," Killany said. "All in all, it was a good trip."

"Dr. Cooper?" Bethany asked. The Doctor was just standing there, lost in thought.

"What? Oh, yes. It was a good trip. Those that survived are a tough bunch. There were fewer medical problems than I expected."

"Those with serious problems died off early," Killany said. "Nature at work. We need to get together and put another team together to go after those things we found that will be of use to us, Gary."

"I'm anxious to get on that, too," Gary replied. "We should do it before winter hits." The two men walked away, discussing the upcoming salvage trip.

Dr. Cooper still seemed distracted as she and Bethany slowly walked along the dock and up onto shore. "Are you all right, Jane? You look… strange."

With a sigh, Dr. Cooper looked over at Bethany, this time focusing on her face. "I feel strange. I've just spent almost two and a half months with a man I can't figure out. I thought I had him pegged from the first, but every time a new situation comes up, I find him doing almost the opposite of what I expect him to do from past observations."

Another sigh. "I even overheard him talking once... He said I'd make a fine wife. I didn't think he even liked me, much less thought I'd be a good wife."

"For him?" Bethany asked.

"No. I guess not. He didn't specify. And he hasn't made any effort to get to know me better."

"You sound like you might accept that kind of attention."

"I don't know... I can't stand him at times..."

"But you've fallen in love with him, despite all that."

Dr. Cooper bit her lip. "I'm afraid I have. Bethany, what do I do?" Dr. Cooper looked at Bethany, a totally helpless look on her face.

"Well, I don't want to hurt your feelings by disagreeing with you, but you're wrong about him not trying to get to know you. Why do you think he finagled you into going along on this trip?"

"But..." Dr. Cooper looked thoughtful. "But... That... that was sort of a mistake. I wasn't offering to go..."

"No, but he made out like you were and you went along with it. I think you both wanted to get to know the other. Two and a half months in close quarters was a good way to do it. You did learn things about him, didn't you? You said he kept confusing you..."

Dr. Cooper frowned. "Well, sure, we learned some things about one another... At least I did about him. But he's so calm all the time and never lets much emotion show."

"Bit of an enigma, I agree," Bethany said. "But that isn't necessarily a bad thing, is it? Sure would make life interesting, being with him."

"But he's always running off!" Dr. Cooper said, almost in anguish.

"But this time, you went with him. What's to stop you going with him on some of his other jaunts? There are bound to be more. You heard what he said. It's the wanderlust in him. It is part of his nature, just as your call to provide healthcare to those that need it."

"I'm... I'm going to have to think about this some more. Could be a moot point, anyway. He can believe I'd be a good wife for someone else, not him."

Dr. Cooper fell silent, lost in thought again and Bethany just walked beside her, until they reached the house. "I'm going to go check in," Dr. Cooper suddenly said. "See how the other medical personnel did while I was gone."

Bethany didn't offer up the fact that all was well. Dr. Cooper needed something to do at the moment.

## CHAPTER ELEVEN

-

After several trips using the Munson and the 'Li'l Gem' as cargo carriers, everything on Killany's list of things to recover was now either at the Farm or at the Properties. The harvest was almost complete and the Thanksgiving celebration was over when the first snow began to fly.

Even the Orem group had returned with stock and seeds, plus three people that wanted to join the Group. Jeremiah had spoken highly of those at Orem, despite having decided to stay here, rather than go back. There was an even exchange in people. Three people went back with the group from Orem.

The Group picked up some additional residents before winter set in. One of the family groups living on the lake contacted by Killany on the summer trip asked to join the Group. Killany took the 'Wanderlust' and the Munson to go pick them and their possessions up and brought them back to the Properties.

The family took up residence at the Farm, when additional housing was brought in. Everyone was glad to have them, the move pointed out a problem that was beginning to crop up.

Though both the Farm and the Properties had prime power generators, and were producing enough biodiesel to keep them running, both places were beginning to run short of power.

At the staff meeting a week before Christmas, the subject came up. Again Killany had a possible answer. "I say we take a page out of one of Tired Old Man's stories and get some windmill generator systems."

"Good idea," Gary said. "TOM would be proud."

Gary laughed, and then had to explain who TOM was. The Major had heard the term a few times and hadn't a clue what the person was talking about each time.

"We're a long ways from the wind farms out west," Gary said, after the explanation.

"Ah! But there are some a lot closer," Killany said. "Saw a report on the tube way back when about Rock Port, up in the northwest corner of the state. They have four wind generators of 1.25 megawatts each."

"Northwest corner of which state?" Bethany asked. Killany had a tendency to think in terms of distance on a different scale than some.

"Missouri," Killany said with a smile. "It's just a little ways off I-29 north of KC."

"One and a quarter meg units aren't small units. How would we manage to get them down, here, and rigged up?" asked Major Tandy.

"I know it won't be easy, but I think it worth a try," replied Killany.

"What if there are people there, using them?" Dr. Cooper asked.

"That's why I plan on going up there and checking the situation out," Killany said. "Won't take long. Should be back in a month or so."

The others, including Killany, were surprised when Dr. Cooper didn't protest. "You going alone, or taking someone this time?"

"Alone. Just a scouting mission. I may check on the Springfield area. We know there are survivors there. I'd like to make contact. And since they aren't responding to any of our radio communication attempts, I think we should try and make personal contact."

"It could be dangerous," Bethany said. It wasn't really a protest, just a statement.

"You know I'm pretty cautious," replied Killany. "I won't be taking any chances. Things are going well, for the moment. And the future looks pretty good. I intend to be around to enjoy things for a long time to come. But all risks can't be eliminated. And some things are worth taking risks."

Dr. Cooper remained silent. They moved on to other subjects. But three days later Killany was leaving the Properties on the Kettenkrad, pulling both tracked trailers behind. A light snow storm was starting to cover the ground with fresh snow.

Dr. Cooper was the last to turn away after he disappeared from sight as the snow began to accumulate.

Killany didn't push it. He knew there was no rush, and his shoulder and leg both bothered him some when he did push things. So it took a few days before he stopped and set up camp outside of Springfield.

For two days he studied the smoke he saw rising, at least, when it wasn't snowing. The third day, Killany broke camp, packed everything away, and drove the Kettenkrad and trailers into a snowdrift. He covered everything with tarps and proceeded to cover the unit with additional snow.

When he was satisfied that the intermittent snows would soon leave no trace of the disturbance of the snow, Killany shouldered his pack, picked up his rifle, and headed for the nearest of the locations that had a continuous column of smoke going up.

He was careful, caching most of his gear, taking only the smaller Kifaru pack that he carried piggybacked on the larger one that held most of his gear and supplies. With his rifle slung over a shoulder, he approached the group of three houses that were emitting the smoke from fireplace chimneys. He noted the huge stacks of firewood, much of it from dismantled structures. "Someone's been busy."

Stopping at a point where he could take cover if the occupants reacted aggressively, Killany called out in a loud voice, "Hello the house! Anyone home?"

Only seconds later there were four guns aimed at him, two from one house and one from each of the other two.

"What do you want?" came a deep toned voice. Surprisingly deep from the size of the man that stepped from the middle house, gun up.

"Just passing through and wanted to touch base. My group is looking for trading partners for our crops, animals, and seeds. Like to set up a link between here and our place further south. Who in this area would I talk to, to organize something like that?"

The man was silent for several seconds. "That would be Carl Manscony. He's sort of the unofficial leader for several families around here."

"Any way you can set up a meeting for me with him? I'd be glad to contribute a bit to your supplies if you help me."

"What are you offering?"

"I've got a little coffee, some lamp wick, sugar, some batteries, some hard candy, a box of canning jar lids. Regular size." Killany saw the man step back and lean his head toward the open door of the house.

"Well, don't mind contacting Carl for you. Won't charge you for that. But we would like to do some trading. Keep that gun on your shoulder and come on up to the house."

When Killany stepped up onto the porch, the man said, "Hold it. Going to take your guns and look in your pack. We aren't going to hurt you or steal your stuff, but I have to know you won't try something while you're here."

"Fair enough," Killany said, holding his arms out so another man could take the rifle and pistol he carried.

"I'm Harold Wilson," said the man that was doing the talking. Killany moved his arms back and down, to let the pack slide free when Harold gripped the pull loop of it. "Over to the sofa there," he added.

Killany went and sat down on the leather sofa, his eyes going to the small group of children and women looking at him from the two doors that opened into the living room of the house. There was a moderate fire in the fireplace and Killany stretched his hands out toward it.

Harold dumped the pack onto the coffee table and considered the objects. "What are you looking for in trade?" Harold asked. "For the jar of coffee, the jar lids, and the batteries?" There were some groans from one doorway where the children were.

"I'll take real silver, say fifty cents worth for the batteries, a dollar for the lids. I'd ask more, but they're getting up in age.

Still look good, though. And a dollar for the coffee. It's getting scarce."

"I'll say," replied Harold. "Been a long time since we had real coffee. But I'm holding on to my silver. What for trade?"

"Meat. Dried fruit. Rice, beans, or lentils. Honey. What do you have to offer?"

"No meat. Need all of it to get us through. Might spare some dried fruit and rice. One pint of honey."

"Sounds fair to me," Killany said. He looked over at the door where the kids were staring at the bag of butterscotch disks on the coffee table. "I'll throw in the candy for the kids. No charge."

There were gasps from the doorway and eager whispers.

"Well... all right. Deal. Betty come get these things and get... What's your name?"

"Killany. Just call me Killany."

"Get Killany a bag of the apricots, pound of rice, and a pint of the honey. And Jude, turn on the radio and tell Carl that there's someone here wants to talk to him."

"Okay, Dad," said one of the older children. He disappeared from view.

A tall woman, very slim, but not looking malnourished, hurried in and picked up the items, including the candy. There was a scramble away from one door to the other, as the children followed Betty into what Killany decided was probably the kitchen."

"How'd you get here, anyway?" asked Harold. "You can't be traveling in this weather with just what you have here."

"No. I have my other pack cached. Didn't know how far I might have to walk to get with the right people. We've had some bad ones down south. How's things around here?"

"Not bad. Just a few of us. Haven't had any raiders since early on. Pretty peaceful around here, and we aim to keep it that way."

"Good. That's the way we are. No one bothers us, and we don't bother anyone. Just wanted to get to know our neighbors. Figure there might be some trade potential. Our Farm is doing okay. We'll have meat come next fall. Enough to start trading for other things."

"There's only one farm around here up and going, and they stay to themselves. Tight fisted. Only have a little to spare, they say, and it's expensive. Wants double what it's worth, in my eyes. We do okay hunting. Now. Slim pickings early on."

"Same where we are," Killany said.

"Dad?" said Jude.

"Yeah, Son?"

"Carl says bring him over."

"He would say that," replied Harold, sighing.

"Let me get my coat and gun and we'll go on over. Only about a mile."

"I'm sorry if I'm creating a problem, Harold."

"No. Just I don't do too good in the cold weather anymore."

"I can go alone, if you want to give me directions."

"Best I take you and announce our presence. The community stuff is at Carl's and it's closely guarded. Don't want to go up unexpected."

"I see," Killany said. He gathered the remainder of the items on the coffee table and put them in his pack, adding those things that Betty handed to him.

"Thank you for the candy," she said. Her voice was soft. "The kids don't get much in the way of treats."

"My pleasure," Killany replied. He put on the pack and took the rifle and pistol when Harold handed them to him.

"Back in a couple hours, Honey," Harold told his wife, and then kissed her lightly on the lips.

The snow had started again, and both men, in their heavy insulated coats, had an accumulation on the coats and their hats when Harold stopped and pointed to a large house, mansion size, actually, with four chimneys, two of which had smoke coming from them.

"We wait here until someone comes to get us."

"I see," Killany said, studying the place carefully. It had the requisite large pile of firewood, and there were a couple of vehicles present, that looked like they were being used. "You have fuel for the vehicles?"

"Yeah. But not much. We only use them for emergencies, or to carry things too big to move by hand cart.

"There's Seymour. We can go on up."

Seymour was standing on the broad, covered porch of the mansion. He had a holstered revolver and a short barreled shotgun. Seymour was silent as he ushered Killany and Harold inside.

Harold un-slung his rifle and put in a rack by the door, and put his pistol on a shelf. Killany did likewise, without waiting to be asked.

Seymour finally spoke when they reached the carved double doors down a short hall from the entrance. "Mr. Manscony will see you now. Please come in." He opened one of the double doors and stepped aside.

Harold went inside first, blocking Killany's view. When he stepped inside himself, and to one side of Harold, he saw Carl Manscony sitting in a wheelchair in front of the fireplace. Wheeling his chair around, he rolled himself over to the massive desk that was the key point of the room.

"Please, sit. So, Stranger, young Master Jude informs me, through Seymour, that you would like to speak to me, in my capacity as de facto leader of our small community here in Springfield."

"That is correct, Mr. Manscony. I'm Killany, a representative from the Properties and Farm located south of here. We'd like to initiate contact and eventually set up a mutually beneficial arrangement between our two communities. Trade, primarily, but also simply association with others to share knowledge before it is lost to future generations."

"I see. We've heard some of your radio conversations."

"I'm here because we didn't get a response."

"Yes. I thought it prudent to wait until we had some assurance that your group would not be a danger to our own. We aren't equipped well enough to do much adventuring. All our resources are being used just to maintain the group in a safe and healthy environment."

"I understand. We are fortunate to have the means to do some moderate distance travel. If you would be willing to let one or more of your representatives accompany me down to our group, say sometime next spring, to check out our operation, we'd be pleased to provide the transport and support they might need. Someone that can evaluate what we have to offer to you."

"I see. That seems reasonable. I will take it up with our council of advisors and we will contact you sometime this winter by radio, if you can give Seymour specific radio frequencies and communication schedule."

"Yes, Sir. I have it here." Killany took a piece of paper out of his shirt pocket.

"Please give that to Seymour on your way out." Carl backed away from the desk and rolled over to the fireplace to the same position he'd been when Killany and Harold had entered.

Harold stood up and Killany followed him out into the hallway. Seymour was waiting.

"I have a set of radio frequencies and a time schedule that Mr. Manscony asked me to give to you. These frequencies okay for your system?"

Seymour took the paper and checked. "Yes. We have this capability. I'll show you out."

With their guns in hand, Harold and Killany left the mansion.

"Uh… Look. I'm sorry about that. Carl is pretty remote. It's nothing personal. He just has so much on his mind. If it wasn't for him and the preparations he'd made, several of us would not have lived through the first year."

"I understand. No offense taken."

They walked the rest of the way back to Harold's in silence. The wind had picked up and it was snowing heavily. When they reached the house, Killany stopped. "I hope to see you again, Harold. I'll be on my way so you can get inside and warm up."

"You aren't leaving in this, are you?" Harold asked, holding out his hand to allow snow to fall on the gloved surface. You're welcome to wait for a while, see if it stops. Can't offer you much, but we can give you a hot meal and a pad to sleep on, in out of the weather."

"Thank you, Harold. But it isn't necessary. I'm well equipped to take care of myself in this weather."

Harold shook his head. "Okay. Your funeral. Have a good trip home."

"I will," Killany replied, not bothering to tell Harold what his immediate future plans were. He trudged off, and Harold hurried inside to the warmth of the fireplace.

It was growing dark when Killany reached the cached pack. He set up the tent and soon had a warm meal in him. Satisfied with the way things had gone, despite Carl Manscony's abrupt manner, Killany crawled into the sleeping bag system and settled in for the night. His last thought before falling asleep wasn't about the meeting today, or the rest of the trip. It was about Dr. Cooper.

The storm wasn't quite a blizzard, but it was close, and lasted for three days. Killany hiked back to where he'd buried the Kettenkrad and trailers in the snow when the storm broke, and the fourth day dawned clear and bright, but briskly cold.

An hour's work with the shovel he'd cached nearby, and Killany had the Kettenkrad and trailers uncovered, and was back on the road, headed north.

Taking his time, watching for other signs of survivors, Killany continued north on US 65 until he picked up I-70 west for a while. Again he swung wide of Kansas City, staying east and going north before he cut back west to pick up I-29.

There simply was no one about that he could determine. St. Joseph was a snow covered ghost town. He spent three days there, resting primarily, but also doing a little salvage work as he often did on the trips he took.

But soon he was back on the way to Rock Port. When he arrived, he did a thorough search of the town and all around it. The four wind turbines were easy to spot. Killany set up camp near them, and investigated the area.

He had to admit that it would take a daunting effort to accomplish the task of not only moving the turbines but the entire system that took the power from the turbines and made it available to the power grid, and then to the consumer.

The more he investigated, the more he began to doubt the feasibility of the project. The wind turbines looked all right. On two-hundred-fifty foot high columns, the three ninety-foot long blades on each of the four units appeared undamaged. But the same couldn't be said for the electrical system it was connected to. From the looks of some of the transformers, EMP had struck the system and struck it hard. One transformer was in jagged pieces, another looked like it had caught fire. Many of the cables and insulators were damaged.

The chances of finding intact equipment elsewhere was slim. But there were other wind power sites fairly close by that he checked. It was the same in each case, or worse. Some of the turbines were down, and all of the major electrical distribution components were damaged by EMP.

Killany decided to head for home, disappointed, but satisfied that the trip had been worth it to find out for sure. There would be other options. He just needed to decide what they might be and where he might find them.

On the way back home, Killany decided to check out as much of Kansas City as it was safe to do. He had his radiation monitors with him, and wouldn't get into any really hot areas. The first thing he did was find a Kansas City Yellow Pages. He then set up camp and took a couple of days while it was snowing heavily to map out the areas where he might want to salvage some items, if the area wasn't too hot.

Just on a whim, Killany checked for solar power suppliers. He was surprised to find a major commercial installer not only listed in Kansas City, but also in St. Louis, Jefferson City, and Springfield.

He couldn't get to the place in Kansas City. It was far too hot of an area. And from the address listed for St. Louis, he had serious doubts that it could be accessed safely, if it was even still in existence.

But he was definitely going to check out Jefferson City on the way back, and make another stop in Springfield.

Since he'd already mapped out some other salvage sites on the outskirts of Kansas City, he went ahead checked them out. He was pleased with the trailer load of items he picked up, and was in a good mood as he went east, headed to Jefferson City.

He made sure he let the Properties know he was running late and would not be home within the month's time he'd planned.

Killany found what he was looking for in Jefferson City, and detected no signs of anyone that might object to the group taking the components to install a large commercial size installation solar photovoltaic system. From the looks of what was on hand, they could probably build five such systems. There were many more components for residential systems in stock, as well.

Eagerly, Killany headed back south to Springfield. He was careful to avoid any contact this time with the locals. He checked out the facility he was looking for, and found enough additional components to build three more large commercial systems and several residential ones, to boot.

With new plans forming in his mind, Killany headed for home. He arrived in the early evening and only Gary, Bethany, and Dr. Cooper were out to greet him. Killany saw Dr. Cooper studying him carefully and returned a long look she gave him.

"You look chipper for someone that had to abandon what seemed like a very good idea," Gary said, distracting Killany from Dr. Cooper.

"Yeah. Well, something else occurred to me, so I checked it out. There are some other options, not as powerful, but with enough to make things much better. I'll lay it all out in the next staff meeting. Right now, I want to unload, get a long, hot, shower, some food, and crawl between some cool, crisp sheets."

Gary and Bethany laughed. Dr. Cooper managed a smile, but it faded when Killany began unloading the Kettenkrad's rear trailer.

"You like a little help?" Dr. Cooper asked.

Killany's movements stilled and he looked over at her. "You sure? You can't afford to bang up your hands. Some of these items are awkward and a little heavy."

"We'll help him," Gary quickly said. He and Bethany both stepped forward to take the first item Killany picked up from the trailer.

Gary, Bethany, and Dr. Cooper were all surprised when Killany looked at Dr. Cooper again and said, "But if you really don't mind, I could use the help. This old body isn't what it used to be, before all the gunshot wounds."

Killany looked quickly away from Dr. Cooper when she looked at him questioningly.

His statement hadn't sounded like he was just talking about the recent wounds. Two didn't really equate to 'all'. But she didn't mention it and simply began to take the items that Killany handed to her. The four took the first load in to Killany's basement apartment and returned for another. It took several trips, and they hadn't started on the Kettenkrad when Killany called a halt. "I'll get the rest in the morning. I really want to get to that shower and food."

Killany stood a long time at the outer door of the garage basement, watching Dr. Cooper head for her quarters in the bright moonlight of the winter sky. He sighed and turned around. Again he went to sleep thinking about her.

Managing to avoid the doctor for two days, Killany rearranged a few things after finishing unloading the Kettenkrad early the next. A few things were put on the 'Wanderlust', some went into cache buckets, totes, and barrels. He would hide the caches over the next few days, before the winter really set in. The rest stayed in the apartment.

The next time Killany saw Dr. Cooper was at the staff meeting. He avoided her eyes as he described the trip and what he'd accomplished. And hadn't accomplished. "I'm glad I went up there," he said. "It wasn't a bad idea, it just didn't work out. I'm not one-hundred-percent sure we could have taken them down, moved them, and erected them again, anyway.

"The PV panels, on the other hand, shouldn't be much of a problem. It looked like everything needed was there, including dry stored batteries with acid, the inverters, and pallet loads of panels.

"The systems you put in here, your place, Gary, and the Farm are carrying most of the load you require. It's the other, expansion, houses and other buildings that need something to replace the generators. Or at least reduce their use, to increase their longevity.

"Commercial units will run several residences with basic power. Individual residential units for those living out on their own now. Our various new Farm buildings, and the new buildings here, would need one of the smaller commercial units, each. But that's only four of the commercial systems, leaving four more.

"That is, if we don't have any trouble getting the ones from Springfield. The place showed no signs of disturbance, but we won't be able to get them without the group knowing. We might want to make an offer for them, to the community. Something reasonable, just to keep things on a friendly basis. I can come up with the necessary funds, as long as Manscony doesn't get greedy. But I would like something in return from the Properties."

"What would that be?" Gary asked.

"There is a piece of land nearby, on the lake that I have my eye on. No one has claimed it yet. I want to assume ownership so I can homestead it. To do that, I'm going to need quite a bit of help. That means pulling people off some of their regular jobs at times. I'd be paying them out of my own pocket, but I'd need the cooperation of both the Farm and the Properties to get what I want done on a timely basis."

"Losing that wanderlust, Killany?" Bethany asked, studiously avoiding looking at Dr. Cooper.

"Some. But mostly I want to get established so I can start conducting some entrepreneurial businesses. I need a place of my own. I plan to get married soon, and hopefully have a couple of kids."

Dr. Cooper thought her heart would break right there. She blinked back tears, but sat straight and proud.

Gary, Bethany, and the Major looked at Dr. Cooper, and then at Killany. Killany's eyes were on Dr. Cooper when Gary asked, "And when would all this take place?"

"Actually depends on the woman," Killany said. "What do you think, Jane?" Killany, eyes having never left Dr. Cooper, took something out of his pocket. It was a ring box. He opened and set it in front of Dr. Cooper."

"Would you marry me?"

"What? But... But... I..." Dr. Cooper was more or less speechless.

"We can discuss children later. But I'd like to set a marriage date today, if you'll accept my proposal."

Gary, Bethany, and Major Taylor looked on, in almost as much shock as Dr. Cooper.

Suddenly Dr. Cooper lunged to her feet and moved toward Killany's chair. Ready for anything, Killany waited for Dr. Cooper to do something. After seconds that seemed an eternity to everyone in the room, Dr. Cooper whispered, "Yes. I'll marry you." Suddenly she was in his arms and the two were kissing.

"I've wanted to do that for so long," Killany said, setting Dr. Cooper back down on her feet.

"I didn't think... I was so sure you didn't even like me," Dr. Cooper said, standing with Killany, her right hand still in his left.

"I've admired and respected you from day one," Killany said softly, his eyes on Jane's. "And as I came to know you, I quickly fell in love with you. I just couldn't let it show. There were too many uncertainties in the early days. And I had to give you the chance to get to know me and my ways, so you could make an informed decision."

"You know, Killany," Gary said, grinning, "These things are usually done in private. Not with witnesses."

"I wanted witnesses for Jane, so she wouldn't have to convince any doubting Thomas' that I actually asked, and she accepted."

"Good point," Major Taylor said. "I don't think I would have believed it. Would have figured it as a practical joke that one or the other of you set up." He shook his head and stood. "Let me be the first to congratulate you."

Major Tandy held out his hand and he and Killany shook hands. Gary was next, as Bethany gave Dr. Cooper a hug, and then Killany.

"I think we can handle everything else tomorrow," Gary said.

Bethany was smiling and agreed. "You two obviously need to talk. Jane, come on back when you get a chance and we'll start planning things."

"Yes. Yes, I will." Jane's hand still in Killany's, the two left the den in the house Bethany had build.

"Well, what do you know about that?" Major Tandy said, shaking his head. "Sure didn't see that coming."

"Oh, Major!" Bethany said, chuckling, "It's been obvious for some time now. For those who worry about such things."

The Major smiled. "I suppose so. My late wife probably would have seen it, too. I'd better get back to the Farm." He let himself out.

"So you can stop fretting about those two now," Gary said, taking Bethany into his arms for a long kiss.

"Yes. I'm glad Killany finally made his attentions known. Poor Jane has been going through agony trying to hide her attraction to him, because she thought he really didn't care about her."

"I'm so glad we didn't have those troubles," Gary replied. Gary kissed Bethany again, but Jamie Ann let out a cry and Bethany went to check on her.

The official announcement for the wedding came the next day. Everyone at the Farm and the Properties got the word that Killany was marrying Dr. Jane Cooper, June 30th, five months hence.

There were a few people more than a little disappointed. Killany and Dr. Cooper both had others interested in them, but neither had seen it, being taken with each other. The couple spent much time together those few months leading up to wedding, learning more about each other, and making plans for the future.

But that time was broken up into small sections, for Killany went on three of his scouting trips while the weather was still bad. He wouldn't tell Jane, or anyone else what he was doing on the trips, but he finalized the deal with Gary, Bethany, and Major Taylor to get the help he needed in the near future to get a place ready for himself and his soon to be bride.

Winter broke and spring came early, allowing the planting to get an early start. Killany made two more trips after the major work was done at the Farm and the Properties. But he was back well before June 30th.

The wedding was the biggest event for the group in some time. A veritable feast was created, and everyone was rotated from the have-to jobs so they could enjoy part of the day at the reception.

As he had Bethany and Gary, Major Tandy married Killany and Dr. Cooper. They stayed for the reception for a while, but soon left to go aboard the 'Wanderlust' for a one week honeymoon.

Things got hectic upon their return. Killany again took off on a trip without Dr. Cooper. This time he was accompanied by Gary, and a team of twelve people, and all of Bethany's maintenance trucks, plus the several semi trucks they had accumulated and put in running condition.

It took three days after they contacted Carl Manscony through Harold again, that their equivalent to the leadership staff at the Properties and the Farm, came to a decision to allow the solar power systems to be removed from Springfield. For a price.

A mixture of food, biodiesel, some skilled labor, and gold was the price insisted on by Manscony. Gary radioed back to the Properties and the Farm for a select crew to bring their tools and join the group already in Springfield.

While the original crew gathered up all the solar power equipment and took it home, the second crew began work on several greenhouses that had been located by the Springfield survivors. Killany did convince Carl to sell him two of the eight greenhouses. There wasn't room for all eight where they wanted the greenhouses to be.

Neither Gary, nor Killany could understand why they had not been erected previously. Harold finally told them that there had been a great deal of debate and hard feelings over who would get the greenhouses, and who would benefit from them. "Carl just put a hold on the project until something could be figured out.

"This way, with you putting them up, they are community property, and we can get started raising some badly need specialty foods."

While the second crew continued to erect the set of greenhouses, Gary and Killany took the salvage crew to

Jefferson City. They saw no one during that entire time. But everyone continued to go armed at all times.

When the last load was on its way, Killany took Gary aside to tell him, "I've got some investigating to do. I'll be back home in three or four more days. Jane knows I was planning this, so she shouldn't be worried when you show up and I don't."

"Okay, Killany. Anything I can do to help?"

Killany shook his head. "No. I've got an idea I want to check out."

"Okay. But you be sure you call in. Believe me, wives worry. Whether they need to or not."

When Killany returned to the Properties, he was smiling and in a very good mood. Much more demonstrative than he'd been before, he picked up Dr. Cooper and spun her around a couple of times. He kissed her and set her down and told her, "Found what I wanted. It's almost too good to be true."

Jane smiled. His enthusiasm was infective. She, too, found herself much more open to people than she had been before meeting and marrying Killany. "So, what do we do now?"

"You just keep doing what you're doing. Taking care of everyone, and training a few to take over when you retire."

"Those texts and other items you salvaged in Columbia from the School of Medicine and the School of Nursing are making it so much easier to teach. At least with them as references, the education can continue beyond what I can impart.

"I don't know what I would have done if Sharon Lee hadn't agreed to help me with the herbal and other natural remedies. She could have been a pharmacist, if she'd received the training." Dr. Cooper shrugged slightly. "I guess she is a pharmacist, in a way. She's making up medications and remedies for me on a regular basis.

"She's taught her girls, and is now teaching Annie and Twilla the intricacies of the art. I'm a lot more comfortable about being able to treat certain things with her creations than I was at first. There are a few things that just don't have good substitutes for the modern versions."

"The poppy plants seem to be doing okay?"

"Sharon say's yes. Fortunately she has some really old texts that describe how to extract the useful ingredients for effective pain killers from them. I'm running really low on those types of supplies."

"We'll look for another pharmacy sometime this summer. Get what we can to supplement what you still have and what Sharon and the others can make."

Dr. Cooper looked around to make sure no one was nearby before she spoke again. "Are you sure we can pull off the clinic idea? I'd hate to get peoples' hopes up and not be able to follow through."

"That's why I don't want it known until we have things completed."

"Things are better medically than I thought they would be when I started making preparations. The idea of having a real clinic wasn't even a consideration then."

"We're slowly progressing. Hopefully the trend will continue and we can bring more and more things back to useable condition. The useful things. Leave behind the old baggage society had picked up."

With the farming activities well under control, and a crew working on installing the PV systems for the buildings in both places, Killany began the work on his and Jane's new place. First, the home site was cleared of trees and stumps, and the ground landscaped the way Killany wanted it, using the earthmoving equipment he'd found and brought in for the job.

Next, the well drilling rig was brought in and Killany paid the men that could run it to drill three wells on the site. All proved out, and they had plenty of clean fresh water for all the things that Killany and Jane wanted to do with the place. An abandoned plumbing shop in Branson furnished the components for a commercial size septic system, and two cistern tanks.

Jason Carpenter, the arborist, began putting in an orchard for the place. Like the others that Killany hired, Jason was paid in silver and gold. There was a small, but steady, stable economy going now, with some trading and buying and selling going on between the groups on the lake, and with the residents of Springfield.

With water and septic taken care of, Killany brought in several semi trucks and trailers that he'd been getting into running condition and the trailers loaded with the things he'd been planning on having at the homestead from the early days after the attack.

A basement and shelter were dug for the house and the concrete for them, with other foundations, poured using the only two cement trucks the local concrete plant had that would run. Fuel tanks from two of the marinas on the lake were transported in the Munson and installed to hold biodiesel, using the RT crane that was part of the equipment Killany had salvaged. The supply of gasoline Killany recovered and treated with his stock of PRI-G was in a fourth tank.

Besides some equipment for use around the homestead, three of the trailers had the components of a log home kit. It had been on the way to Los Angeles for shipment overseas from North Carolina when the HEMP attack stopped the trucks in their tracks.

That was simply a fortunate find. The house was a gambrel roofed two story log home, a simple rectangle comprising a total of a little over twenty-one-hundred square feet of floor space. Killany had not been able to determine the final destination from the papers in the trucks, but he was pretty sure it was headed some place with severe winters.

The bald cypress logs were a milled D profile, with double tongue and groove mating surfaces, six inches high and twelve inches wide, in random lengths, resulting in a fairly high R-factor even before the inside was insulated and finished. The corner dovetail joinery would make an exceedingly strong building. The roof was high quality baked enamel finished steel, green in color.

The house was complete, down to windows, fixtures, appliances, electrical components, plumbing, and an external wood/coal burning furnace that included its own solar system to power the fans and pumps of the unit.

The building didn't stop there. Killany had found a log home kit manufacturer north of I-70, east of Kansas City. He'd scouted out what he wanted from there, but had not had a chance to get everything loaded up and ready to move.

So he took a crew up and dismantled several display structures. He also took all the milled logs that were ready for use. All that was left when the last truck pulled out were a few odds and ends of damaged product.

The companion log buildings Killany brought back to the homestead included two three-bay one-and-one-half story garages, of conventional styling. The other buildings were all gambrel roof style like the house. Three bungalow cabins, a work barn, animal barn, garden barn, a studio type building, and a six stall horse barn. The studio building would be Jane's clinic when Killany recovered all the medical equipment he'd scouted out and earmarked for the community.

The construction of the buildings, using the labeled components, with an excellent set of plans for each structure at hand, went quickly. Despite that, the work took all summer and had to slow down for the harvest. But everything was completed before the first snowfall of the season. Even the barns were stocked with hay and feed, though there were no animals yet.

The additional logs and things from the log home kit manufacturer were stored away for future building projects that Killany had in mind.

A trip to Branson with a semi truck and two trailers came back loaded with furniture for the house and the bungalows.

The day before an open house that Killany and Jane held a week before Thanksgiving, Killany disappeared on the lake, with the Munson. He got back to the dock that had been installed at the new place and unloaded three horses. A stud and two pregnant mares. A second trip brought a boat load of tack the family no longer needed.

"It's your house warming gift from me," Killany explained to Jane. "I worked a deal last fall for them."

Jane, three months pregnant, was absolutely glowing, according to Bethany as they visited during the open house. "You don't look so bad, yourself," Jane said. Bethany was pregnant again, with hers and Gary's second child.

All the medical personnel were ecstatic about the new clinic. Though the manufactured housing unit that was the old clinic was functional, the new clinic had much more equipment, in a much larger space, and had adequate power.

The power came from one of the residential solar arrays he'd bought from the group of those from Springfield and Jefferson City. The rest of the homestead was powered by a commercial size array from the same source. Each building did have a separate, stand alone solar power system for basic power loads.

The clinic also had two ambulances that Killany had located and got running while looking for medical equipment and supplies to salvage. One was kept at the farm and the other at the clinic for use at the Properties and the residential section across the road.

Killany spent the rest of the winter, with the help of the three families he hired from the groups on the lake, to bring in the remainder of the things he'd found on his scouting and salvage trips. The two couples and one family with two teenage children took up residence in the three bungalow cabins Killany had moved to the homestead.

The work barn was equipped as a comprehensive shop for both metalworking and woodworking tasks. A side structure to the building was a blacksmith shop. A trip to a couple of welding supply shops in Springfield provided a heavy duty diesel engine driven welder, MIG/TIG units, and welding gases and other supplies that would last for a lifetime.

The garden barn, with the greenhouses next to it, was stocked with tools taken from farm and garden stores. Killany and his crews also took every component and item useful for gardening from the stores.

The animal barn was likewise equipped, but Killany wouldn't begin his stock operation until the following spring when he could buy some breeding stock from the farm.

## CHAPTER TWELVE

-

Killany worked most of the spring in the metal shop, repairing items, mostly from the Farm, worn out or broken over the years. He was also training three people, including one of his hired hands, in the basic skills needed to do like work.

A young bull and three cows; two boars and six sows; a rooster and twenty-five chickens were brought over from the Farm and took up residence at the Homestead. The mares foaled, bringing the Killany horse herd up to five.

There were five other births that spring. Jane gave birth to a strapping eight pound three ounce boy, named Sebastian. Bethany, a few days later gave birth to her and Gary's second child, also a boy, Arthur. Three other women gave birth, the births all going well with healthy babies being born.

Orem did another major trade, though no people changed locations on this trip. A few things were traded with Springfield, with mostly surplus stored food and the means to grow more, sent to Springfield, with permission for three more unrestricted salvage trips in return.

The crops were in and doing well, as the mild spring turned into summer. A few days before the Independence Day celebration Darren Evens, the teen on radio watch called excitedly on the local radio network for the staff to come running.

Killany was the first one to reach the Martain house. He'd been returning home after delivering a part to the Farm and was just passing the house when the radio call came in. Gary and Bethany were there next, and Jane joined them a few minutes later. The Major was on another radio, ready to be included in whatever it was going on.

"What's up, Darren?" Gary asked.

"It's another group! They want to talk to the leaders here! On the forty meter band."

"Okay. Good job. We'll take it from here," Gary said. He sat down in the chair that Darren vacated.

"You don't want me to run the radio for you?" Darren asked, obviously disappointed.

Killany quickly said, "We need you to stand by. We may need you to go get some things."

"Oh. Okay. I'll be right outside."

Killany turned back to watch as Gary keyed the mike and made contact with those on the other radio.

"This is Gary Martain, one of the staff of a group on Table Rock Lake in Missouri. Who are you?"

"This is Miles Cassiday. I'm the leader of a group living at the Twin Bridges State Park on the Grand Lake O' The Cherokees. We need some help. Our doctor is sick. He just passed out yesterday and we've been trying to find a doctor anywhere close. No one has answered our radio calls. You're our only hope. We've heard you on the air a couple of times when conditions were right. Can you help us?"

"Standby one," Gary said and set the microphone down. He looked at Jane. "I can get you there in the Seawolf."

"Could be a trap," Major Tandy said. "If they've heard us, they know we're doing okay. Kidnapping our doctor, under false pretenses... they know good and well we'd give almost anything to get her back."

"I'm inclined to agree," Bethany said. "Why haven't they contacted us before, if they know we're here?"

All eyes turned to Killany and Jane. "It's up to you," Killany said softly. "I'm going, either way."

"I'll go," Jane said. "Let me talk to them a minute. I might be able to tell if they are making up something, just to get me there."

Gary let Jane sit down. She picked up the mike and keyed it. "This is Dr. Jane Killany. What are your doctor's symptoms?"

There was a notepad and pencil on the table and Jane began to write down what Miles was saying. She asked a couple of questions, and seemed satisfied with the answers. Setting the mike back down, she turned to look at the others.

"Either someone there has medical training and came up with this, or it is legitimate. The description of the abdominal pains and other symptoms jive with appendicitis. I'm a little surprised that the doctor wasn't able to tell them what was wrong before he passed out. That's the only thing that has me worried. "If it is real, we need to hurry. He won't have much time."

Gary looked at Killany. Killany gave a tiny nod. "Okay, Jane," Gary said, "get what you need and meet us at the hanger."

"Come on. I'll help you," Killany told his wife and they hurried out.

"Major," Gary spoke into the other microphone. "Get Strotskey and Monahan on the way over here. Armed for bear."

"Will do. Out."

"Okay Darren," Gary then said, seeing the young man looking into the room through the door that Killany had left open. "Back on the radio. Once we get airborne, we'll be using the aircraft band radios. Listen close. If there is trouble, you tell Mrs. Martain and the Major immediately."

"Yes, sir! Is there anything else I should do?"

"Just monitor everything. If you hear any type of transmission that could be someone setting up an ambush, call on the aircraft band to let me know and then let Bethany and the Major know."

"Yes, sir! I will." Darren took the chair when Gary stood up.

Gary and Bethany hurried out of the room. "I'll help you get the plane ready," Bethany said, trotting beside Gary.

Jane fretted a few minutes as they waited for Dudley and Roger to arrive. As soon as they were there, Gary got them aboard, followed by Jane, in the rear seats. Killany flew co-pilot with Gary.

Gary had them in the air in just a few minutes, headed almost due west. Killany quietly filled in Dudley and Roger while Jane studied two of the medical texts she'd brought with her. The flight seemed interminable, but finally Gary picked up US Highway 60, and followed it the rest of the way to the Lake O' the Cherokees.

When they spotted the state park, Gary made a high pass as the other three men checked it out carefully through binoculars. Two more passes, each lower than the last and Gary, having heard nothing ominous from the spotters landed the plane on the lake.

Instead of approaching the shore where a group was standing, watching the plane, Gary took them up the shore for a ways before beaching the Seawolf. Gary and Killany were quickly out of the plane, rifles ready for action in case of trouble.

Dudley and Roger were next out and they stationed themselves in defensive positions. Jane handed her kit to Killany and climbed out of the plane. When Killany saw Gary get ready to go with them, he said, "Gary, I think it might be a good idea for you to idle the Seawolf back out into the lake. Keep an eye on things from out where they can't sneak up on you."

Gary hesitated. But Killany was right. They would be in deeper trouble if they lost the plane. Gary nodded and got back into the plane. The others pushed him back into the water and he turned the plane, and taxied toward the middle of the finger of the lake they were on.

Jane and the three men had barely stepped into the forest when two men burst into sight. They came to a sliding stop when four rifles were pointed at them. "Hey! Hey! It's okay! We're just here to help you get back. You missed the landing zone."

"We didn't miss," Killany said, studying the two men. "We weren't about to go into a situation blind. Could be an ambush. Still could."

"No. Oh, no. There's no ambush! Our doctor is sick and we need some help. Is one of you a doctor?"

"I am. You lead the way. And don't try anything. I'll shoot you to protect myself and these other three. Only thing different was I'd try to patch you up again after I shot you."

Both men went pale at the seriousness of Jane's statement. "Okay. Believe me," said the second man. "We won't be doing anything dangerous."

"Let's go," Killany said. "We don't want to be too late."

The two men turned around and headed back to the campsite. As Killany went on into the group of tents with Jane, Roger and Dudley took up positions in the edge of the woods surrounding the camping area.

"You're not joining them?" asked one of the men.

"No," replied Roger. "We'll just hang here until they are done and we know they are still safe."

"You guys are paranoid!" said the second man. But both of them turned and went into the camp.

Dudley and Roger immediately split up, finding positions where they could each help the other if needed, and both help Killany and Jane, were that required.

They were getting a bit worried when Killany neither called on the radio nor showed up. But his orders had been to stick tight, but not do anything unless the situation called for it. But two hours after they'd arrived, Killany's voice came over the radio. "Come on in. Everything is fine."

"You sure?" Gary asked.

"Copasetic," replied Killany. It was a long standing agreed upon safe word. If Killany had responded 'hunky-dory,' it would have signified things were just the opposite and to act accordingly.

Still, Roger and Dudley entered the camp cautiously, guns held muzzle down, but ready for quick use. Gary edged the Seawolf up to the beach, his eyes scanning the area. When Killany, one arm around Jane, waved him in, Gary eased the Seawolf up onto the beach and cut the engine.

Gary climbed out of the plane and joined the other three. A small group stood to one side. One man stepped forward to greet Gary. "I'm Miles Cassiday. I can't thank you enough for bringing your doctor to help."

"Quite all right. Is there some place we can talk?" Gary asked.

"Sure, come over to my trailer." As Gary and the others followed Miles, the group began to disperse.

"Keep an eye out on the plane," Killany told Roger and Dudley when they reached the long fifth-wheel travel trailer.

"Excuse the mess," Miles said after ushering Gary, Killany, and Jane inside. "I'm a bachelor now. Lost my wife to the radiation."

"Quite all right," Gary said, taking a seat on the sofa in one of the trailer's slide outs. Killany and Jane took seats across from him.

"Thank you again," Miles said, taking the remaining chair of the small grouping. "I don't know how we'll ever repay you. If we had lost Samuel, I don't know what we would have done."

"He's not out of the woods yet," Jane said. "There is always a risk of infection. I took all the precautions I could, but in situations like these, one never knows."

"Well, still, he's in a lot better shape than he was before. The three assistants he was training should be able to take care of him, with the instructions and the medications you gave them."

"Just have them contact me if something comes up."

Gary spoke up in the pause that followed. "How did you all manage to wind up here? You obviously couldn't have survived the radiation and ash fall in these trailers."

"No. It just seemed to happen. Everyone here survived the attack, ash fall and first winter here and there in this area. Basements, mostly. As we each went looking for food we began to group up. We decided to try and stay together for safety.

"This place just seemed logical. It had the facilities we needed, like the showers and restrooms. We cleaned up the trailers and motorhomes that were caught here in the attack. When we got a pickup running, we started moving more trailers in. Got a generator and then some solar power units to power the water pump when the generator quit. It just grew, people that we ran into in the early days when we salvaged for food just joined up for protection."

"I'm curious why you hadn't contacted us before. We've been trying to make contact with everyone in the area we can find. Mutual aid type things, as well as trading. Seed and animal swaps for genetic diversity. Sharing of skills, like we just did."

Miles sighed. "I wanted to, but the group was afraid to make the contact. We had two guys stagger in here once that said there was a group on Table Rock Lake terrorizing everybody else."

"That wasn't us," Gary quickly said. "As a matter of fact, that group attacked us and we eliminated the problem. I wonder if the two that came here could have been part of that group."

"That would explain some things. We wound up running them off a month after they arrived. They were trouble, for sure. I think now the rest of my group will be willing to open up a dialogue with you. We are in desperate need of some things. But we've done some salvage work and have things to trade you might find useful."

"That sounds promising," Gary replied.

"But I don't know how we'd do the exchanges. Sure can't carry much in your seaplane. And we only have half a dozen working cars and pickup trucks. I don't think anyone would want them to leave the area."

"We have the means," Killany replied. "Since Highway 60 bridges are still up, we can handle pretty much anything that will fit across the bridges and not be too heavy for them."

"I can't think of anything that big we might have." Miles looked thoughtful.

"Now probably isn't the best time to discuss it," Gary said. "If you want, we can set up a communications schedule and, as they used to say, my people can talk to your people. Exchange needs and wants, versus haves."

Miles nodded. "I'm going to have to convince the group. They prefer to keep things pretty tight to home. We had some trouble early on with lone wolf raiders. Lost seven people right after we all got together after the radiation faded and the ash quit falling. They were out trying to salvage along I-44 on three different occasions. We gave up that salvage work after the third time. Only salvaged things locally."

"I see," Gary replied. "Haven't had much trouble lately?"

"No."

"I might be interested in doing some salvage work on I-44, if we can come up with some kind of split arrangement." Killany said.

Miles eyes widened. "I... I don't know. I guess if the others agree, we might work out something."

"I'll be in contact," Killany said and then leaned back in the chair, Jane's hand in his.

"I think that wraps up things," Gary said. He stood up and Killany and Jane did, as well.

"Okay. Thank you again," Miles replied. He opened the door and followed them out of the trailer.

Over near the Seawolf, Roger and Dudley were talking to a small group of people. Mostly female. Jane was grinning when she asked Roger, "What is Annie going to say?"

Roger turned red. "Nothing. We're just talking here."

A couple of the women frowned. One said, "They said there are more men than women around your place. Is that true?"

"It is for a fact," Jane said, still smiling. "If things work out, some of them might be doing some work over here in the future."

There were several sighs of relief from all the women. The two men with them looked a little sour.

"Come on you two heartbreakers," Killany said. "Let's get the Seawolf back in the water."

Once the plane was floating again, the five boarded and Gary had them airborne in a few minutes. "I take it the operation was successful," Roger said.

"Yes," Jane replied. "Was fairly simple, but it is a good thing we got there when we did. The doctor's appendix was close to the bursting point."

"Things are a little strange there," Dudley said. "People are terrified, seems like."

"They lost people to raiders early on. Been keeping just to the park for the most part, apparently," Killany said. "Hopefully, contact with us will open them up and they'll gain some confidence."

"And gain some weight," Jane added. "Several of them were entirely too thin for good health."

"One of the women we were talking to said they mostly had fish from the lake. Very little wild game, except for migratory waterfowl. And their gardens aren't doing well. The hybrid seeds they've been using and saving aren't very viable anymore. We need to make sure they get at least some good seed and probably some beef and pork."

Gary sounded sure of it when he said, "Frank, Colette, and Major Tandy will figure something out."

"I don't think we can just give them things," Killany said. "Unlike some of the others we've dealt with, I believe they would simply take what we offered and then begin to expect the same on a regular basis. What do you think, Jane?"

"I'm afraid you're right. There was something of that attitude in the ones I dealt with. Those three trainees of the doctors that helped with the surgery all seemed to believe that they were entitled to the things I'd brought with me, since they were running short and I had plenty."

"Going to have to be careful not to let them become dependent on us," Killany said.

That was the last of the conversation until they arrived back at the Properties. As soon as they landed Jane headed home to check on Sebastian while the four men saw to the plane. That task done Dudley and Roger headed back to the farm and Gary went to his and Bethany's house to fill her in on what happened and then spend some time with the children.

The contact with the Twin Bridges group turned out less than ideal. It was just as they'd discussed on the way back from the mercy mission. It was a constant effort to get the group to do anything beyond just the minimum effort in return for any that was done for them. And the goods they had for trade were not nearly as useful or numerous as Miles had implied.

Killany only made three salvage runs that summer, and decided the hassles of dealing with the group weren't worth the effort. And Miles, though the declared leader of the group, seemed to have very little influence on any of the group. Killany found it difficult to keep any of what he salvaged. The group wanted ninety percent of what was recovered, though they'd had plenty of chances to go out and recover the items themselves for the last two summers.

There was a call every few days requesting help in one form or another. When it was made clear that enough fuel to get there and back, plus some sort of payment for the services and goods was required, the requests tapered off to something reasonable.

It seemed, however, that the increased radio chatter opened the door for several other individuals and groups to make themselves known. There were three more groups on Table Rock Lake, beyond the areas that Killany had investigated. Two groups on Bull Shoals Lake contacted the Properties, and several more small groups spread over the eastern Ozarks, and the southern Ozarks in Arkansas.

Each seemed to be making it all right, though each also was short of one thing or another. Trade was established with all of them, and Killany supervised several trips to take the requested items to the sites, and bring back whatever the particular group had in excess in trade.

A couple of the groups were well supplied with gold and silver, and preferred to pay rather than trade. As Killany and the others continued to seed the economies with gold and silver, the other groups, with coins available, began to value items based on the precious metals. A year later, all the associated groups were on Killany's gold standard.

Gary asked him one day how he'd accumulated so much of the coinage. "Oh, I had quite a bit before the attack. But one of my main salvage goals was to get hold of every silver and gold coin that wasn't obviously owned by a survivor. I've been hitting every place I could find that had, or even might have had, coins.

"I also have accumulated quite a bit of bar type bullion gold and silver, plus quality jewelry. When the time comes to add more coinage, I'll process the jewelry and bullion into sheets, punch coin blanks, and then mint them."

Gary looked surprised. "You can do that?"

Killany grinned. "I own a machine shop and blacksmith's shop. I have everything I need to refine the gold and silver, alloy them, and form them. Yes. I can do that."

"Wow! Had no clue. You're saying we can have our own coinage?"

"That is what I'm saying. There isn't a need yet. But if it comes before I pass on, I can get things set up and running in a short time. Hopefully we'll have a state or federal government re-established that will be producing coinage before the local need requires it."

It was almost prophetic. Less than a year later, on July first, a strong signal, broadcast on several frequencies at once, had Gary and the other staff gathering around the main radio, after Darrel Evens called them together much as he had when the Twin Bridges group had radioed in.

"They've just been announcing an important message to be broadcast at the top of the hour." Darrel sounded excited. "I've been running the bands. It's on at least two or three of the frequencies in each Amateur band, the call frequencies on the aircraft and marine HF bands, even the NOAA weather radio frequencies."

Gary looked at his watch. It was five minutes before one in the afternoon. "We just wait, then," he said.

Darrel looked pleased when Gary didn't take over the radio. He quickly set about not only just looking busy, but getting the cassette recorder set up to tape the message, and tuning in two other radios to different frequencies so they wouldn't lose the signal if any one band faded due to conditions.

"This is Joel Smith speaking," boomed the voice. Darrel reduced the volume just slightly. "I am speaking to you from Austin, Texas. I am the leader of a group of patriotic United States Citizens attempting to resurrect the Constitution of the United States. I call for all groups of survivors, no matter how large or small, to send representatives to a New Constitutional Convention next July, to be held at some point in the central US to be determined, to re-write the Constitution so we can begin to rebuild the country as a national entity.

"I ask you to spread the word to anyone that might not be hearing this announcement, and keep them informed of the progress of the task. For the next three months, we will entertain all thoughts on a likely place to hold the Convention so as many people as possible can make the trip during these difficult times.

"We know how short fuel supplies are. We now have a refinery in production and will make fuel available for anyone that attends so they can make it back to their location after the Convention.

"You will be able to contact us, dependant on atmospheric conditions, on the frequency to which you are currently tuned to. Please be patient. We expect many replies to this broadcast, so it could be some time before we communicate directly with each and every individual group.

"That is all for now. This message will be rebroadcast every day at this time to allow the notification of others so they can tune in and hear the plan for themselves."

The strong carrier went silent. There was a jumble of attempted replies, but as Joel had said, direct contact was going to be a matter of catch as catch can. Darrel looked up at Gary and Killany. "You want to try to get in now?"

Gary and Killany were both shaking their heads. "Going to be too hectic," Gary said. "We need to discuss this, anyway. Get the Farm and ask Major Tandy to join us."

"Yes, sir," Darrel replied. "I'll do that and then keep monitoring and take down anything that comes across."

"Very good, Darrel," Killany said. "Make sure you have someone monitoring twenty-four seven."

Darrel nodded and then turned back to the radio. After the Farm acknowledged the request, Darrel put on a set of headphones to allow him to hear better some of the weaker stations trying to make contact with the Austin station.

The staff went up to gather in the den in the house Bethany had build, to wait for the Major. Bethany and Jane checked on the children and left them in Annie's care, before joining Gary and Killany in the den.

Killany studied the large globe in the room while they waited. Gary, Bethany, and Jane chatted quietly, not wanting to start the discussion before the Major arrived.

When he did show up, the five got right down to business. "I heard the broadcast," Major Tandy said immediately. "You think it could be bogus? A trap to bring in gear and supplies that a group wants to take over?"

"It's possible," Killany said. He was leaning against the large desk in the room, his arms crossed over his chest. "But it feels legitimate to me. It would pay to take precautions, but I think the hazards on the road would be of more danger than the meeting."

Gary nodded. "I'm inclined to agree. I don't think it is a scam. Might be someone with visions of grandeur, but it could be true. I'm hoping it is. We've just about reached the limit of what we can do in this area. Outside cooperation would be great. Particularly for road maintenance."

"We really need to get some schools open. Home schooling is fine for general education. And most of those reaching adulthood are getting some type of training from their parents or the community. But doctors, nurses, dentists, and some other specific fields need real schools. I'm doing the best

I can, but I simply don't know enough of other fields to produce a good, well rounded doctor on my own." Jane looked intense.

"I agree," Bethany said, joining the conversation. "Higher education in many fields is needed. Infrastructure across group spheres of influence, like a regional power grid and the roads, like Killany said."

"Don't forget airports and rail," Gary said. "Aircraft are fast for those things that need it. And rail can move so much more for less fuel use than trucks."

"Okay. There's a need for more than just our local area cooperative agreements," Killany said. "The meeting is a good idea. Where? The geographical center of the US is near Lebanon Kansas.

"Not a lot of facilities there, and the further you go north, the more ash fall there was. We haven't heard much of anything from east of the Appalachians. Or the west coast."

"That's true," Gary said, "but they might just be keeping a low profile the way we did at first."

"Jeff City is still in decent shape," Killany said thoughtfully. "Not far off I-70, probably the main east west route still open to a major degree. Got the state capital buildings that might be in good enough shape to hold the meetings."

The others were looking around at one another. "What do you think?" Gary asked. "We suggest Jefferson City?"

"You realize that if Jefferson City is voted on and chosen by those planning on attending, we're probably the closest to it with the means to get some things set up and going." Major Tandy shook his head. "Could be a real drain on our resources."

No one commented for long seconds. "We vote on it?" Jane asked.

"I'm for it. We'll find a way to control costs," Killany said.

"For it," Bethany said.

Then Gary and Jane both said the same. The four looked at Major Tandy. "Okay. I was just playing Devil's Advocate. I'm for it, too."

"We'll get our recommendations and offer to help host the meeting to Austin when communications allow it," Gary said.

"Might be a good idea to run up there and take a look around, before we submit our suggestion," Killany said. He looked over at Jane. She gave him a tiny nod of permission. "I can leave right after the Fourth of July celebration."

"You sure?" Bethany asked.

"He's sure," Jane said. "Things seem to be different now. Not as dangerous."

"For the moment, anyway," Killany said. "That could very well change. No matter which site is picked, there are going to be all sorts of ne'er-do-wells, and outright villains, attracted to the area to get what they can. I think one of the main suggestions will be for every group to be armed. At least let them know that whoever we send will be armed as a matter of course."

"I agree," Gary said. "I'll get with Darrel and figure out a good time to submit our ideas."

The group broke up, and began the task of informing everyone in the area of the event. Gary joined in, letting those at the Properties know about it.

Killany took a small team with him to Jefferson City three days later. It didn't take long to decide that, though the place needed some work, it would handle any reasonable number of attendees to the convention.

So Gary finally made the contact with the group in Austin and volunteered the Missouri Capital Building for use as the Convention meeting place. He also offered to get it ready and prepare places for delegates to stay. He assured Joel Smith directly that they would have the place ready in time for the convention.

In return, Gary, at Killany's urging, asked to have a moderate amount of gasoline and several trailer loads of AvGas delivered to the Properties when the Texas contingent came up for the Convention.

There were many other offers, with many of the sites wanting the convention in their area, so they wouldn't have to travel far. But none of them, other than Austin itself, would guarantee a spot suitable for the entire convention the way Gary had.

A few days after Thanksgiving, it became official. Jefferson City, Missouri would be the site of the New Constitutional Convention, and it would be hosted by Gary and Bethany, with the backing and help of the people from the Properties and the Farm.

That winter the plans to do what was needed were discussed and formulated. Work would start as soon as the weather became reasonable enough in the early spring for the work to be accomplished.

Besides those that would be doing the work, a small group was selected to represent the interests of the Ozark Mountains. A member from each of the groups in regular contact with the Properties would go, With Gary as the primary delegate. Bethany and Killany were going, while the Doctor and the Major stayed to keep everything running smoothly at home. Jane and Annie would be taking care of the Martain children while the parents were gone.

So, on a cold, crisp, sunshiny day in late March, a small convoy left the Properties, on the way to Jefferson City. Twin Bridges and Springfield would be sending their own teams to the convention, independent of Gary's group. Both groups had declined to help with the preparations, though they both asked for help getting their large delegations to and from Jefferson

City. It didn't take much discussion among the staff to decide that the two groups were on their own.

Bethany's was the fourth vehicle from the front of the convoy, the Topkick motorhome and trailer brought out of storage for the trip. Killany was next in front of Bethany, in another of the vehicles he had managed to acquire and get running. It was the Boone County, Indiana Cadillac-Gage V-150 armored car.

Killany had found it, abandoned, on I-70 about halfway between Columbia and St. Louis. According to the way a US highway atlas was marked up, someone from Boone County, perhaps a police officer, perhaps not, had taken the V-150 to try to get to relatives in Colorado.

The fuel tanks were empty when Killany ran across it, but after adding fuel to them, and priming the diesel engine, it started right up. Killany had hauled it back to his place, along with some other equipment, on one of his equipment trailers.

The V-150 had no weapon systems, but two men were riding with Killany, with personal weapons that could be used under the armor protection. It would be the ambush buster if anyone was foolish enough to try and take on the convoy. It was no secret in the area that Gary and Bethany's group were the ones setting up Jefferson City for the convention.

Out front were two experienced riders, on powerful Harley-Davidson motorcycles, scouting for any hazards on the road including possible ambushes.

It took two days to make the trip, with an overnight camp at the rest area on I-44 northeast of Springfield. They arrived without incident and set up a semi-permanent camp on one of the open areas adjacent to the Capital Building.

Killany put his crews to the preliminary work of getting the Capital Building cleaned out. Several doors had been left open and ash had filtered inside, along with some animals. Not much was done to the damage on the exterior building, but the inside was repaired as needed to avoid actual hazards. Cosmetic work wasn't attempted.

The building's backup generator system was intact, though out of fuel. One of the semi tank trailers with fuel they'd brought with them solved that problem. Once they had electrical power in the building, things were much easier to accomplish.

Gary had two work crews he was supervising working on facilities for the delegates to stay in. There were several tall buildings close to the Capital Building that were suitable, if they limited things to the first and second floors. Generators were located to provide primarily lighting for the buildings.

City services such as water and sewer were beyond the group's ability to put back in service, so Sani-huts were rounded up from around the city and set up for use by the delegates. A potable water tank truck was cleaned up and put into running condition. It would haul water from a well that had a working pump powered from yet another portable generator, to the buildings to distribute water.

Getting things ready took the group two full months. With a small team left behind to keep an eye on things, everyone else went back to the Properties and Farm for a break and to catch up on things.

But they didn't stay home long. Radio reports were coming in from various groups already on the move toward Jefferson City. Some of them were getting close. Again a convoy headed for Jefferson City, rather smaller than the first, but with enough people to keep things running, hopefully, during the days the Convention would be going on.

Things were just as they'd left them when Gary and the others returned. Again they set up camp near the Capital Building. A few more little details were taken care of, and then everyone simply made themselves comfortable and waited for people to start showing up.

When they did, despite all the efforts they'd made, there was still near pandemonium. Most of the groups were prepared to take care of themselves at the Convention, but some were not. They seemed to expect a Las Vegas Convention set up.

Gary had been adamant in all of his communications with Austin that the delegates would have to be able to fend for themselves during their stay, with only sanitation, water, and habitable space provided.

More than one group arrived having used up their provisions on the trip, with nothing for their stay, much less to get back home on.

Killany had suggested that it would be thus. It was one of the very few times Gary and Killany didn't see things eye-to-eye. "I'm telling you, Killany, that these people will be prepared. How can they not be? They survived so far. And I've told Joel several times that everyone would have to bring their own supplies. I've heard the radio broadcasts from Austin to the parties involved. They all stated the same things. Bring what you need for the duration."

"Okay, Gary. But, unless you strenuously object, I plan to make some things available. At a price."

"Go ahead," Gary said. "But don't be surprised if you have to haul everything back home."

That had been early in the discussions. After the third group arrived and asked where they could get something to eat, Gary admitted that he was wrong. "You were so right, Killany. I simply did not believe it would be like this. I'm glad you made preparations for this."

Killany grinned. "No big deal, Gary. I'm a lot more cynical than you are. And have dealt with Springfield, Twin Bridges, and a couple other places quite a bit more. It just seemed inevitable that some of the same kind of people that wanted a nanny state before everything happened would survive by happenstance and want someone to take care of them.

"They might have had to take care of themselves, but if the opportunity arises, they'll go back to their old ways."

"I guess you're right. I'm just disappointed at the way this is starting off."

"I know. But we just have to wait and see. I do have high hopes we'll get some good things accomplished. The kind of people we've been talking about are the minority. They just stick out because they are so vocal."

"Yeah. Okay. I plan to do my best to see that the country goes back to the old values that made us great for so many years."

"You'll do it, Gary. I have great confidence in you."

"Thanks. Now, what do we do about those that don't have enough supplies?"

"Got it covered," Killany said with a grin. "Just have to activate plans B and C."

"Plans B and C?"

"Setting up a bank to make collateralized loans to those that don't have enough to get what they need, and a chow line to feed those that don't have enough of their own. All for a small fee, of course."

"You never stop thinking ahead, do you?"

"I try not to. Now, if you'll excuse me, I'll go put those plans into action before we have a small riot on our hands."

There was more than a little grumbling by those that came without proper preparations, but Killany stated his rules for loans and access to the chow line, and wouldn't budge. People began to break out trade goods and precious metals. Others pledged labor hours to Killany to get the money to buy what they needed.

Killany held them to their word. Much of the work to keep the area clean and tidy was done by those owing Killany labor hours. But, as he intended, the process got some coin flowing, and the idea of a precious metals currency system took hold.

It was one of the early discussions on the re-writing of the Constitution. A gold standard currency; a balanced budget; and the absolutely clear declaration that owning firearms and weapons of all sorts was an individual right, not subject to federal, regional, state, or local jurisdiction restrictions.

Each was enumerated as a separate clause in the Constitution. There would be no multiple groupings as in the original. All other clauses were individual as well, as the original Constitution and Bill of Rights were discussed and evaluated, and changed as needed based on past histories of abuse. And the responsibilities of citizens pertaining to each right were included in the clause.

Things would not be ambiguous. A compendium of the reason and rational behind each element of the new Constitution became a legal companion document to the revised Constitution. It would not be open to abusive interpretations.

It took until early fall to get the documents hammered out. Another week to set up the manner and means of elections to be held the following year to elect regional representatives to a federal government that would, by unanimous decision, be housed In Jefferson City.

The City would become a Federal District. And though the concept of States was retained, they would not become effective in the overall scheme of things until the population increased and began to spread beyond the local borders of the groups represented at the Convention.

For the next two decades the various groups would be autonomous territories, subject to their own laws and rules, with only the new Federal government as higher authority. And that authority was strictly limited in the new Constitution to only those few things spelled out in detail in it. Everything else was an individual right and responsibility, except what the territories might wish to cede to a future State Government.

States would be limited much like the new Federal Government, barred from usurping or denying any of the few federal rights and responsibilities the new Constitution enumerated as individual rights and responsibilities. Only those powers that the citizens of the State, in their own State Constitution, gave to their State Government would apply to the State's residents. All citizens would still retain all the rights and responsibilities outlined in the Federal Constitution.

A simple head tax was implemented, to provide funds for Federal use. It was not tied to the right to vote in any manner. When it became possible, import tariffs would be the second source of income for the Federal Treasury. For the moment, the gold that the former Federal Government had in storage would be minted and used for Federal projects.

It was a tired, but mostly happy, group that broke up to head for their individual homes before winter caught those with long distances to travel. A small group made up of members of several of the groups would stay in Jefferson City to continue the work to improve things. They would be paid for a year from the funds loaned by Killany to the new Federal Government until the nation's gold could be recovered and additional coins for circulation minted.

Though he had not actually campaigned for any type of office during the Convention, the way Joel Smith had, Gary was one of those in the running the next year for President and Vice President.

There was no actual election for Vice President. The person with the most votes for President became President, and the person that came in second was Vice President. It was close. Joel, as the person behind the whole idea, beat out Gary by a few votes. Gary, with forty-six percent of the votes became Vice-President.

The few other Federal elected offices were, for the most part, single candidate races. There weren't that many people that wanted to be burdened with the extra work that the officials took on to do their job, usually on top of taking care of their own family.

Representatives and Senators were elected at the Territorial level and the winners met at Jefferson City for the First Post-War sitting of Congress.

As much as his friends tried, Killany refused to run for any office. But that didn't stop Jane. She ran for and became, with Bethany, their groups Federal Senators. Killany wasn't completely absent to the political scene. He was a major contractor for a large number of projects that were funded by Congress to bring the country back together.

And the country did come back together... slowly. It was over thirty years before States began to form again. The new national map was much different when drawn than the old one, with only fifteen states total. Only four of the lower forty-eight states remained intact as states. New York, Florida, Texas, and California.

Other states, with strong ties to one another, formed larger regional states. There was North New England, South New England, The Mid South, The Deep South, East Heartland, West Heartland, North Heartland, The Dakotas, The North Mountains, The Western Mountains, and The Pacific Northwest.

Bethany and Gary, and Killany and Jane, never gave up their prepper lifestyle. There were still too many 'What If?' possibilities out there.

THE END

# MEET THE AUTHOR

Jerry D Young was born at home, in Senath, Missouri July 3, 1953. At age 5 the family rented a small farm house on an active farm 40 miles southwest of St. Louis. While the family weren't farmers, they lived something of a homestead type life, raising a milk cow, sometimes two, and calves, a pig or two, chickens, and the occasional goat. Along with the stock, a large garden helped to feed Jerry's three brothers and two sisters for several years. Fishing and hunting contributed to the pantry, as did foraging the wild edibles on the property.

At the age of 14, the family, minus a brother and two sisters that were now adults and on their own, moved back to Senath. Having been encouraged from an early age to read, Jerry was a regular patron of the Senath Branch Library.

A love of a good story was born within him, and shortly before graduating high school, for a lack of stories that he liked at the library, he began to write short vignettes, and started taking notes for stories that he wanted to tell. Jerry eventually began to write in earnest and now has more than 100 titles to his credit including Prep/PAW stories, Action/Adventure, and a few of the romance type stories that first got him started.